the Night Parade

KATHRYN TANQUARY

sourcebooks
jabberwocky

For grandparents, especially mine.

Sourcebooks and the colophon are registered trademarks of Sourcebooks, Inc.

Published by Sourcebooks Jabberwocky, an imprint of Sourcebooks, Inc.
P.O. Box 4410, Naperville, Illinois 60567–4410
(630) 961–3900
Fax: (630) 961–2168
www.sourcebooks.com

Library of Congress Cataloging-in-Publication data is on file with the publisher.

Source of Production: Worzolla, Stevens Point, Wisconsin, USA
Date of Production: November 2015
Run Number: 5005036

Printed and bound in the United States of America.

WOZ 10 9 8 7 6 5 4 3 2 1

CHAPTER 1

From the backseat, Saki sent another desperate message on her phone. The reception bars dipped lower, and her palms slicked with sweat as the Toyota turned around a bend. The green mountains rose outside the window, but Saki's eyes were fixed on the screen. The hum of the air conditioner muted her father's snores while her little brother played a video game. His button tapping had the same force as a small typhoon, each burst louder and more frantic than the last. Her mother halfheartedly hummed to a radio station that had been cutting out since the song began. The static drowned the buzz of Saki's phone when the reply came at last.

She opened the message with a swipe and skimmed Hana's text.

going 2 odaiba 2nite, ttyl (^o^)

Saki frowned at the screen. She hadn't waited almost an hour for reception to get a message like that. She flopped back against the seat with a glare that could have set fire to the trees outside. Back in Tokyo, her friends were out shopping, eating crepes, and talking to high school boys two years too old for them. But instead of the summer vacation she wanted, Saki was forced to spend a week at her grandmother's creaky house in the middle of nowhere.

Hana had only made it worse. Her so-called best friend had found a new punching bag in Kaori, another girl in their circle. Before the summer break, Kaori had been seen talking with a boy Hana liked. When the news got back to Hana, she had gone on the warpath. Of course, Hana acted normal while Kaori was around, but the messages she sent Saki and the other girls in private were anything but friendly.

Saki thought that Hana was being unfair to Kaori, who was on the student council and had to talk to everyone in class, but if Saki spoke up and tried to remind the other girls of this fact, she'd risk Hana being mad at her too. Saki just wanted the whole thing to be over. She didn't want to have to agree with Hana's tirades anymore or watch her trying to sabotage Kaori's student council projects. After thinking it over, Saki decided a boring message was better than the alternative.

She faked an enthusiastic response and punched the send key. Her reception bars flickered and died. Saki stiffened in her seat then launched herself toward the front seat.

"Mom, stop the car!"

The Toyota jerked as it took a curve in the road, half a meter away from a tumble down into the river below, but Saki's mother kept her hands firmly on the wheel. "Saki, sit down and stop shouting. Do you have your seat belt on?"

"What? What's the matter?" Her father yawned and rubbed his eyes behind his glasses, stirred awake by the raised voices.

Saki leaned around the seat and showed him the red error message. "My signal is gone! We have to go back!"

"It's probably just the elevation." Her mother turned off the radio, which had become more static than music. "Calm down and try sending it again at Grandma's house."

"But that's, like, an hour. Hana's leaving *now*. If I don't answer, she's going to think I'm snubbing her on purpose!"

Her mother checked the time. "We passed Tatebayashi forty minutes ago. We'll be there sooner than you think. Hana can wait for a while, can't she?"

"Uh, *no*. She can't. You don't know what she's like," said Saki. "Come on. It's really important."

"Listen to your mother." Her father angled the GPS mount. "And put your seat belt on."

Saki slouched down and crossed her arms. She did not put her seat belt on but pulled her knees up and rested her feet on the edge of the seat. Her family was useless, as always. She'd expected that, but what really hurt was realizing that her friends didn't seem to care she'd be gone. Not one of them had bothered to ask when she'd be back. They had all of their adventures in the city planned out, and none of those plans included sparing time to think of her.

The car lurched around a hairpin turn on the narrow road. Saki drew in a breath through her nose to keep her carsickness at bay. Small, ragged shops began to appear on the edge of the forest.

"There it is!" Her father's voice broke her concentration as he shifted forward in his seat. "That's the last gas station. It's the next right."

The next turn took them down a road only wide enough for one car at a time. If the tires veered too far on either side, they'd slide into the wet rows of a rice paddy or a muddy patch of garden. The houses were so far apart that the only other sights to interrupt the panorama were a smattering of persimmon trees and the aging community center. Their car passed it at a crawl, as if the family needed a better view of the water stains on the concrete.

"Look at how many people are getting ready for the festival." Her mother leaned over the steering wheel to peer at the villagers putting up plastic tarps and hauling grills for their food stalls. "Doesn't that seem like fun?"

Neither Saki nor her brother responded. There was no phone signal, no shopping mall, and absolutely nothing to get excited about out here in the middle of nowhere. Not since Grandpa had died anyway.

Grandma was her father's mother. Her father's father had died three years ago, and now Grandma lived alone in a tiny village along the Watarase River. Both Saki and her brother should have been enjoying a month without homework and sleeping until noon. But instead of vacation, they'd had to wake up with the sun and drive out to the countryside to celebrate the Obon Festival, three full days of boring ceremonies to remember ancestors she hadn't even met, awkward talks with old people, and snail-pace traffic all over the Kantō Plain.

Her mother's parents lived west of Tokyo and thankfully never did much for Obon, but her grandmother who lived in the country believed in tradition. It wasn't fair. None of her friend's parents had forced them to go anywhere to celebrate Obon. It was true that most of their families had been born and raised in Tokyo for generations, but that didn't mean it was *fair*. Saki made a tortured face out the window as familiar landmarks appeared along the road.

Fewer than a thousand people lived in the mountain village. There was one convenience store, two noodle shops, and no karaoke parlor. The junior high school had a grand total of forty-two students, and the high school students had to commute almost an hour to the town down through the valley. Saki couldn't imagine growing up in a place so dull. She watched a patch of sunflowers sway as the car continued east and the road shrank to little more than a dirt trail.

Grandma lived in a house halfway up the mountain, a fifteen-minute hike from the village. There was a deserted Shinto shrine up near the top, and Grandma's house overlooked the only Buddhist temple in the village. An old graveyard took up most of the temple grounds, where the ancestral gravesites of every family in the village rested.

When Grandpa was still alive, he had taken care of all the temple chores and even a few at the small, forgotten Shinto shrine. As a priest, he officiated ceremonies for births and deaths, always complaining that there were fewer of the former every year. He also kept the grounds, including the vast graveyard. Grandpa knew every corner of the temple and every crevice of the shrine on the mountain. He kept the paths swept, the buildings in good repair, and the offerings fresh and neat. After he died, another priest from a nearby village would come down once a week to tidy up, rake the leaves, and take care of official business, but it had never been the same.

From the window, the tall stone monuments of the graveyard poked out from behind the trees. Saki's mother pulled up to the side of the huge thatched-roof house. Her father opened his door, and a rush of sticky heat from outside spoiled the breezy chill of the air-conditioning. Her mother turned off the engine and pushed back from the wheel.

"Well, we're here. How's your phone?"

Saki didn't move from her slouch. She had checked the signal on the way up the road. "Why do we have to leave *every* year? Everyone else I know is still in Tokyo." Saki's last visit to the village was the first Obon they'd spent without Grandpa. Obon was supposed to be a time to celebrate the spirits of the dead, but spending the three days of the festival in a place so close to his memory only made the loss sharper and more painful.

"That's not true. And you didn't complain last year."

"Last year we weren't in the middle of nowhere!" said Saki. "At least *your* hometown has entered the modern era."

Her mother leaned over and pulled off her brother's headphones. "Jun, we're here. You both can help your father with the luggage."

"Mom, I don't want to do Grandma's laundry again," Jun said with a whine. "Why do we always have to do chores?"

"Grandma doesn't even have a computer," Saki joined in. "How am I supposed to keep up with everyone else?"

"I had to touch her underwear." Her brother emphasized the point with a stab of his finger.

"I can't even send messages to my friends!"

"Her *underwear*, Mom."

Their father rapped his knuckles against the back window. Saki and Jun both snapped their mouths shut.

"Out. Now."

Grandma appeared to greet them in a gray yukata with a pale-blue flower print, her smile wrinkling the sides of her face. On a vacation in Hawaii, Saki's parents had bought Grandma a souvenir T-shirt. But Saki had never seen her wear anything except a yukata or kimono outside the house. They were all old and had been worn so many times that the fabric was soft like velvet.

"Saki, Junnosuke, look how big you've gotten!" Grandma gave each of them a sesame candy and hurried them inside. "This weather is so hot. Even when the sun goes down, I feel like I'm going to melt. You should leave your things here and cool off for a while."

Saki and her brother exchanged looks behind their parent's backs.

Grandma's house had no air conditioner. It was more than a hundred years old, built before electricity. All of the wires and plugs stuck out from the walls like sagging veins. The house stood above ground level, lined with vaulted wooden walkways. The inner floors were covered in tatami mats, except the kitchen, which had been remodeled with hideous orange linoleum four decades earlier. The sliding doors were screened with shoji paper that was peeling at the corners, and the thatched roof gave off a musty smell. It probably hadn't been changed since before Grandpa died.

Saki and her brother dragged their bags to the little room near the back corner. At least they were together in their misery. Saki slid the door open with her foot, heaving a heavy sigh. Jun took off like a shot.

"I'm taking the futon by the fan!"

"Uh, no. I'm older, so I get to choose first."

"I'll play you for it." He turned and held out his fist for a round of janken. With a roll of her eyes, Saki did the same. She threw rock, but Jun had his hand stretched out for paper. With a crow of victory, he flung his duffel atop the nearest stack of bedding.

Saki ignored him and put her bag next to the pile by the outer wall. The sliding doors to the outside had been opened wide to let the room air out. Only a few steps from the house, the forest rose up all around them. The trees were so thick that it was hard to tell one from another. Saki thought she could make out a path winding toward the mountaintop, but when she blinked, she saw nothing but a cluster of trees. A summer breeze stirred against her cheek before she slid the door closed and followed the sound of Grandma's aging radio back for tea.

CHAPTER 2

They drank cold barley tea as Grandma worked in the kitchen to finish dinner. She stuffed them with thick homemade miso, cold noodles, and chilled tofu with soy sauce. When Saki refused a second helping of eggplant, Grandma tried to sneak a little more into her bowl when Saki turned her head toward the open doors to the forest.

"You're so skinny," Grandma said. "You can eat as much as you want while you're here."

"Make sure to finish everything," Saki's mother warned her. "We're lighting the Welcome Fire as soon as everyone's done with dinner. I don't want you two leaving food to waste and then complaining later that you're hungry."

"Right away?" Saki stopped halfway through a sip of tea. "We just got here."

"It's the first day of Obon. If we don't light the fire today, when else would we do it?" Her mother raised an eyebrow, the silent answer to her own rhetorical question. "Besides, I heard someone complaining in the car about hating to be bored…"

Saki bit her tongue and stabbed her chopsticks into the noodles.

"Saki, dear, can I ask you to do a little favor for me?" Grandma pressed her hands together around her tea cup and smiled.

Saki shifted her legs on the floor. So this was how their vacation would begin. "Um, sure…"

"We'll need a branch for the Welcome Fire tonight. Your father and your brother are helping chop the wood for the pyre, so if you wouldn't mind… There's a special group of sakaki trees in the grove around the shrine. One of those branches would make the perfect centerpiece for tonight." Her eyes turned soft. "Grandpa used to get sakaki branches from the shrine every year, but my knees just aren't up to climbing that steep path. Do you think you could help fetch one for the fire?"

The rest of the family was looking at her. She couldn't exactly refuse. "Uh, sure? I'll…try to find a dry one."

"Oh, if you could, please get a fresh branch. We want to welcome the ancestors with something green and full of life. I'll give you my gardening scissors to take with you. You might have to stretch a little, but I'm sure you can do it. You've gotten so tall."

"Okay, Grandma. Whatever you say." Saki tried to return Grandma's smile, but there was an empty space in her heart. She recalled a vague memory from when

Grandpa was still alive. She used to ride on his shoulder as he went up the path to cut a sakaki branch, her fingers swatting at the leaves overhead. Now that he was gone, she didn't see any good reason to trudge all the way up the path for a piece of wood. They would just burn it anyway.

When they were finished with dinner, Grandma cleared the dishes and Saki's father took her brother around the side of the house to the woodpile. His voice drifted into the twilight calm of the forest as he explained the basics of building the fire. Saki stood on the stairs outside the front door and craned her neck toward the mountain path up to the shrine. A piece of cool metal tapped the bare skin of her arm.

"These are the sharpest cutters I could find," her mother said. "Make sure you get back down before you lose the daylight."

Saki took the gardening shears with a grimace. "What if I get lost?"

"Follow the path. It might be a little overgrown, but it shouldn't be that hard. Grandpa used to take you up there all the time."

Shooting her mother a dark look, Saki shoved the scissors into her back pocket and jammed her feet into her sneakers. The path to the shrine jutted up through the trees, and she had to quell the urge to kick every rock she came across. The trail cut up the side of the mountain in a steep zigzag, turning this way and that in no particular pattern.

The path was overgrown with weeds and vegetation, just as her mother had predicted. Visitors only came to the shrine on New Year's Day to make a wish, and without a dedicated priest like Grandpa to clear the path, it had grown wild and unruly. None of the forest animals feared humans. More than once, she had to step over the snakes slithering home after a lazy afternoon sunning themselves on the weather-worn rocks.

Saki scowled as the dust on the path coated every clean bit of her new white sneakers. As she climbed, the haze of the heat and the rhythmic cries of cicadas drowned out every other thought. Even through her breaking sweat, her eyes drooped with fatigue and boredom.

Saki hopped over a little brook at a bend in the path and veered around a fallen trunk of bamboo. A fat frog jumped out onto the trail, and Saki snapped to a halt, her foot frozen in the air. With a low croak, the frog hopped away, unaware of how close it had come to getting trampled.

"Excuse you," she called after the creature. "Why don't you watch where you're going?"

She climbed closer and closer to the sinking sun, yet the path turned dark as the forest thickened. Only little patches of sunlight streamed through the shifting leaves, twisting and reappearing before her eyes. Her breath came quick and raspy, the cries of the cicadas dropped off to a dull murmur, and Saki brushed her fingers against the handle of the gardening scissors in her pocket just to make sure they were still there.

Finally, the sharp form of a torii gate appeared between the trees, its bright red paint faded and peeling where it met the earth. The symbolic gate was made of a round pillar on either side of the path, with two beams raised across the top to mark the entrance to the sacred grounds of the shrine. It was small compared to the huge torii gates of Tokyo shrines, and her father could have easily touched the top of the first beam, but it barely fit beneath the treetops on the mountain. Though it was the newest of the gates, the looping calligraphy of her family's name was faded and worn. Older gates, each more battered than the next, continued up the narrow path.

The last torii gate had no paint. The beam across the top had been rounded down by rain and wind. Moss clung to the base, as if nature meant to reclaim it for the forest. Saki stopped to catch her breath against one of the rough-hewn pillars, the wood humming beneath her fingers.

The shrine grounds rested below the mountain summit, a tumbledown collection of sticks and weeds before the underbrush and a treacherous slope overtook the peak. The handful of neglected structures dotted the open area, all in various states of disrepair. Halfway across the grounds, a stone water basin waited to purify visitors. The water was still and stagnant but didn't look too dirty. When Saki had come up with her grandfather, he'd taught her each step of the washing ritual. She picked up the ladle and sloshed a little water over her fingers on one hand, then switched to wet the opposite one. She didn't clean out her mouth, the last of the three steps, but no one was around to see.

Saki passed the empty donation box in front of the main shrine building and the rusted prayer bell dangling from the overhang. The first of the sakaki trees sat on the slope behind the structure. The tree was dead and lay half-eaten by termites, their paths carved out in the bark. Beyond the rotting stump grew the rest of the grove, the living trees' smooth bark unblemished by decay. Some of the trees' shiny, oval leaves had fallen to the ground and shifted with every step Saki took. Yet even in the midst of the greenery, her nose caught the thick odor of the rotting tree.

Farther into the grove, the branches grew a full arm's length above her head. Saki tilted her chin up into the last slanting rays of the sun and groaned.

"Ugh. Are you kidding me?"

She stretched to reach the lowest hanging leaves. When she finally caught a branch, she bent down to slip the gardening scissors out of her pocket. With a snap, the leaves in her hand tore away from the branch. It whipped up, leaving Saki holding nothing but scissors and a handful of leaves.

"Fine, I didn't want yours anyway… Jerk."

As she toiled, the wind caught her scent, and a host of mosquitos descended on the grove. The pack swarmed around her exposed arms and legs, and Saki threw the leaves in her hand as she swatted the bugs away. She tried to lose them by moving to a tree higher on the hill, but the swarm found her wherever she went. Every time she stopped to reach for another branch, she had to fend off a cloud of bloodsuckers raring to eat her alive.

She was too slow to land a swat on any of the winged things, so she kicked the trunk of the closest sakaki tree.

With a rustle of leaves, something fell from the branches and plopped onto her head. Saki shrieked and brushed an eyeball-sized tree crab out of her hair. It scuttled across the ground and disappeared underneath a pile of leaves.

"This is disgusting! I'm going home!" she shouted to the woods. The forest answered with an indifferent breeze.

Saki trudged back to the shrine. On her way there, she passed the fallen tree, one ragged branch still poking out from its carcass. Saki slipped the gardening scissors back into her pocket. She wouldn't need to cut a branch that was half fallen-apart. With one foot braced against the softened wood, Saki held the base of the branch and yanked it off the tree in one pull. A pair of sick, yellow-tinged leaves fell to the ground by her feet. That would be good enough. A fresh branch wouldn't burn right anyway, and what Grandma didn't know wouldn't hurt her. Holding the branch away from herself with two fingers, Saki shuffled back to the main path in front of the shrine.

As she left the shrine grounds, the underbrush stirred. Something moved behind her, but when she whirled around to check, the wind had only blown a crunchy leaf across the sharp edge of a stone.

She hurried down the hill until she reached the very first torii gate. The view of the shrine had disappeared behind the darkening trees. A wind picked up and whistled past her ears, stirring the hair on the back of her neck. She jogged the rest of the way down the hill to Grandma's house without looking back.

❧ ❧ ❧

Saki tapped her foot. The rest of the family watched her brother pile up the cedar wood that their father had cut, piece by agonizingly slow piece. Their father stood behind

and waited until the tower fell apart before he showed
Jun and Saki both how to fix a proper pyre. After years of
practice during his childhood on the mountain, her father's technique was flawless, but Saki could see his hands
hesitate as he placed the wood, uncertain movements in
his eyes as he tried to recall the distant memories.

The bare earth was far enough away from both the
forest and the house, but her mother had scattered water
buckets all around to be certain there was no chance of
a stray ember catching the wind and setting the whole
mountain alight. When the pyre was ready, Grandma
came forward and placed the withered sakaki branch at
the very top.

"Bit smaller than usual, don't you think?" Saki's
father asked.

Grandma squinted at the branch but waved his concern away. "Oh hush. Saki got the best one she could.
Now don't take too long or you'll be praying to my
ghost too."

With a laugh, her father struck a match and lit the
kindling. The rest of the tinder burst into flames.

They fanned out to watch the fire catch on the cedar
logs. The wood cracked and shifted, but the forest noises
seemed to hush as Saki's father recited the invocation.

"Now is a time to remember those who have come
before us, as well as those we have lost. Even though

Grandpa won't be with us this year, tonight we light this fire so that he can find his way home. Let's hope his spirit will continue to watch over us in the future."

Grandma smiled and clasped her hands together. She stood in silence for a moment, her eyes reflecting the hopping flames, then excused herself back to the house.

As Saki stared into the fire, her father put a hand on her back.

"Thanks for helping Grandma out. I know it seems silly that she wanted a branch from those particular trees, but it was very kind of you to go to all the trouble. You made her pretty happy today."

She couldn't tell him the truth, not after that praise.

Saki had always wondered why her father had left the countryside. There were times when she'd seen him look at the forest with regret. After her grandfather died, he seemed to look that way more and more. The village was as boring as a rotten log, but a part of her wanted to know what he was seeing.

Grandma returned with a plate of watermelon slices. Saki hung back, still watching the fire. There was a roiling knot in her stomach that wouldn't let her feel hungry.

"It's so nice of you to wait for everyone else, Saki," Grandma said when she came around with the plate. Saki's parents had their hands full trying to keep her brother from poking sticks into the pyre.

"I guess," Saki replied, looking down at her shoes. "It's not like there's a hurry or anything."

"Yes, yes, that's exactly right." Grandma tried to catch her eyes. "I have a present for you. Would you hold out your hand?" Grandma put the tray down on a stack of the unused cedar logs and felt around for something in the sleeve of her yukata. "Oh, dear... Now where did it run off to?"

"That's okay, Grandma. I don't need a present."

"No, no. I want to give it to you."

Saki hoped it wasn't a porcelain cat or one of those folding fans that Grandma collected.

"Oh, here it is." Grandma placed something small and cool in Saki's hand. "This belonged to your grandfather. I think he'd want you to have it."

Saki uncurled her fingers. It was a tab of flat iron about as long as her little finger. The metal was inscribed with a long verse of calligraphic characters that Saki couldn't read.

"Grandpa always carried this good luck charm with him when he took care of the mountain shrine. The mantra engraved on the front is supposed to protect you. Grandpa strung this charm on his prayer beads until the string snapped... But here, look, I made a little strap so you can hang it on your phone. Your mother told me that you like things like this."

The strap was a pretty silk brocade from one of Grandma's old kimonos. It showed part of a moonlit reflecting pool.

Saki blinked and brought her face closer to the delicate patterns and the silver thread of the moonlight on the water. It was stunning.

"Wow, thanks, Grandma." For once, the enthusiasm wasn't feigned. "It's really pretty." Saki wove the threaded end of the strap through the loop on her phone. The polished metal gleamed in the light of the fire and clinked against the edge of the plastic case.

"Let's just call it your reward for helping me with that branch, all right?" Grandma smiled.

A knot of guilt twisted in Saki's stomach. "Oh, right. Yeah."

They ate their watermelon, letting the seeds drop freely on the ground. When the fire was low and everyone was ready to leave, Saki's father grabbed a pair of her mother's buckets and sloshed the water over the logs until not an ember remained. Saki went inside to wash the smell of ashes off her face before she changed for bed. She still felt guilty, but there was nothing she could do now.

On her way back from the bathroom, her towel and toothbrush in one hand, Saki passed another door that Grandma had left open to the woods. The wet summer air sank into the folds of her clothes as she braced her hand against the frame to slide the door shut. Away from the city lights, the moonlight coated the forest. The leaves rustled in the wind and looked like silver fish scales in a black ocean. Her body was hot, but she shivered. She blinked and thought she saw it again: the path winding up to the mountaintop. Another breeze shifted the leaves, and the path was gone.

Saki shut the door.

CHAPTER 3

After a heavy breakfast of brown rice and pickled vegetables, Saki lay with her brother on the floor beside the fan until their parents started to shout for them to get going. Outside, their father had the rakes hoisted over his shoulder, and their mother had stuffed a few rags in one of the empty fire buckets. Once Saki and Jun had kicked on their shoes, they all began to walk the short distance to the temple. Down the road, the cars parked in a line as families arrived for the annual grave cleaning.

Grandma had arranged the grave offerings on a tray— simple foods that included many of Grandpa's favorite dishes. She straightened as far as she could with her crooked back and gave Saki a smile.

"It's so nice to have the four of you here again this year. I know Grandpa will be glad that you've come to visit."

Saki and her brother looked at one another.

"Yeah, Grandma, it's great," Jun said. "Hey, do you think I could catch a bug and put it with the offerings?"

"Junnosuke, what in the world are you talking about?"

their mother asked. "If you have so much energy, then you can scrub the stones."

"No, come on! That job sucks!"

Their father shot a warning glance over his shoulder.

"I mean, I always used to go collecting bugs with Grandpa, right?" Jun said, mischief at work in his eyes. "So if I'm going to leave an offering, it should be something that has a good memory attached to it."

Grandma smiled. "I think that's a wonderful way to celebrate Grandpa, Junnosuke. He'll be very happy to receive a gift like that from you."

Saki rolled her eyes. "Mom, come on. He just wants to play around while the rest of us are working."

"Saki," her mother warned. "Don't talk like that around your grandmother."

"But, Mom!"

There was no room for argument. Saki trudged the rest of the way to the edge of the graveyard enduring Jun's maniacal grin. Inside the low stone walls, people from the village had begun to gather around their family plots. Incense burned and filled the air with a heavy musk. Grandma struck up a conversation with almost everyone she came across, though the solemn ritual of the grave cleanings spared Saki from an endless parade of introductions. The old villagers simply smiled, bowed their heads, and went on their way.

Only one face caught her off guard. As Saki dragged her feet through the rows of gravestones, a girl with long, straight hair glanced up from the stone she was scrubbing and smiled. Saki was too surprised at seeing another girl her age in the crowd of old people to return the gesture. When she looked again, the girl was laughing and talking with her own family, and the chance was gone.

At the family gravesite, Saki's mother and father exchanged only paltry words as they decided who would rake the leaves around the gravestones and who would sweep the smaller debris into piles. Jun had long since disappeared on his quest for the perfect beetle, and Saki was cursing her luck once more when her father tapped her on the back of the head.

"Up all night on your phone again?"

Saki opened her mouth to protest, but he saw the rebellion stirring in her eyes and cut her off.

"Hang up the daydreams for now and bring some water for scrubbing."

With a sigh that would have made Cinderella roll her eyes, Saki trudged toward the tap on the far side of the graveyard. Wooden buckets and ladles for purifying the graves were stacked in the far corner near the old temple compound. Before he died, Saki's grandfather had been the priest in charge here too. He had woken up at dawn every morning and come to the temple, cleaned the grounds, and maintained the buildings. Judging by the peeling shoji paper in the temple's doors and windows, his replacement wasn't up to the task.

Saki picked out the cleanest ladle and tried to fill a bucket from a hand pump near the wall. The water sloshed against the wood with every press and splashed all over her legs. It was cold and crisp, pulled from some underground mountain spring that filtered through the ground, and it was soaking all the way down into her socks. Just her luck.

"Do you need help?" The smiling girl from earlier stood behind Saki with her own empty bucket. Her hair was black and smooth, and her face was very pretty. When she spoke, every word was polished and polite. "The water pushes the bucket around sometimes. I could show you how to do it, if you like."

The girl seemed too perfect to be real. She stood dry and serene as she watched Saki struggle with the water pump, waiting for a reply. It was mortifying. Saki's cheeks burned with annoyance at being hovered over like some helpless tourist who couldn't do anything on her own.

"I'm fine," Saki said with a grunt. Another pump of water made it only halfway into the bucket. The rest of the water pooled on the ground. At least she'd kept it off herself this time.

"Are you sure?" The girl smoothed the skirt of her plain gray dress and leaned in.

"I said I'm fine," Saki told her. "Besides, you don't even know me."

"Our families do. My dad was friends with your dad back when they were kids. I'm Maeda Tomo," the girl said. She bent her head into a little bow.

"Yamamoto Saki. Sorry, I'm kind of busy..." Saki turned her head for a split second, then looked up at the girl once more. She didn't like being stared at like an animal in a zoo exhibit. "Just because I'm not from around here doesn't mean I'm helpless, you know."

The girl turned away as Saki finished filling up her bucket, her cheeks bright red. Saki bit her tongue. The words sounded sharper out loud, but at least she'd gotten her point across. Until the last pump, they both remained silent.

Saki held the brimming bucket with both hands and hoisted it up. She shuffled sideways like a crab, and the water spilled over the sides, soaking her shoes and socks again. She was halfway back before she realized that the ladle had gone missing, and she had to set the water down to retrace her steps from the pump.

The village girl held the missing ladle out to Saki without a word. She had abandoned her own half-filled bucket under the water pump.

"Thanks," Saki muttered. She snatched the ladle back and retreated before Maeda could see her flush in embarrassment.

The family gravestone was swept clean by the time Saki arrived with the water. Half of the bucket had sloshed over the sides on the way from the pump, but Grandma insisted that there was enough to wash the stones. She took the ladle from Saki, who was more than happy to give it up. Without a splash or a splatter, the rivulets of water trickled down the polished rock.

❧ ❧ ❧

The sun dipped below the trees, but evening was just as sticky and hot as the daytime. After a light dinner, Saki was the last one to the car. She sat between Grandma and Jun, wedged into the backseat like rush-hour commuters as they drove down the mountain and into town. The corner of her phone dug into her ribs, the little iron-etched charm dangling outside her pocket.

Every year, the community center by the river held a fireworks festival above the dam. They passed dozens of people on bikes and on foot, all headed to see the fireworks. As the crowds grew, so did Saki's dread of the forced conversation and the many prying eyes.

A few makeshift food stalls stood around the edge of the concrete square selling yakisoba, baked sweet potatoes, and baby castella cakes in what was usually the community center parking lot. A gaggle of younger children huddled in a circle near the center's front door, lighting sparklers and racing to see whose would snuff out first. Jun pressed his nose against the window to watch as they drove toward the festival parking area, while Saki kept her hand over her pocket just in case her phone buzzed. She had promised her mother she'd leave it at Grandma's house, but the middle of the village was the only place where the reception was reliable enough for Saki to be sure she wasn't missing any important messages.

The parking lot was an empty field down the road, where the Toyota wedged into a spot between a small white truck and a rusty motorcycle. The air outside was stifling, even with the sun gone. Saki left her jacket in the car and trudged after her family through a shortcut between two rice paddies, the water between the rows of plants reflecting the heavy moon overhead.

At the community center, most of the people gathered for the fireworks were dressed in yukata. Saki and her family, still in Western clothes, stuck out like red beans in white rice. As the eyes turned their way, Saki lowered her gaze. Grandma had offered to dress her in a yukata, but Saki had put off the favor with endless excuses. Maybe refusing her grandmother hadn't been the best idea after all.

"I want sparklers!" Jun turned on his heel. "Dad, can I have money?"

"We just got here. Can't you wait a bit?" Their father

slipped a hand into his pocket but didn't pull out his wallet.

Grandma took a coin purse from the sleeve of her yukata. "Oh, let me. What kind do you want, Junnosuke? Grandma will buy you and Saki both some sweets too."

"Really? Yes! Grandma, you're the best!" Her brother dragged the whole family around the square to the castella stand as more and more villagers arrived.

Bigger fireworks flared and fizzled as two gangs of unruly kids chased each other with sparklers. Her brother, his mouth full of castella cake, tried writing his name in the air with the tip of his.

"You're not eating your cake, Saki. Does your tummy hurt?" Grandma asked.

"Huh? Oh no, I'm just not hungry." Saki rolled one of the small cakes between her fingers. It was shaped like a superhero cartoon character she'd watched when she was little. She squished the head between her fingertips.

"I know how much you like them," Grandma continued. "We can save them for later, but we'll have to hide them from your father and brother. It'll be our secret, okay?"

"That's all right, Grandma. Jun can have them if he wants. I'm on a diet anyway."

Grandma leaned closer and poked Saki's arm. "What? A diet? You're too young to worry about that."

"All of the girls in my class are on diets," Saki explained. "It's normal. Besides, you can get cavities if you eat too many sweets."

"Oh yes, that's true. I didn't eat cake either when I was your age. We didn't have many chances when I was a girl. You're so lucky to be young in such an exciting time."

Saki shifted her weight. What was she supposed to say to that? Grandma was trying to be nice, but they just had nothing in common. "Sorry, have you seen my mom? I need to ask her something."

"Hmm, I don't know…"

"That's okay. I'll find her."

Saki hurried out of Grandma's sight and ducked behind a group of parents to check her phone reception. The signal strength was barely there, but the phone connected. The few messages that had filtered in were all invitations sent en masse to things happening back in the city. She sighed.

A firework exploded nearby, and a toddler began to wail. Saki took a step back and shoved the phone into her pocket. A few stalls away, her mother was browsing a secondhand knickknack booth. Saki came up from behind and put on a deep frown while her mother bent to inspect a collection of porcelain cats.

"Mom, this is boring."

"Oh, Saki." Her mother picked up one of the

tortoiseshell cats and flipped it over to check the price. "This is cute, isn't it? I was thinking I could put it on the shelf by the front door at home."

"Mom, I want to go get my jacket."

"It's summer, dear. Aren't you warm enough?" Her mother raised an eyebrow. "You were telling me it was too hot an hour ago."

Saki crossed her arms. "I changed my mind. Can I go get my jacket?"

Her mother shook her head and fished the car keys from her purse. "Make sure to lock it when you're done, okay? Hmm…I think I'm going to get this." She put the porcelain cat down to dig for her wallet.

Saki walked back to the car, where the sounds of the festival were loud but not deafening. She lingered long enough to glance over her shoulder and then continued down the road toward the center of the village. If she hurried, she could be back in less than thirty minutes.

There were no streetlights or any houses close enough to illuminate her path, but she took out her phone, and the light from the screen bathed the pavement in enough electric blue to see two steps ahead. At a three-way intersection, Saki took a right and headed down the street to the convenience store. With all its lights, it shone like a beacon of deliverance in the middle of the pitch-dark town. The eerie hum of cicadas buzzed all around. Even with sweat beading on her back, Saki picked up her pace and closed the distance at a trot.

The mechanized swish of the automatic doors sounded like Tokyo. The convenience store looked just like every other chain store across the country. The products were arranged in different places, but they were the same chips, the same cans of coffee, the same packaged salads. Even the employee behind the register could have been the same bored high school student from the convenience store down the street from her family's apartment.

"Welcome." The employee was reading a magazine behind the counter and didn't look up when she passed.

A burst of laughter floated over the aisles from a group of teenagers in the corner. They didn't wear school uniforms, but they had blond streaks in their hair and too much attitude to be anything but the popular crowd. The two boys and two girls had spread out in a circle in the rear by the refrigerated drinks, their backs to Saki.

She kept her distance. She scanned the magazine rack by the front window, picked up a celebrity gossip tabloid, flipped to the most sensational article, and pretended to read.

The group of town kids laughed as a quiet voice tried to speak under their noise.

"I'd like to go now…"

"Come on, give us a preview of tomorrow night's

dance first," a loud girl insisted. "Your mom is on the festival committee, right? So it's your civic duty to perform for us."

"Looks like she's a little shy, Yuko," a boy said to the loud girl. "Come on, just a step or two? Be a good sport, Maeda."

That name…Maeda was the name of the girl at the grave cleaning. In a town so small, it must have been the same girl.

A plastic bag crinkled, and another boy said something about potato chips, but Saki wasn't listening anymore. Instead, she was squinting to see if she could make out a clear reflection in the window glass.

"I'm sorry. I told you, I have to get back to the fireworks." Maeda's voice was so small, Saki wasn't sure she'd heard half the sentence.

"But we're all going to a concert in Ota tomorrow, so we'll miss all the dancing. You should show us what it looks like now," the girl called Yuko continued. She seemed to be the leader of the group. She had the same sneer in her voice as Hana when she'd locked on to a target.

"Oh, please. We won't tell anyone," the second girl added. She was less noisy than Yuko, but her voice was twice as shrill.

The two boys in the group shifted and started talking in low tones. They were snickering. In the watery reflection of the store window, Saki could see the hem of the same gray dress Maeda had worn that morning. She'd been right; it was the same girl.

"Jeez, I give up," said the second girl. "She's never gonna do it."

A moment after she spoke, the girl gave a yip of pain, as if someone had elbowed her into silence. Yuko was beginning to resemble Hana more and more.

"I'm not asking you," Yuko said. "I wanna see you dance, Maeda. We all do."

"Yeah, me too."

"So do I."

"There's nobody here. Relax."

Saki took one step sideways to get a better view. As her foot settled on the floor, a burst of music sprang from her pocket. Her message tone. Of all the terrible times... In the reflection in the glass, the village kids turned to look at Saki for the first time since she'd come in. It was too late to disappear. Saki buried her nose behind her phone screen, pretending to be busy looking at the message Hana had just sent.

The employee behind the counter didn't even stir when the village kids came over to her. Panic fluttered in Saki's chest. If she took too long, her parents would know that she wasn't really looking for her jacket. But if she ran away now, she'd look like a baby. Whatever happened, she didn't want to be in Maeda's position. All she'd wanted was a few minutes alone in an air-conditioned convenience store. Why did it have to come to this?

"Hey," one of the boys called out to her.

Saki didn't turn. She kept her gaze focused on the phone screen.

"Hey," he said again. "Are you one of the kids from up the hill?"

After the second question went unanswered, Saki felt a tap on her shoulder. She turned to see a girl with bright blond highlights.

"Hey, we asked you a question. You're not from around here, right?" The voice belonged to the girl named Yuko. Over Yuko's shoulder, Saki could see Maeda wedged into the corner of the store, holding a bottle of unpurchased tea. Saki took a deep breath.

"Sorry, didn't hear you," she lied. "But yeah, I'm visiting my grandma."

Yuko leaned forward until her nose was uncomfortably close to Saki's face. "She's the old lady who lives up the hill, like, by the graveyard, right?"

Now was the perfect opportunity for Maeda to slip away. To Saki's increasing frustration, the other girl did nothing but huddle in the corner. If she was going to be such a doormat, she deserved the treatment she was getting. Yuko noticed Saki's gaze.

"Oh, you know Maeda?"

Saki shrugged and tried to look elsewhere. "Not really."

"That's weird," Yuko said. "Because Maeda told me she knows you. She said you were a stuck-up city girl from Tokyo."

Maeda stirred from her spot in the corner. "I never said that. Don't confuse me with you, Yuko."

The spark of fire that had gathered in Maeda's eyes was soon extinguished by a withering gaze from Yuko.

"Anyway," Yuko continued, "I don't think you're like that. I'm glad we could run into you. I'm Yuko." She smirked and tilted her head up. The other village kids watched like a pack of hungry dogs.

Saki had no choice. If she was going to survive the next few days in the village, she didn't want a girl like Yuko against her. She smiled back.

"I'm Saki."

"So, what's it like?" Yuko asked.

"What's what like?"

"The graveyard! At night when nobody's around, do weird things happen or what?"

The village kids moved in closer, and Maeda was forgotten. Yuko and her friends blocked Saki's view. Either way, she had problems of her own. The village kids seemed to think she was interesting, but whether that was a good or a bad thing, Saki couldn't tell.

Saki shrugged. She'd never felt the urge to go sniffing around after dark. "I don't know. No one goes in at night."

"Lame," said the second girl in Yuko's group. "I want to see ghosts."

"You can't see ghosts," a boy replied. "They're invisible."

Saki shifted her weight. They may have been delinquents, but kids like Yuko and her friends would know how to get out of the village to someplace more fun. "It's probably not half as cool as other places you've gone."

Yuko gave her a sly look. "You busy tonight, Saki?"

It was exactly the opportunity she'd been looking for. Saki brushed a strand of hair behind her ear, trying to keep cool. "I've got some stuff to do, but…"

"What are you doing right now?" Yuko said.

"Like, right this second?" Saki froze. This wasn't part of the plan.

"Yeah."

"Talking to you…?"

The town kids looked at one another. One of the boys stifled a laugh. Saki tried not to smile, because Yuko didn't take well to the joke. She was losing points fast. Hana had always liked her ego stroked…Yuko couldn't be all that different.

"What did you have in mind?" Saki asked.

From the wicked smile on Yuko's lips, this was a more satisfying response.

"We want to go see that graveyard," said Yuko. "We've been talking about it forever, but now we have the perfect chance. That old lady almost never leaves."

"Wait a minute." Saki held up a hand. "Can't we go someplace…I don't know…cooler? It's just a bunch of old rocks."

Yuko didn't bat an eyelash to Saki's suggestion. "We all decided. If you don't want to come, that's your business."

"No, I'll do it." Saki had learned from Hana that saying no to girls like Yuko was never easy. And if they went up there and made a mess… "We just have to keep quiet, okay? My grandma's house is right down the road, so if anyone hears us, we're done for."

Yuko gave her a flat look. "Uh, duh. That's why we're going while they're all down here. Honestly, we're not going to *do* anything. We just want to check it out. Nobody around, when all the ghosts are supposed to come out… We could have a séance or something."

The second girl in the group shivered. "Ooh, freaky."

Yuko slapped Saki on the shoulder. "I knew we could count on you. Tokyo girls aren't wimps. We just have to grab some of our stuff, okay? Wait for us by the gate in ten minutes."

"All right." Saki did her best to play it cool, though a sick anxiety began to creep into her stomach. "See you then."

The other kids gave tacit good-byes as Yuko led them

41

all out of the convenience store. They struck up another conversation on their way out, but Saki couldn't catch a word. She'd held up well against Yuko, better than she ever did against Hana. If she played her cards right and showed them she wasn't scared, they might invite her to that concert tomorrow. Ota wasn't much of a city, but it was better than four days stuck with her family in Grandma's crusty old house.

Maeda moved out of the corner. She'd been waiting in the store the entire time with her bottle of tea. She came up the aisle, her shoulders squared. Her face was impassive, but she gripped the plastic bottle so hard that it bent out of shape.

Saki wasn't sure how to greet her. She opened her mouth, but Maeda spoke first.

"I hope you realize that they're not trying to be your friends."

Saki closed her mouth and turned away. She didn't need a lecture from a doormat. "Better than being their target. Besides, I don't need friends. I have friends in Tokyo. I just need people to hang out with for a few days so I don't die of boredom."

"And that's exactly how they see you. You're just a passing attraction to them. A toy. If you're leaving anyway, why do you care so much about what people think of you?"

"What about you? You don't have any pride. Why

would you just stand there and take that? No wonder they don't respect you."

"I don't want their respect; I just want them to leave me alone. One person's opinion isn't the end of the world," Maeda said. "But maybe Tokyo people do things differently."

"Yeah, it must be because we're all stuck up."

Maeda tried to break in, but Saki wouldn't let her.

"And in case I didn't make it clear before, I don't need any more of your help. I can take care of myself."

In a huff, Saki stormed out of the convenience store, leaving Maeda behind at the magazine rack. She walked fast and didn't even take out her phone to light the path. There was no way she would let Maeda catch up. Saki didn't think she could stand the sight of that ugly gray dress for one more second. Some country girl had no right to spread rumors about her. Saki gritted her teeth as she stomped down the road to the base of the hill.

The festival would go on for another hour at least. Her mother would spend most of the time browsing and chatting with the other families. Her father would have more than enough to do among the locals, reminiscing about their childhoods. She didn't know what Jun would get up to, but it would likely be noisy enough to keep Grandma after him all night.

They'd never even miss her.

CHAPTER 4

The village kids were late. Saki waited at the foot of the hill in the shadow of a tree so she wouldn't be seen from the road. Insects buzzed in her ear, and the anticipation in the air made her sweat more than the muggy summer heat. She had a constant, gnawing sense of being watched by something just behind her. It was the same foreboding she'd felt on the path down from the shrine. But no matter how many times she turned around, there was never anything there.

Where *were* they? She considered bailing, but after she'd gone to all the trouble of sneaking away, she couldn't just go back. For all she knew, this was the only chance she had to impress them. She wouldn't give Maeda the satisfaction of being right.

Saki waited for almost twenty minutes before her resolve faltered. As she turned to leave, a quartet of voices came laughing up the road. The village kids' silhouettes moved between the trees as they wielded their phones as flashlights. None of them seemed to notice her until they were right in front of the gate, shining the bright light into her eyes.

"I was starting to think you guys wouldn't come." Saki had a sharper remark ready, but she kept her temper in check as she squinted against the phone lights.

The tallest boy took a step up the hill toward the grave-yard. "Come on, then. Let's do this."

Saki trailed behind and tried to keep the annoyance from showing on her face. She pretended to smile, but her pride stung every time they burst into laughter over a joke she was never in on.

At the flat part of the hill, the headstones gleamed in the moonlight, fresh from the morning cleaning. Offerings lay spread out on each family grave. The heavy scent of incense still lingered in the air as the group fanned out on the main path.

"Whoa, this place is totally creepy," the tall boy said, awe in his voice as he snapped a quick photo. "It's like the ghosts are going to pop out at any second. Check this stuff out!"

The other boy in the group inspected the offerings. "This is still good to eat, right?"

"Ew." Yuko scrunched up her face. "That stuff's been out in the sun, and bugs have probably crawled all over it."

"Gross!" the second girl squealed. "I dare you to do it."

Saki struggled for what to say without telling Yuko off. She still hadn't forgiven them for keeping her waiting, and if anything happened to the graveyard, Saki's family would be the ones to clean it up. "If they're offerings, I don't think we should eat them. Didn't you promise that we weren't going to mess anything up?"

Four pairs of eyes sized her up.

"I mean, what if they curse us or something, right?" Saki added.

"Exactly," Yuko agreed. Such a quick response was the last thing that Saki had expected. "Just shut up and remember the plan, okay?"

The boys stifled their laughter and hushed one another. Saki certainly didn't remember hearing about any "plan." She pursed her lips and kept close to Yuko. That way, she could keep an eye on all of them.

The village kids combed over the graveyard, whispering in conspiratorial tones.

"If the Obon stories are true, that means we probably have a hundred ghosts watching us right now," said the tallest boy.

Yuko snorted, and the second girl shivered, hunching her shoulders. Saki's eyes darted from the village kids to the trees beyond. How long before her parents realized she was missing?

Yuko slapped her on the back. "You scared already, Tokyo?"

"N-no." Saki bit her tongue to curb the stutter in her voice. "I'm not scared."

"Is that so?" From her bag, Yuko took a rolled-up sheet of paper. She looked at Saki the way a cat would look at a goldfish. "If you're not scared, we should play a game."

The other village kids huddled close. Yuko propped up her phone and unfurled the paper to show a circle full of words and characters. The center had numbers from zero to nine, along with the words *yes* and *no*. In a circle around the center, each character of the alphabet was written in heavy black lines.

"We're going to play Kokkuri-san?" Saki asked, raising a brow.

"It's just a little fun," one of the boys said.

"Isn't that a kids' game?"

Hana and her other friends had talked about it before. The players summoned a ghost to answer their questions, like who they would marry or what day they would die. It didn't seem like fun, least of all with a group of delinquent village kids.

"If you're bored, you can leave." Yuko turned up her nose and turned her back, boxing Saki out of the group.

Saki swallowed and sidestepped until she was a part of the circle again. "Fine. But I've never played before."

"You don't have to do anything. The ghosts do all the work," teased the tall boy.

Yuko stuck out her tongue at him. "The rules are easy. We just have one special one for tonight."

The village kids exchanged glances. From the looks of it, none of them had heard about the special rule before either.

"What are you talking about?" the second boy asked.

"The penalty, of course," said Yuko. "The first one to get scared has to do a penalty."

"Wicked," the boy replied with a nod of appreciation.

"Ooh, Yuko, that's such a good idea," the other girl cooed.

The penalty would be decided by a vote at the end of the game. Yuko and the others discussed the prospects with sadistic enthusiasm as they stole glances Saki's way. None of them expected to lose. Why not have a little fun with the new girl? Maeda's words at the convenience store wouldn't stop repeating in her head, but before Saki could open her mouth to protest, the others were all settling down around the fortune paper.

They sat in a circle on the path at the center of the graveyard. Saki ended up sitting opposite Yuko, framed in the shadows of the old temple building. The tall boy to Saki's right took out a pencil and handed it to Yuko, who placed it at the center of the paper.

"Everyone puts a hand on the pencil. Even a few fingers will work," she explained. Her gaze was aimed at

Saki. All of the other kids nodded along, already familiar with the rules. "We each take turns asking a question. You can ask anything you want."

"Just not something dumb," said the shorter boy.

"Well, that leaves out all your questions," the other boy replied.

Saki forced herself to smile as everyone else laughed, but her heart wasn't in it. The whole idea of the game was dumb. Why even bother playing if they'd already decided she would lose?

"You got it?" Yuko asked.

Saki nodded. She put her hand in first and grabbed the base of the pencil. She wasn't going to let them walk all over her. If she was going down, she would go down with a fight.

"No problem," she answered.

A bit of respect flickered across Yuko's face. She curled her fingers around the eraser end, and the others joined them.

Yuko closed her eyes, and the village kids followed suit. Saki left her eyelids open a crack, enough to see the pencil, the board, and the wrists of anyone who tried cheating.

"Kokkuri-san, Kokkuri-san, please descend." Yuko's even tones lifted into the night air.

The pencil moved, but Saki knew one of the boys was

only trying to mess with them. She had her grip on the base, so she could tell when one of the others was pushing or pulling. They'd have to try harder than that if they wanted to scare her.

"Kokkuri-san," Yuko continued, "please descend and show us the truth."

The wind tugged at Saki's clothes and hair. An unseasonal cold crept up through the stones below and settled in her bones.

"If you have descended, give us a sign," Yuko finished.

The invocation was complete.

All of their eyes snapped open. The tip of the pencil hovered between *yes* and *no* on the fortune paper. For a long time, nothing happened.

A sudden jerk brought the pencil to land on *yes*. The movement happened too quickly for Saki to pinpoint just who had guided the pencil. The town kids were all fixated on the answer, except for Yuko, who stared across the board at Saki. When Saki raised her eyes to meet the gaze, Yuko let her focus drift slowly back down to the board.

Saki didn't like being made the butt of the joke. Yuko and her gang weren't as cool as they seemed to think. In Tokyo, they didn't have to make up such stupid games to have fun. She would show them all that she wasn't going to be played with. From here on out, she would be the one in control.

"Kokkuri-san, when was I born?" Saki asked before anyone else could claim the first question. A small smile curled at the corner of her lips from the bewildered faces of the village kids. None of them would be able to answer. So much for all-knowing spirits.

The pencil glided across the game board, but Saki could feel Yuko moving everything from the top end. The tip of the pencil hovered by the numbers. Instead of watching to see what numbers the pencil pointed to, Yuko's eyes were once again fixed on Saki. None of the others seemed to notice the strange behavior; the pencil and the board had their full attention. Saki glanced back and forth between Yuko and the game.

The tip of the pencil rested on the number five. Saki's stomach did a flip.

Saki tried to shrug off the coincidence. The number five was the closest to the middle, an easy target. Yuko had a one in ten chance of picking a number that would mean anything. She couldn't guess the other two. Saki took a slow breath, keeping her face as neutral as possible. She fixed her eyes on Yuko's wrist. A wrong flick of her glance or unconscious gesture could give away the last two numbers.

The pencil drifted toward the number one. Saki's calm façade crumbled. Heat rose up her neck, and her fingers struggled to keep a firm grasp on the pencil. After lingering for a moment, the tip reversed course and landed on the number four. Saki looked up at Yuko. The other girl stared back at her without a hint of hesitation.

May 14, Saki's birthday, had been mapped out on the board.

"Was that right?" the tall boy asked her.

Saki opened her mouth to lie, but she couldn't make a sound.

The second girl wrapped her free arm around herself. "Ooh, creepy. Let me go next. Kokkuri-san, is anyone here going to die?"

The pencil moved to *yes* before resetting itself in the middle of the board.

The tall boy scowled. "What a stupid question. Everyone dies eventually."

"Oh no, you're right! Let me ask another."

Yuko broke eye contact with Saki to stare at the other girl. "No. You are finished."

Yuko looked around the group, her eyes open just a little too wide. The hair on the back of Saki's neck prickled. No one else spoke as Yuko asked the next question.

"Kokkuri-san, do you sense death around us at this very moment?"

Once again, the pencil pointed to *yes*.

The tall boy opened his mouth, but Yuko cut him off. "Kokkuri-san, who in this circle is closest to death?"

Every second seemed to take minutes. Saki's vision narrowed to the pencil, the board, and Yuko's wide eyes.

The pencil kept moving down the board. Saki broke into a cold sweat, but she never let the pencil out of her grip. It passed out of the outer circle of characters until everyone's hands were dragged to the edge of the paper. A shiver worked up her spine and shook her to the core, but the pencil moved slow and steady. When she thought her chest would burst from the breath she held inside, the pencil came to a stop before Saki.

She pulled her hand back as if she'd been burned. The circle erupted in a flurry of chatter.

"Penalty!" one of the boys called. "You have to do a penalty!"

Saki blinked, her heartbeat thundering in her ears. They all looked so far away, their voices distant and distorted. Had that really happened? No, it had to be a trick.

Yuko smirked and joined in the chants of "Penalty! Penalty!" and the too-wide eyes were gone. It was as if she'd never been acting strangely at all.

The town kids pulled Saki to her feet and away from the game board, deeper into the graveyard. Brooding in the shadows, the old temple loomed at the end of the walkway. The disrepair was hidden by night, but Saki could still feel the age of the building as the wind raked across the yellowed shoji paper and the tiled roof blocked out the light of the moon.

"Your penalty is to go into the main chamber and ring the monk's bell," Yuko hissed into her ear.

The others nodded their heads, biting back giggles. They watched for her response. Saki didn't give them the pleasure. She kept her mouth closed and her eyes forward. But inside, she shuddered. The game was over, yet she still felt the tip of the pencil pointed toward her.

A death curse, her fears whispered. That was the price she paid for disturbing the spirits here… She shook her head to clear the ominous thoughts, but they hid in the back of her mind between her fears and doubts. They lurked in the half-seen shadows of the trees that pressed in from the forest beyond the wall.

Her feet climbed the steps, and the wooden staircase teetered under her weight. Yuko and the village kids coaxed her from behind, but over the dreadful beating of Saki's heart, their voices were no louder than the buzz of the cicadas.

Saki stepped into the open chamber. A gust of wind at her back slammed the doors shut. She froze. She didn't dare turn her head. She took her phone out of her pocket with shaking hands. It cast a meager glow, not even the span of a full step. The walls glinted with statues and altars cloaked in the darkness that pressed all around. The bell was supposed to be in the very back of the room. If she walked straight from the entrance, she would find it.

One step. One step, then another. It would be fine. It was only an old building...

No sound disturbed the deadly silence of the temple but the whisper of her footsteps on the floor. The wooden beams groaned beneath her. Saki kept her head down, away from the eyes of the statues on the altars.

Her knees hit something hard, and she dropped her phone with a gasp, breath too short to scream. The pale light disappeared before Saki knew that her hand was empty.

She fell to her knees, feeling for the smooth plastic case until her fingers brushed the metal charm. The suffocating darkness pressed against her chest. She tried to swallow, but her mouth had gone bone dry. Another gust of wind raged down the mountain and shook the wooden walls.

A window over the altar burst open. The moon, heavy and round, filled the temple with silver light. The bell gleamed, and Saki stuffed the phone in her pocket as she summoned the courage to stand. Only a few seconds more. She took the bell in one hand and gave it a single, solid shake.

The chime rang through the air. The breeze through the window brought an earthy smell, like her grandfather's temple robes.

Then the wind blew harder. It rustled the trees, picking up speed until it was howling through the walls and the floorboards. Saki pushed the bell back onto the altar as her hair whipped across her face. Behind her, screams pierced the air, and the front door flew open with a clatter.

The village kids had their backs turned as they ran back to the gates and stumbled over the walls. They disappeared, no bigger than ants scrambling down the mountain road.

A shadow passed over the moon, bathing the room in darkness once more. A deep, ominous weight settled over Saki's heart. A voice in the back of her mind repeated the words *death curse, death curse.*

The wind began to push the doors closed again. Saki took off like a rabbit, tumbling down the stairs and sprinting along the path through the gravestones. The temple moaned behind her as the wind cut through the trees and tried to push her back.

A bright light flashed on the road. It bobbed up and down in the dark, the wandering soul of some ancient spirit. Saki shrieked and swerved, tripping over a headstone and scattering the offerings across the path.

"Who's there? You think you little punks are funny, do ya? I oughta—" The angry words stopped short. "Saki?"

Saki shielded her eyes from the flashlight and squinted through her fingers until she made out her father's face.

She began to pick herself up off the gravel path, but her father reached down and hauled her up. Saki yelped.

"Ow! That hurts!"

"You tell me exactly what you're doing out here, young lady."

"Me? What are *you* doing here?"

"Finding my daughter desecrating a graveyard." Saki's father swept his flashlight over the scattered offerings. His grip on her arm tightened, and the rough sounds of his country accent slipped into his words. "Come on, back to the house. I'm calling your mother."

"No!" Saki dug her heels into the gravel path, but her father pulled her along. "I wasn't doing anything, I swear!"

"You swear? You already lied to your mother once tonight. Are you gonna start lying to me too?"

Saki winced, her cheeks flushed with shame. "I'm sorry…"

"Who were those kids with you? The ones that took off down the hill."

Saki bit down on her tongue as her father marched her across the road to Grandma's house. The car was parked to the side, her father's keys in the ignition and the doors wide open. "It wasn't my idea! I tried to stop them, but they wouldn't listen…"

"If one more excuse comes outta your mouth…" He

stopped in front of the door and stared down at her. "The names, Saki. Tell me their names."

Saki's eyes darted from his harsh gaze. She blinked back tears and tried to keep her voice from breaking. "I don't remember," she lied.

Her father gave her a dark look and hauled her up the steps. "Sit down." He pulled a phone from his pocket and punched the keys with a deep frown. "Eri? Yes, I found your wallet… No, it's not that. It's Saki. She was up here in the graveyard." He paused for the reply, watching Saki with a hard, unwavering stare. "Messing around with some local kids. They made a mess of the offerings and broke into the temple… No, I heard them ringing the bell… I don't know; she keeps lying to me."

"I said I was sorry…" Saki shrank from her father's gaze. The trees surrounding the house whispered through the night.

Out in the darkness, two pinpricks of light blinked at her like glowing eyes. Saki stiffened again and bolted upright. "There! There's something out there! It's coming to get me!"

Her father swore and lowered the phone. "There's nothing coming for you except a grounding if you don't pipe down." Back to the receiver, he said, "She's either worked herself up or she's doing a good job of faking it…

Yeah, I'll stay up here. Don't tell Mom anything about it yet. The stress isn't good for her condition."

Saki tore her eyes away from shifting leaves. "Condition?"

Her father ignored the question and finished his conversation with her mother. "Take your time. Yeah, see you soon."

Saki glanced once more at the trees from her perch on the stairs. "What's the matter with Grandma?"

"Her heart's weak. Since your grandfather died, she's had to do everything on her own, and it's been getting worse."

Saki's panic began to settle, replaced with a creeping dread. "Why didn't you tell me?"

"Because your grandmother didn't want you kids to know. She wanted you to come and have good memories here, not tiptoe around because you felt bad for her." Saki's father eyed her up and down, the disappointment written all over his face. "But maybe a little guilt might do you good."

They passed the few seconds in silence. Her father readjusted his flashlight and turned back to the graveyard. "I'm going to clean up that mess you made. Stay here. You move so much as a centimeter and I'll know."

Saki braced herself on the wooden steps to stand. He wasn't going to leave her alone here, was he? "I can help. I swear, it was an accident."

"You've done more than enough already. Sit down and

wait for your mother." The light of his flashlight bobbed up and down in the dark until it disappeared behind the headstones and the low walls around the graveyard.

Saki sat with her knees to her chest in the circle of light by the door. The moon hung heavy in the sky, watching and waiting. Saki shivered in the sticky summer heat, and the wind through the leaves whispered in her ears.

"There's no such thing as curses," she said to the darkness. She put her hands to her head to block out the sound. "There's no such thing as curses…"

CHAPTER 5

The rest of the family didn't take long to arrive. Saki apologized with every other word, but nothing would move her father. He stood over her shoulder as she told the story to Grandma, but the look in her grandmother's eyes was worse than any of her father's scathing words. Her mother had also wanted the names, but Saki kept her mouth shut. She'd gotten in enough trouble; she didn't want to be a target for Yuko and the village kids too.

The argument went back and forth until Grandma put a hand to her chest. She declared she was tired and that the rest would sort itself out in the morning. After the yelling finished and she was banished to the back room with Jun's gloating laughter, Saki stared at the ceiling until she drifted into a shallow sleep.

In the dead of night, she woke to three cold fingers on her neck.

Saki blinked in the darkness. The sliding door was open to the forest. The fingers pressed against her jugular, and bright, thundering panic surged through her body.

The fingers curled down toward her throat.

She tried to open her mouth to scream, but her jaw was locked shut. Her hands groped for her phone under the futon. Before she reached it, she touched her grandfather's worn-out charm. The three fingers retracted, leaving her skin cold and bloodless.

"Oh good, you're awake." She heard her brother's voice.

Saki flipped around. Lying on her back, she stared up into a pair of eyes.

It was not her brother.

It knelt next to her on the tatami floor, knees brushing the edge of her pillow. Her brother's futon was empty, and the blankets were flung around the room. It may have been Jun's body kneeling there, but whatever stared back at her was not her brother.

The clouds shifted, and light fell through the open door, burning moon-blue on everything it touched. Her not-brother's eyes reflected the light like a will-o'-the-wisp.

"I thought you might sleep through it." The creature smiled. Her brother's teeth seemed sharper than usual.

Saki touched her hand to her jaw. It unlocked. Her voice was little more than a whisper. "Sleep through what?"

It leaned over. She stared into its will-o'-the-wisp eyes.

"The Night Parade, of course."

With a single movement, it was standing by the crack in the door. The forest stretched on into the night.

"Get up, get up! We're late already."

Saki scrambled to her knees. She pulled a blanket around her shoulders and clutched her phone to her chest.

"W-what have you done to my brother?"

It rolled her brother's eyes around the room and licked his teeth. "Impressive, isn't it?" It opened its arms and looked down at the body it had taken. "Of course, beautiful maidens are traditional, but we must work with what we have, no?"

Saki eyed the backpack in the corner. It was heavy enough to swing in a pinch. "If you touch me, I'll scream."

The creature with her brother's body became very serious. "Oh no, that won't do any good. They won't hear you anyway. This is your burden, little one." It barked out laughter, eyes wide open, reflecting the moon.

"This is crazy. Jun, if you're playing a joke, it isn't funny. I'm telling—"

"Why do you refuse to believe what you observe to be true?" it asked. "I don't know what sort of game you're playing at, girl. You invited me here."

Saki blinked. "What?"

It dropped on her brother's knee beside her. "Don't you remember? On hallowed ground, you put your hands to the summoning table. You called out our names. You rang the bell. So we came to you, as we must. Well, *I* came to you."

"You're Kokkuri-san?"

"No and yes. I am the first of three. The others will be along later."

"Others?"

"Oh yes. I'm always the first, whether I like it or not. The third you will like very much. Everyone likes him. But the second..." It covered her brother's mouth as a malevolent glee twinkled in its eyes. "Oh my. I daresay you will not like him at all. Very...scary." It curled and uncurled her brother's fingers.

"No," Saki said. "No. No, no, no, *no*." She pulled the blanket over her head and rolled into a ball on the floor. "This is crazy. This is insane. This is not happening. I am asleep and having a dream. When I wake up, it will be over."

The creature sighed. "Very well. If that is your final decision..."

Saki waited underneath the blanket. The wind whistled through the cracks of the old house, but after more than five minutes, she heard no sounds of the stranger anywhere. Bit by bit, she peeled back the blanket and peeked over the top.

Her brother slept soundly on a mess of tousled blankets. His face squished against his pillow as he drooled a bit down the side. His eyes were closed and didn't shine at all in the moonlight. Saki wrapped her blanket around her shoulders as she rose to shut the open door.

On the wooden walkway in full moonlight sat a fox with four tails.

Her fur was the color of rusty gold, and each of the silver tips on her tails swayed in a different rhythm. In her eyes was that same will-o'-the-wisp glow. Her black lips curled, but she did not open her mouth.

"Is this better? Seeing my true face?" she asked. "Though I miss having thumbs…"

Saki dropped the blanket down to the floor. A pressure built in her chest until she remembered she needed to breathe. The next lungful of air felt like her first.

"You…you're a…" Her own voice sounded foreign. She pinched herself, hard. The pain certainly felt real. "This is really happening."

The fox flicked all of her tails at once. "Of course. That's what I was trying to tell you. Are we ready to begin now? We'll have to move quickly."

"Wait, stop." Saki held up a hand and retreated back toward the wall. "I still don't understand. I'm sorry if I called you without meaning to, but we were just playing a game. It wasn't serious. I don't want to go to any parade. I don't want to go anywhere. I'm already in a ton of trouble."

The fox stared at her with burning eyes. "Oh yes, you're in quite a bit of trouble, I'd say. A death curse looms over this house. I see it hiding in your shadow even now."

Saki turned. There was nothing behind her but blankets. "Those guys, they moved the pencil on their own. It wasn't..." Her voice broke, betraying her. *Death curse.* She'd heard it before, but she didn't want to believe it. "You're...you're lying to me."

"Am I?" the fox asked. Her tails billowed around her, and she raised a dainty paw. "How very silly of me to go to all of this trouble then. Do you think I enjoy this, girl? I'm here because I am bound by contract, nothing more."

"What kind of curse is it?" Saki shivered. "If you really knew, you'd be more specific."

"We see what we see, but there are those who can see more. They can even combat such afflictions. Of course, to find them, you'll have to go through the Parade..."

Saki bent down to gather the blanket. "No way. It's the middle of the night. I'm not going out in the woods. It's dangerous."

"More dangerous than staying in this house, waiting for whatever curse that follows you to catch up? That story never ends well. Or do you think you're the first human to walk with us?"

Saki looked to the woods beyond the door. Tinkling music drifted through the air between the towering trees, unlike anything she had ever heard before. The forest was awake with sounds, alive and eager. It called to her, drawing her closer to the door. One look, just one. If anything seemed off, she could slip back inside and shut all the doors.

The fox turned and hopped to the ground. "Follow me. There are many things that can be found during the Night Parade, even the power to lift the darkest of curses."

Saki crept across the room as goose bumps rose on her skin. She set one foot onto the walkway. The moment her other foot touched the wood outside, the door to the house slammed shut. Saki turned back and pulled, but the door wouldn't budge.

"It's locked! There isn't even a lock on this door." Saki eyed the fox. "You did something."

"Come now." The fox stepped toward the forest with a chuckle in her voice. "It's a long way to the shrine."

Saki crossed her arms and didn't budge from the walkway. "I don't have any shoes." She nodded her head to the dusty earth below. "And I am not going barefoot. Forget it. My shoes are inside, so you're going to have to unlock the—"

The fox stopped and turned her head back toward Saki. "Use that pair underneath you."

On the dirt below the walkway, where nothing had been before, sat a pair of wooden geta.

"Where did you—?"

"Put them on and hurry up. There's no time to waste." The fox bounded away from the house without a second look back.

"Where are you going?"

The fox kept moving, and Saki shifted from one bare foot to the other. The door was still shut tight, and without the fox's otherworldly glow, the dark shapes of the trees closed in overhead.

"W-wait for me! I'm coming!" Saki slipped her feet over the unpolished wood of the geta. The straps, which at first seemed like simple pieces of black fabric, were made of shadows. Saki could see her skin through them, and when she walked through the darkness to catch up with the fox, the straps disappeared until she stepped again into the moonlight.

"Hold on! We're going the wrong way!" Saki called to the fox as she caught up. For a forest creature, the fox didn't seem to know her way around very well.

The fox stopped and peered up at Saki. "Which way do you want to go?"

"If you want to go to the shrine, you'll have to take the road up the hill. Over there." She pointed left.

The fox laughed with a voice that sounded like a bark. "That way? Oh no. The way we're going is much more reliable."

"But we'll be walking into the forest any second now. I'm a human, you know. I can't just go running off between the trees. We have to go up a road."

"That seems like quite a disadvantage to your species…

But if you like, I'll take you on the Pilgrim's Road." The fox entered the edge of the forest and disappeared behind a tree. "Come on, follow along. Don't you see the way all lit up?"

Saki edged around the same tree and brushed a branch away from her face. Suddenly, she knew where she'd seen the path before. It was the same one that had appeared through the trees when she'd first looked out the door of Grandma's house. Saki stared down the path and blinked. This time, the path stayed put.

A round red lantern hung from the farthest tree. The path was too narrow to walk together, so Saki trailed behind the fox's four tails. She raised her eyebrows as she glanced around.

"Is this supposed to be a road?"

"Patience, patience. Save your breath for the climb," said the fox as they passed beneath the first lantern.

"So what is this 'Night Parade,' exactly?" Saki asked.

"The Night Parade is the biggest celebration of the year," the fox explained. "Spirits travel from far and near to pay homage at the shrine on the mountaintop. At least, that's the idea…"

The lanterns they passed glowed with an odd light, far steadier than a candle flame but without the metallic glow of electricity. Saki brushed her hand on the trees as they walked but felt no cords or wires. Each lantern was painted like a daruma doll: a fat little man with a thin, inked beard. Their right eyes were filled in with black circles, but their left eyes remained white. All of Saki's questions about spirit business faded away under the lanterns' glow.

"Who put up all of these lights?" She touched the delicate paper of the body. The warmth spread around on both sides.

"Oh, many people. There aren't as many as there used to be though. It's such a shame." The fox sighed. "You'll just have to watch your step."

Saki didn't always understand her answers, but at least the fox didn't seem to mind the questions. "Why do some of the lanterns only have one eye?"

"Because those are the ones yet to be fulfilled. They're wishes, you see. They light our path, but they have to be pure. So many aren't anymore. Do you recognize any of them?"

Saki thought for a moment. "Last year, I wished for a new bag for school. There's a brand that all my friends—"

The fox interrupted her. "Oh no, a silly thing like that won't be here."

Saki frowned, but she didn't have time to dwell on the insult. Up ahead, the outline of a small wooden stall appeared.

The fox licked her chops. "Wonderful, simply wonderful. I was craving a bite. Weren't you?"

A yellow lantern hung near the entrance of the minia-ture noodle shop. A blue-and-white half curtain fluttered underneath the shop's name, which was written in scroll-ing, old-style characters that Saki couldn't read properly.

"Let's go in," urged the fox. "This is my favorite shop."

Saki stuck her hands in her pockets. The metal charm on her phone made a noise against her fingers. "I don't usually sleep with my wallet."

"My treat then. If you hope to make it through the night, you'll need your strength." With the brush of one soft tail against Saki's leg, the fox darted underneath the curtain.

The little shop hardly seemed big enough for an animal, let alone a fox and a human girl. Saki bent down, pushed the curtain away from her face, and took a tenta-tive step inside.

The shop was ten times bigger inside than out. The fox sat on a stool at the empty counter and nodded at Saki to take the neighboring seat.

"This place is huge!" Saki leaned over the counter. "It looked so much smaller in the dark."

"Many places are different once one looks inside," the fox said.

Savory smells danced on the air and tickled Saki's nose. As she inhaled more of the delicious aroma, her mouth watered and her stomach let loose a growl. The fox laughed her barklike laugh.

There was no bell to ring, and no waiter came. "Where do we order?"

"We've already ordered. This shop has only one specialty."

Before Saki could open her mouth for another question, the vapors of a piping-hot soup brushed her nose. On the counter in front of her seat, which had been empty only moments before, was a bowl of thick, doughy udon noodles topped with lush green onions and fluffy fried tofu skins. A pair of wooden chopsticks rested near her hand. The fox began slurping up her own bowl of noodles with a note of satisfaction. Suddenly the question of how the food had gotten there seemed much less important.

The fox gave her a sidelong glance, a twinkle of something else in her eyes. "Well, what are you waiting for?"

Saki dipped her chopsticks into the bowl and picked up a steaming udon noodle. Flecks of soup broth splattered her nose as she slurped. "This is delicious!"

"Of course," said a voice across the counter. Saki looked up with a mouth full of noodles and nearly choked. Another fox, dressed in a shop owner's coat, stood behind the counter with his paws folded. "That's fox udon, the very best recipe. It's been passed down through my family for centuries."

Saki glanced to her guide.

"I'm sorry, how terribly rude of me," said the she-fox, patting her mouth dry with her paw. "I was so delighted with the food, I forgot to introduce you. This is my good friend, the shopkeeper, and this is the human girl who summoned me. The fox udon at this shop really is the best." She nodded her head and continued eating as if she gave the recommendation to humans every night.

The shopkeeper fox didn't seem surprised. He smiled at Saki through his yellow eyes. "Very pleased to meet you. I can't remember the last time I served a human in my shop. You must need something very badly to pass by this way on the night of the Parade."

"I'm not really going for a parade," Saki explained. "I'm just going to get a little problem taken care of, and when I'm finished, I'll go home. It won't take a lot of time...will it?"

"I see... That question is best left to the guides. I wouldn't know the first thing about it." The shopkeeper refolded his paws. "But good luck. Sometimes finding one's way during the Parade can be a little difficult. Take care not to get lost." He watched Saki as she finished her noodles.

"Shall we go?" the she-fox asked when the last drop of broth was settled in their stomachs. "There is so much to do and so very little moonlight left." Her nod to the shopkeeper fox was cordial and polite, but there was a will-o'-the-wisp gleam in her eyes that sent a prickle down Saki's back. "By the night's end, I'll come again to settle my tab."

"I look forward to it," the shopkeeper fox said. He bowed as they passed through the blue-and-white curtain and back into the night.

CHAPTER 6

The path wove among the trees until it took a sharp turn and merged with a road wide enough to accommodate a few elephants. More painted daruma lanterns illuminated the night, but this path seemed to give off a kind of glow. Saki saw the forest in a new light, as if she'd become a kind of night creature. Far in the distance, other shapes bobbed up and down on the road ahead. The tinkling music grew louder.

Saki leaned forward for a closer look. "There are more people here?"

The fox flicked her tails, and a grin spread across her pointed face. "Others, but none of them human."

"What was in those noodles?" Saki asked. "Things look…different…somehow."

"Or perhaps you're finally seeing them as they really are. Have you thought about that?"

Saki hadn't, and she decided not to press any further. "Your friend in the shop was nice. It wouldn't be bad to meet more spirits like him."

"Yes, he's very nice." The fox tilted her head. "But be careful. Not all of the other spirits will be kind to a human girl lost in the Parade."

"But I'm not lost. I've got you, right?"

"Hm. Yes, I suppose."

The fox pressed forward, leaving Saki alone under a tattered lantern. She glanced back through the trees and down the path they'd climbed up. Even with the daruma lanterns, the trail twisted through too many trees and too many shadows. If she took even one wrong turn, she'd never be able to find her way back. In the corner of her vision, the fox's glow drew farther and farther away.

"Hey, don't leave me!" She rushed forward again but stopped short a few steps behind the fox's shining tails.

As they stepped from the forest to the Pilgrim's Road, Saki turned her head in wonder. More spirits than she could count stretched as far as she could see, filtering in from a dozen smaller trails. The fox sprang forward, and Saki leapt to catch up. If she focused on the dusty gravel at her feet and not the hundreds of pairs of eyes that watched her as she darted past, she might not be so afraid. The fox slowed with the rest of the traffic as another pair of trails joined the Pilgrim's Road. Saki let her gaze wander over the procession of spirits climbing up from the other side of the mountain, giant boars with charms and wind chimes dangling from their silver tusks. But these weren't even the strangest of the lot.

The Pilgrim's Road drew creatures of every color and shape. Some had the head of one animal and the body of another. Some looked more like rocks or trees than any breathing creature. Most, however, were nothing more than vague shapes that would fade in and out as if they were tricks of the light.

"This is the crossroads," the fox explained. "All of the paths converge here. This is where the Parade truly begins."

Saki wrapped her arms across her chest and tried to keep herself from shaking as a half-transparent figure with three heads lumbered by. "It seems pretty crowded…"

"Oh yes, and sometimes things get a little…rowdy." The fox's tails flicked, as though they had caught wind of something. "Look out, behind you!"

A pair of wet blue hands pushed Saki aside. She fell into the dirt as a slick-skinned kappa sprinted past. His webbed feet slapped the ground as he waddled along, leaving soggy footprints in his wake. His pointy face was scrunched and twisted, which might have been his normal face, until he turned his head to mutter curse words behind him to whatever spirit he was quarreling with. Saki recognized the water bowl he held atop his matted hair from the picture books her parents used to read to her as a child. The stories said that if the kappa lost his water, he would be robbed of all his powers. They were also supposed to have a weakness for juicy cucumbers.

A gust of wind blew Saki's hair across her face, then whipped past her in the direction of the kappa. Chattering laughter filled the air as the sharp edges of the wind tingled against her skin. She caught a glimpse of three grinning weasels with razor-sharp claws riding the waves of the gust. None of her childhood picture books had ever talked about spirits like these. Their giggles chased the kappa, who shrieked back watery threats behind him.

Saki laughed in disbelief and trotted after the group to see what would happen. Spirits fought and argued, just like human beings! She passed the fox, who said nothing, and cut the corner at a bend in the road.

There was a sudden flash of scarlet before Saki toppled to the ground. She blinked to clear her vision, but when she looked up again, an ogre nearly three times her height stared back down at her. She tried to swallow, but the movement got stuck in her throat.

He was shaped like a man, but his skin stood out bright red. Two horns curled from the gray hair on his head, and two sharp teeth hung below his lip. He wore a simple black-and-white pilgrim's robe, and in one hand he held a wooden club. The ogre watched Saki for a moment. He blinked slowly. Then he looked toward the fox with drooping yellow eyes. The more Saki stared, the more she realized how old the ogre seemed. His red skin was wrinkled and cracked, his horns were twisted, and his teeth were yellow. His robe couldn't even cover all of his sagging shoulders because so many holes had been worn through the fabric.

The fox slid up to Saki's side and made a throat-clearing noise.

Saki took a deep breath and bowed. "Sorry…" was all she could manage before her voice withered into a whisper.

The old ogre grunted and plodded forward along the road. His body swayed from side to side, and his arms swung back and forth. His form disappeared in the tide of spirits, though his gray horns bobbed up and down among the crowd.

Saki remained on the ground for as long as it took for her heartbeat to slow down. She'd had enough close calls for one night. When she could finally breathe regularly, she tried to stand up on quivering legs.

"I thought he was going to eat me," she confessed to the fox.

"He might have if you hadn't apologized," the fox said. "Ogres aren't my sort of creatures. Much too blunt. Well, don't just stand there. We must move on."

They continued down the Pilgrim's Road, where every sight was stranger and more spectacular than the last. Many of the spirits ignored Saki, though some stopped to pay respects to the fox. Sometimes Saki felt eyes watching her, but she could never catch any of the creatures in the act. Perhaps the fox was right, and there had been other humans before her. Or perhaps it had been so long that the spirits had forgotten what a real human looked like. Either way, she had no words to describe the kind of sights she was seeing. Even if she could, no one she knew would ever believe her.

An enormous torii gate, bigger than any Saki had seen before, straddled the spirit road. The pillars on either side were as thick as a train car and as tall as two of them stacked end to end. The bright red paint shone as though it had been put on yesterday.

"This is the first gate," said the fox. "We'll need to go through all of them before we're even close to the shrine."

"Wait, are you sure this is the right way?" Saki asked. "The torii gates leading to the shrine don't look anything like this."

"What a silly question. Just because it looks different doesn't mean it is different. Look, over there!" The fox pointed with her four tails to one of the shining pillars. "That's your name, isn't it?"

Scrolled across the base of the torii pillar was indeed her family's name in vivid black calligraphy. She ran her fingers over the characters, half expecting the paint to rub off on her skin.

"This is impossible." Saki gaped.

"Perhaps," said the fox, "yet you can see it for yourself. Shall you believe your own eyes, or shall you cling to what you think you ought to be able to see?"

Saki had no answer.

"Don't think too long, or at least move your feet while you do it. Come on, we mustn't dawdle. I have other things to do tonight, you know, so the sooner we finish, the better."

They passed through other gates, each just as bright and shining as the first. None of the paint looked chipped or faded. They passed half a dozen gates before the last one appeared far ahead.

The final torii gate was unpainted, just as it had been that morning, though it had grown ten times in size to accommodate the girth of the Pilgrim's Road. The wood rose smoothly out of the earth, as though the gate was somehow crafted from living trees. A queue of spirits formed at the mouth of the gate, and each spirit waited its turn to pass. Perched on the horizontal beam between the pillars was a creature covered in long black hair that dangled in clumps over the road. Behind the hair peered a blue face with a wide, twisting mouth. The guardian's claws braced against the edges of the beam, ready to pounce at any moment.

Saki and the fox stood at the end of the queue, waiting

for their turn. Saki fidgeted on the path and twisted the hem of her nightshirt between her hands as even more spirits joined the line behind them. How could all the others be so calm and collected as they walked underneath the hairy blue spirit? Its claws seemed to get bigger and bigger with every step Saki took.

"Listen to me," the fox instructed. "The guardian atop the gate must verify that all walkers in the Night Parade have purified themselves."

"But the water basin is inside the gates," Saki said, her eyes fixed on the hairy spirit.

"Only humans use the water. Spirits have our own way of preparing for the Parade. Our world, our rules. Remember that." The fox stopped to sniff at Saki's hands. "You visited the shrine early this morning, did you not? The purification of that visit should still be in effect."

Saki nodded, though she felt a clench of fear creep up her throat.

The fox continued the instructions. "After you greet him with a bow, the guardian will first ask you to show your right hand and then your left. He will nod once, and you must say: 'Thank you for your vigilance.' As you say this, you must bow and face the ground for five whole seconds. After you have finished, quickly move on to allow the next creature in line to begin. Do you understand?"

"Um, yes?"

"I shall go first, and you may follow me. I will wait for you on the other side. All right?"

Saki nodded and wiped her sweating palms against her shorts. When their turn came around, the fox stepped forward and bowed to the gatekeeper.

"Show us your right hand," the burbling voice of the gatekeeper asked. Its lips quivered, and its yellow eyes rolled around to watch the fox.

She extended her right paw and held it up for the gatekeeper to see.

"Show us your left hand."

The fox repeated the gesture with her opposite paw. The gatekeeper nodded, and the fox spoke her words of thanks and bowed once more. After five seconds, she rose and crossed the threshold of the gate. Her tails flicked behind her as she ascended the last incline before the shrine.

Saki stepped forward. Dozens of spirits turned their eyes to follow her. With all of their attention focused on her, Saki was trapped. Even if she wanted to run, there was no way to escape now. She tried to remember the steps the fox had taught her. The gatekeeper stared down through its bramble-tangled hair and curled its lips. Saki bowed.

"Show us your right hand," said the gatekeeper.

Saki's palms were sticky with sweat, but she was afraid to wipe them off again or do anything else that might upset the ritual. She held out her right hand. For a moment, it seemed as though she was seeing someone else's wrist and fingers shaking in the muggy summer air. She was half-outside her own body when the gatekeeper spoke again.

"Show us your left hand."

Repeating the gesture, she took a deeper breath. Her heart stopped racing, and she relaxed some of the tension in her shoulders. The gatekeeper dropped its shaggy head in a slow nod. A surge of triumph burst through Saki's worries, and she tried to bite back her smile. The ordeal was almost over. She could be in and out of the shrine without another care.

"Thank you for your vigilance." She duplicated the fox's words and bowed again.

A chill snapped through the air. Still bent in a bow, Saki focused on the ground as the shadow of the gate-keeper rippled and contorted. She counted down the sec-onds in her mind…

Three…two…

A roar like an overflowing cistern bubbled over every other sound near the gate.

"Lies! Lies from the unclean mouth!"

Saki felt the air move as the gatekeeper leapt from its perch on the gate beams.

She scrambled back, away from the gate, as the spirits

behind her pressed in for a better view. Her foot caught on a hard, scaled claw and she toppled backward to the ground. Her hair fell over her face, and the dust from her fall clouded the air around her. The gatekeeper hit the road with a thump. Through the whirling of the dust, it stretched open its gaping mouth and smacked its lips.

The spirits around them began to shout.

"It's a human! A dirty human's sneaked into the Parade!"

"The fox brought it! It's her fault!"

Saki struggled to her feet and burst into a run. She darted toward the forest, away from the road and the gatekeeper's open maw. She ran through the curling tendrils of the underbrush and the prickly little plants hidden between the trees. Branches grabbed at her arms and face as she sprinted past. She tripped over a rock and stumbled to keep her balance as her eyes searched frantically for the fox. The fox would know exactly what to do. But Saki couldn't turn back, not even to check if the gatekeeper had followed her. Her heart was beating too fast to hear anything but her own blood pounding in her ears.

When she felt as though her heart would burst, she fell against a tree and gasped for breath. The woods around her were empty. There were no lanterns to light her path or any path at all to lead her back to the spirits. The darkness pressed around her like a heavy liquid. After so many haphazard rights and lefts in order to escape, she was completely and utterly lost. The slope in this part of the forest was so gentle, Saki couldn't even tell which way led back down the mountain. The only thing left of her guide was the wooden geta on her feet.

After a little while, she hugged her legs to her body as hot, desperate tears stung at her eyes.

CHAPTER 7

"Feeling sorry for yourself?" The cool voice of the she-fox floated through the trees.

Saki's head shot up. Beneath a sagging bough, the fox sat prim and proper. Saki pushed off the ground and scrambled to her feet.

"You came! I was so scared you'd left me..."

"I ought to have left you." The fox's yellow eyes narrowed, and her four tails thrashed behind her. "Now every sentry in the temple complex will be after you and after *me* as your accomplice. I've been shamed in front of everyone. Do you have any idea of the mess you've made?"

Saki withered at the sharp words. Her shoulders slumped, and she twisted the hem of her nightshirt between her hands again, fighting back a second round of tears. "I'm sorry...I thought it would be enough. I did do the ritual! I just...I just..."

"You couldn't be bothered to do it properly, or you couldn't be bothered to tell me before I put my reputation on the line for you? These spirits think of me poorly enough without you adding fuel to their fire."

"I said I was sorry…I don't know what else I can do…"

"There is one thing you can do."

Saki glanced up. She wiped the tearstains from under her eyes and straightened. "What is it? What do I do?"

Under the shifting branches overhead, the fox's glow shone brighter than the moon. Her gaze leveled at Saki as her whiskers gave a twitch. "Hidden somewhere on this mountain is a power that can unravel any problem, unlock any door."

"Can it lift my curse?"

"No. It holds no sway over the mysteries of life and death. But with it, you may reach the heart of the shrine where the prince dwells, and he may grant your wish."

"Okay." Saki nodded, her determination grappling with her nerves. "How do we find it?"

"*We* do nothing. It is you who must undertake this task alone."

"Alone?" The blood drained from Saki's face. Her courage wavered, a leaf against a strong wind. "Why can't you come with me?"

"I'd be chased away with a cleaver the moment she caught my scent," said the fox. "You, on the other hand, are precisely what she'll be looking for."

"She? Who's she?"

"The mountain witch, Yamanba." The fox stood and took a step back, her yellow eyes glimmering. "Search every inch of her lair. Whatever form the artifact has taken, it will be the only thing untouched by decay. If you can take it from her, I might be inclined to help you again."

"Wait!" Saki followed the fox a step into the forest. "I don't understand! How do I find her?"

The fox's voice floated back through the trees, low and laughing. "Patience, girl. You are alone, scared, and so very *human*. She will find *you*."

Saki only closed her eyes to blink, but the fox had vanished. For minutes Saki waited, but no one came. She stood alone in the dark, only three heartbeats away from panic, when another light bobbed up and down between the trees. She turned her head and squinted into the forest. The light came closer every few seconds, heading straight toward her.

A chill ran down Saki's spine, and the wooden geta began to pull her feet away from the point of light. She held out a hand to steady herself against a tree before the shoes could drag her through the woods. With all of her weight pressing down on the geta, the tugging sensation dulled to an itch.

"Hello? Is someone out there?" a voice called through the trees. It sounded clear and grounded. It sounded human.

Saki swallowed, her throat like sandpaper, and wiggled her toes at the itching of the geta. The shoes kept trying to nudge her away.

"Hello? I thought I heard someone crying out here…" The light moved closer, until it lit up the face of the little old woman who carried it.

A wave of relief calmed the nervous thumping of Saki's heart. The woman was half her height and looked like a strong breeze might knock her over. Saki raised her hand and waved. "Excuse me! I'm very lost!"

The old woman jumped, and the oil lamp she held rattled in her grip. The light bounced back and forth off the tree trunks as the woman leaned forward and squinted. She was dressed much like Saki's grandmother, in an old-fashioned yukata that had been worn thin by the years. "My, my, so someone really was out here! Come here, dear. Whatever are you doing out here so late?"

If she was a witch, she didn't seem like a particularly fearsome one. And the warm glow of the light was so much more inviting than the dark shadows of the forest. Saki moved toward the halo of the old woman's light, fighting the pull of the geta. They were telling her to go another way, but the fox's command was still firm in her mind.

"I was walking, but I got lost. I can't find the path anymore."

"You poor dear. Just follow me, and I'll take you somewhere safe and quiet."

Saki nodded and trailed two steps behind. The old woman led her back to a dirt path identical to the one the fox had first shown her, though all the daruma lanterns had been torn to tatters. Only the light of the old woman's lantern shone through the woods, casting long, twisted shadows through the trees. Saki hugged her arms closer.

They walked for a few minutes before they reached a little thatched hut tucked between the trees. A nervous energy filled Saki until words began to fall from her mouth.

"Is that your house?" she asked. The hut didn't look any more like a lair than the old woman looked like a witch.

"Indeed it is, my dear. Come sit with me for a while, won't you?"

"Um, okay…but only for a while." All Saki needed was enough time to figure out whether the fox's words were true.

The woman took Saki inside and made her take off her wooden geta just inside the door. The pulling sensation ceased the instant the sandals left her feet, but somehow that didn't make Saki feel any less anxious.

Inside the one-room hut, a small fire burned in the stove pit at the center of the room. There were no electric lights, nothing that needed batteries to run, not even a radio. The corners of the room were dark and empty, except for the farthest corner, where a young man in a tattered yukata sat facing the wall, his features hidden from sight.

"That's my son. He's very quiet," the old woman explained. "Just leave him be, and he won't bother you. Would you like some tea?"

After running, crying, and trying to reason with the fox, Saki's throat was parched. "Sorry for the trouble…"

The old woman waved her concerns away and set the lantern down to fix some tea. The walls were water-stained, the wooden beams warped, and even the woman herself seemed to be in an advanced state of decay. But if this was the house, was this little old woman really the mountain witch?

They sat together on lumpy straw mats by the fire, where the old woman handed Saki a chipped earthenware cup. The tea was still too hot to drink, so Saki set it on the floor by her knees.

"Where are you from, my dear?" the old woman asked, sipping her own tea with a tiny smile.

"My grandmother lives in the old house across from the temple. We're visiting her from the city," Saki replied. "She never told me about anyone living up here on the mountain…"

The old woman laughed. "Oh, I've been here for as long as anyone can remember, dear. I haven't seen your grandmother in quite a long time, so no doubt she's forgotten all about me, but I know this mountain like I know myself. But dear, whatever were you doing in the dark at this hour?"

Saki blushed and mumbled her response. "I was following a fox…"

"Oh no, dear, that won't do at all! Foxes are notorious tricksters. You should never trust a fox to lead your way; they'll always lead you into trouble. What good luck that you found me."

"May I ask you something?" Saki began. "How is it that you found me in the dark so late?"

The old woman gave a wheezy old laugh. "I was looking for some dinner. When you get to be like me, going out in the sun is so overwhelming. Better to go out at night, when everything is nice and cool." The old woman finished her tea and set the cup aside. "Now, if you don't mind, I'd like to go out and finish gathering the seasonings. Would you stay here, dear?"

Saki nodded with a little hesitation. She didn't want to be left alone with the old woman's son, who had not moved from his place in the corner, but it was the best way to search for whatever the fox wanted her to find.

The old woman noticed Saki's gaze shifting about the

room and said, "Oh, don't be frightened. My son wouldn't hurt a fly. He loves his old mother and keeps watch over the house, but you needn't pay him any mind. You're welcome to anything in my house, the loom, the mending, the kitchen. You may even clean if you wish. I do hope you find something to occupy your time, dear. I'll have such a time preparing for the meal that it only seems fair, yes? In fact, I gathered some mushrooms earlier. It would be such a help if you could chop them up while I'm out."

The old woman leaned in, and the fire glinted in her eyes. "And whatever you do, please stay out of the closet. It's quite dirty, and my son gets rather upset when anyone disturbs his toys. You do understand, don't you, dear?"

The old woman shuffled over to take her oil lantern and closed the door behind her. Once the footsteps retreated into the forest, Saki left the hot teacup and rose to wander the dark room. Every so often, she would glance at the silent, still figure in the corner. Saki positioned herself at every angle she could imagine, but not once could she catch a glimpse of his face.

Everything in the house was falling apart. The tatami on the floor was moldy in patches and worn to dust in others, the kettle over the fire was rusted inside and out, and even the walls had a thin film of grime that came away on Saki's fingers when she brushed them. Only the knives and cleavers set out by the fire were sharp and shining, but even their wooden handles were growing soft with mildew.

The closet. That was the only place she hadn't checked. There must have been a reason for the warning; the closet was where a witch would keep her magic.

Saki glanced over her shoulder to check on the woman's son. He sat in the corner, position unchanged. She reached out and slid the closet door open a crack. A small army of spiders scuttled out through the cobwebs, and Saki bit her tongue to keep from screaming. They had built webs all over the closet and above the two moldy futons stacked on the top shelf. The bottom shelf held an old bucket and rags, also infested with spider nests. Half an arm's length away sat a square box the size of a birthday cake.

With a gasp of courage, Saki kneeled and fished the box out from the maze of webs. The dust came off beneath her fingertips in thick gray smudges. One deep breath blew more of the dust away, revealing the shining black lacquer underneath. The box had no latch, no lock, and no resistance to Saki's fingers as she popped up the lid and slid the panel back.

Old children's toys were stacked on top of one another in a jumble of colored wood and string. The rush of excitement Saki had anticipated dropped to a dull disappointment. She rifled through the small toys without enthusiasm until she noticed a very peculiar doll. The shape and design of the doll seemed normal, but its wooden body and cotton clothes were rotten and half-gone. What had the woman's son been doing with a doll in the first place? The deeper Saki dug into the box, the older the toys looked.

Buried at the very bottom of all the toys was a small leather pouch tied with a drawstring. When Saki lifted the bundle from the box, the contents of the pouch made a sound like glass clicking together. She untied the string with delicate movements, taking care not to make too much noise. She forced open the mouth of the pouch with two fingers and tilted the bag over on her lap. A handful of brightly colored flattened marbles, the kind of toy Saki and her brother used to play with when they were small, tumbled over her folded legs. The game was as simple as flicking one piece into another and winning more marbles than the other player. It was a very old game, her grandmother had told them, played by Japanese children for hundreds of years.

Saki couldn't tell how old the flat marbles were, but the glass was as clear as if it had been melted that very day. The swirls of color within the clear glass shimmered in the firelight. She moved one of the marbles between her fingers, flipping it over and twirling it around her hand. Not a speck of grime, dust, or rot anywhere to be found. It may not have looked the part, but she was sure this was what the fox had spoken of. Saki refilled the bag, tied the string, and stuck the pouch in her pocket. She placed the lid back on the box, opened the closet, and returned it to the spiderwebs.

As soon as the closet door shut, a smooth voice came from the corner.

"You opened Mother's box," said the old woman's son.

Saki froze and turned her gaze to the figure in the corner. Her heart began to pound.

"You took something of Mother's." He spoke without making a single movement.

"I-I just wanted to have a look. I'll put it back. I just need to borrow it for a while."

He shook his head in slow, heavy strokes. "Too late. You'll be punished like the others. She'll take your treasure and munch your bones."

Saki edged backward to the entrance of the hut. The pounding of her heart turned her chest into a drum. She kept her eyes on the figure in the corner as she slipped her feet into the shadow-strapped geta. Her nerves buzzed with the urge to run. The sandals were pulling her back to the woods, away from the house. Saki surrendered to the instinct and pushed against the latch of the door.

The door was locked from the outside.

The figure in the corner shook his head again. "Mother

told you. She told you. You can't leave. You can't get out."
He moved his entire body as he turned.

He had no face—only pale, white skin where the face
should have been. No crest of a nose, no hollows for eyes,
not even a slit for a mouth. Only a smooth surface, like
the shell of an egg. The faceless man watched her struggle
with the latch. His skin was so pale, it was colorless. He
rotated his entire body to face her, then stood.

"You can't leave. Not now. Not ever."

Saki slammed her body against the door. The soft, old
wood buckled, and the door burst from the latch. She
squeezed through the opening, splinters and jagged edges
catching on her clothes, and pulled herself out onto the
dirt path. The faceless man's hands groped through the
shattered door, but his shoulders were too wide to follow
her through the narrow hole.

Saki's feet pounded the ground. She ran through the
woods, past the trees, through the underbrush. She ran
until she was out of breath, until her muscles ached. There
was no path, no light. Everything was shadows, darkness,
and the bitter taste of fear. The moon watched her through
the breaks between the leaves. Maybe, just maybe, she was
close enough to a phone signal to call for help.

Saki slowed and ducked behind a tree, her breath
coming in gasps. She pulled her phone from her pocket,
but the electric glow of the screen distorted the shape of

the forest. Curves and bends grew larger and smaller, and the texture of the plants twisted and warped. The reception fizzled in and out. Strange icons that she'd never seen before flickered on the screen.

Hair stood up on the back of her neck. She raised her eyes from the phone to the darkness beyond the wood. The old woman stood between a pair of trees, watching her with hateful eyes.

"What are you doing?" the old woman shrieked.

"I-I just needed to find…" Saki stammered and held the phone to her chest.

"Put it away! Put that wretched thing away! I can't stand the smell of it!"

Saki shoved the phone back into her pocket. The flattened marbles she'd stashed away clicked from the sudden movement. The old woman narrowed her eyes and inhaled through her nose.

"What have you got there, dear?" The old woman came closer.

Saki took a step back. "Nothing…"

"You looked in my little chest, didn't you? Even after I asked you nicely, you still disobeyed me. That makes Grandmother very unhappy."

Saki took a step back and scraped her legs on the bark of the tree. The fear twisted into anger. "You're not my grandmother! You're a creepy old witch!"

Saki pivoted to run the other way, but the faceless man stood blocking her other side.

Behind her, the old woman smiled. The grin curled up to the tips of her ears. "Now dear, there's no reason to fuss. Come back inside, and I'll make a nice little meal…"

The old woman took a step forward. In the moonlight through the canopy, the sleeves of her yukata began to smolder. With a pained cry, the witch burst into blue flames, and the smooth voice of the faceless man cracked and rose to join her screams.

From out of the dark woods, the fox with her four rippling tails bounded up to Saki's side.

"Quickly," the fox barked. "The foxfire illusion won't last. Follow me!"

Saki's legs were frozen. She tried to move, to scream. The soft muzzle of the fox brushed her hand, and a sharp tooth pricked her little finger. Saki gasped in pain and came back to her senses. The fox bounded away between the trees, and Saki followed as fast as her legs would take her.

The fox's voice carried through the wood. "Did you find it?"

Saki fumbled for the pouch tucked in her pocket. "I think so!"

"Use it on the creatures behind us!"

"How?" Saki would have asked more, but the sprinting

cost her all her breath. Somehow, she didn't think the witch and the monster were going to stop trying to eat them to play a game of marbles.

"Just throw one! The magic knows what to do," said the fox. "Hurry! And don't look back!"

With utmost care not to spill the pouch while she ran, Saki picked out a single marble and held it between her fingertips. Against the fox's orders, she turned her head over her shoulder.

The old woman's jaw had disconnected from her face, dangling by two thin strips of flesh at each ear. The faceless man hurried behind her, clawing at the air. Saki nearly stumbled but caught herself just in time to toss the flat marble back.

The glass hit the ground and started to inflate. The firm glass of its surface softened into liquid, like a trembling soap bubble. The mountain witch and the faceless man ran headlong into the trap as the barrier absorbed them with a thick sucking noise. Inside the gigantic bubble, their movements slowed, and their feet floated above the ground. As they drifted to the center, another quiver shook the sphere. The soft walls had hardened back into glass.

CHAPTER 8

Saki's muscles throbbed as she followed the fox through the winding forest paths. After tromping through the woods long enough for the frantic pace of her heart to slow, they came upon a narrow trail. The fox veered left at every branch.

As Saki batted leaves away from her face, out of the corner of her eye she caught glimpses of a building, shining as though lit from within. But whenever she turned to stare, the image disappeared into shadows. If she made sure not to turn her eyes and keep the wall only in her peripheral vision, she could tell that the structure stretched taller than the trees. They wouldn't be able to get over, even if they could see it clearly. The fox must have been leading them around.

Saki quickened her pace and gave up on stealing glimpses of the phantom walls. "Are we going back to the main road or is this some kind of shortcut?"

The fox sniffed the air. "We're through with the Pilgrim's Road. Right now, I'm searching for a gap in the wall to sneak inside."

"Are you sure that's a good idea? We just got in a lot of trouble at the gate."

"*You* did, you mean."

"Maybe we should just go back. I can't take much more of this." Saki's nerves were still jumping from their last two narrow escapes. Now they were going to sneak in?

"How do you suppose you'll lift the curse without visiting the shrine?" the fox asked, moving faster. "Don't be stupid."

Saki struggled to keep her footing in the dark. "You said this Night Parade goes for three days. Why don't we try again tomorrow?"

"Don't tire yourself with worry. As long as you have those marbles, the guards won't even notice us." The fox winked and left the matter at that.

Saki dipped her hand into her pocket and pressed her fingertips against the pouch of flat glass marbles to reassure herself they were still there.

They rounded another leg of the path, and the fox stopped in her tracks. "Ah, here we are." She put her nose to the ground and took a deep sniff.

Saki smelled the air. There was the heaviness of earth, the sticky summer humidity, and the sweet aroma of tree leaves. All normal forest smells, nothing remarkable about them. Only on her third or fourth breath did she pick up on the acrid base note settled over the wood.

"The grove is a short way up. The wall should be easiest to break through there." The fox continued down the path, her ears perked in alert. "The spirits of the trees are old in the grove. They confuse the barriers of inside and outside. That's where we can slip in." The fox walked for a few more minutes before breaking from the path and heading straight through the trees. "We'll need to get as close to the wall as possible. Take out the marbles."

"I don't see a wall. It's just trees."

"Of course you don't. Humans are so—" The fox broke off with a short growl. "Never mind. Just do as I say. Everything will be fine."

Saki readied one of the glass pieces in her hand.

"Now listen," the fox instructed. "On my count, take the marble and throw it straight in front of you. Eye level. Do you understand?"

Saki nodded, though she didn't really. She felt a little stupid winding up to throw a marble at a wall she wasn't even sure was there, but the fox seemed to have some sort of plan.

"Three...two..."

Saki blinked in the middle of the countdown. As her eyelids were about to shut, the high stone wall rose directly in front of her. She snapped her eyes open again, but the image was gone.

"Now!"

Saki lobbed the marble forward. Halfway through its arc, it smacked into a point in the darkness two feet from the ground and dissolved into the black. A ripple spread through the air where it had hit. Out of nothing, the wall shifted into view. Made of old, dark stone, it stretched so high above their heads that the top blocked out the moon and the stars. Only a single blemish marred the smooth stone, a small hole hewn into the rocks, big enough for a fox or a girl to fit through.

A flame of blue fire flickered in the fox's yellow eyes. "Wonderfully done! I'll slip in first to make sure the way is clear. Wait for me back on the path."

Without pausing for a reply, the fox dove through the wall and disappeared. Saki tiptoed to the mouth of the hole and squinted. A tiny point of light in the distance wavered near the end of the tunnel. She touched the dark stone with wary fingers. How much would it hurt to run into an invisible wall? Given the rest of the strange things she'd seen that night, she'd probably have kept on walking through the trees without ever knowing it was there.

Saki wandered back to the dirt path to wait. The night was darker without her guide's ethereal glow. A branch from one of the trees in the grove—a sakaki tree—brushed Saki's arm. She had been here before, she realized, when she'd trudged up the mountain to get a branch for the Welcome Fire. She'd ended up cutting corners on that too, as she'd done with the purifying water at the gate. Maybe she was just getting what she deserved. Saki shook her head, but the thought lurked in the back of her mind, a needling, uninvited guest.

A warm glow pulsed at Saki's back, and she nearly jumped out of her own skin. At the base of one of the healthy sakaki trees sat a little child with roots curling out the end of its toes and a crown of leaves threaded through its hair. It looked up at Saki with a curious frown.

"You remember us, don't you?" The tree spirit stood up, little more than half Saki's height. "Have you come to stay a while?"

Saki struggled to find her voice. "Sorry, no. I'm just passing through… I'm looking for something, actually. I won't bother you for long."

The little spirit averted its gaze. "Oh. That's too bad. You must be very busy. You were busy last time too."

"Yeah, I'm sorry about that." Saki rubbed her sweaty palms on her legs. "But I have to wait for someone, so I'm not going *right* away…"

The spirit smiled. "That's good. We wanted to spend time with you the last time you came, but you left in such an awful hurry."

Saki scratched the bug bites she'd gotten that morning as the color rose to her cheeks. If they'd been watching her the whole time, they'd have heard all the ridiculous things she'd said. "I had an errand to run."

"Here." The little spirit held out a hand. "Come this way. I want to introduce you to my cousins. Most of them are older than I am, but we all love to have visitors."

Another little tree spirit, taller than the first, stepped out from behind its tree. "Most people only stop at the shrine, if they even come at all," the second voice chimed in.

From all the corners of the wood, tree spirits poked out their heads to watch the human girl. Some of them laughed, some blushed, but all seemed excited to wake up to a new face. One of the tallest spirits, nearly Saki's height, held out a closed hand as if cradling a precious treasure.

"I have something for you. I've been saving this all summer. I kept it up at the top of my branches where nothing could reach it. I wanted to give it to someone special, and you're the first human we've seen in such a long, long time... Here, please take it."

Saki cupped her palms together and received a short branch covered in tiny white blossoms. The sweet scent of the flowers wafted up and filled the air with soft memories of spring.

"For me? Wow...thank you." Saki's smile was slow to bloom, but when she looked up to put the branch behind her ear, she saw it mirrored on the faces of every spirit in the grove. They were only flowers, but the sincerity of the smiles made them feel like so much more. The tall spirit clapped its hands together in delight, and for the first time since Saki began her journey, the trouble seemed worth it.

The spirits led her farther into their grove, but Saki made sure to keep track of where the road had been in case she heard the fox return. The spirits took her past a bank of older trees. Once more, a decaying stink polluted the air.

"What's that smell?" Saki cupped a hand over her nose.

The spirits exchanged glances and frowned. The first spirit she'd met pointed to the border of the grove. Through the shadows, the outline of a fallen tree jutted out against the vibrant landscape. All the soft colors of the evening stopped at the perimeter, and as with all of the trees, the fallen tree was much larger than it had seemed in the daytime. Though the form was obscured by darkness, Saki could see well enough to glimpse the writhing, twisting shapes that wove in and out of the decaying wood. The smell turned bitter, and Saki retreated a few paces back into the living grove. An uneasy guilt twisted in her stomach.

"I should go back to the path and wait. I need to meet someone…"

A burst of foxfire flared through the trees near the path. The soft light of the moon darkened, and the sky near the walls filled with great pillars of smoke. Saki narrowed her eyes for a better look. The plumes morphed and reshaped, spreading and sinking closer to the ground. The shape drew closer, and she realized the sky wasn't filled with smoke but with hundreds of beating wings. Vibrations shook the trees and the earth beneath her. One by one, the tree spirits disappeared into the safety of their roots.

Saki's eyes were fixed on the swarming sky when fox fur brushed against her leg. The she-fox's tails all stood at attention. Her ears were pushed back flat against her head. She bared her sharp teeth, and her inky black lips curled. Clenched tight in her jaws was an old metal key with a long tassel. She lifted her slitted eyes to the cloud of wings buzzing above them and growled.

"What are those things?" Panic crept into Saki's voice. She shielded her head with her hands and bent low to keep out of sight. "They won't follow us into the shrine, right? Let's hurry! Show me the way."

The fox turned and backed farther away from the wall. "Bad news." The key in her mouth distorted the words. Everything came out sharper and colder than before. "Those are insect soldiers. They *came* from the shrine. They certainly won't be letting us back in."

"But you've got a key there. That means there's a door somewhere, right?"

The fox spun and faced the girl. Her teeth were still

bared, the key clenched between them. A cold sweat ran down Saki's back.

"This key isn't for you," the fox growled. "Humans are always so selfish. Why can't I do something for myself for once? I'm stuck with this task every time one of you bumbles around with the summoning as if it's some sort of game. I'm through with it! Now at least I have compensation for all of my unpaid service." She turned and bounded away in the direction opposite the swarm. Her strides were long and purposeful. Saki took off after the swishing tails, the only beacons of light in the moonless dark.

"Hey!" Saki called, her words half-stolen by the wind. "Hey! Don't accuse me of being selfish! You made me use one of my marbles because you said it would help me lift the curse!"

"I never said that," the fox retorted. "You assumed that. Besides, those marbles don't really belong to you. You stole them from the mountain witch."

"You told me to!"

They were sprinting together down the side of the mountain. Gravity helped Saki's tired legs keep going, but the fox seemed to float, unaffected by any law of nature.

"It's…not…fair!" Saki gasped out the words. She couldn't afford any more breaths to argue her point.

The fox barked in laughter. "Fair? Why are humans

so concerned with fair? If you didn't need my help, there would be nothing stopping you from slitting my throat and placing my pelt up on your wall as a trophy."

Saki had only enough energy to keep her legs pumping down the path. There was no room left for argument or to insist that fur was garishly out of fashion, so the point lingered in the air as Saki gasped for breath.

They pushed through an overgrown patch of shrubs. The sharp blades cut at Saki's legs and arms, stinging as they passed. The fox took a hairpin turn that dropped them back onto the main road. The number of spirits had grown tenfold, and Saki was forced to push against the flow of traffic as the nimble fox leapt farther and farther away.

Saki bumped against spirits of every shape and size. Sharp-elbowed spirits left smarting pains on her arms, wet spirits slicked her skin with ooze, and some spirits she went through altogether, though they stopped for a moment to give her a scandalized look before continuing onward. The tide never ceased. A dizzying number of creatures marched along the road without an end in sight.

Saki's legs were weak from running, and she could hardly breathe stuck in the middle of the crowd. A lion-headed beast pushed her to the ground with its furry haunches. She tried to scramble to her feet again, but after pushing her body to its limit, the muscles in her legs went as limp as a wet piece of paper. A band of visiting tree spirits gave her a disdainful look as they filed by with little sacks of earth slung over their backs. Long, spindly legs from another spirit headed right for her. They were connected to a tiny body the size of Saki's head, and the sharp tips speared the earth with a whisper like a sword being sheathed. The spider spirit fixed her hundred eyes on the girl and thrashed her mighty jaws as each leg brought her body closer.

A firm presence lifted Saki up from behind and hoisted her over the crowd. The spider spirit turned its eyes to watch and brushed a hairy leg against Saki's geta sandals, but the flow of the procession kept it marching with the rest. Saki turned to see the ogre with the broken horn holding her up, one spike of his club hooked on the back of her nightshirt. His face was set in the same yellow-toothed grimace, but he set her down next to him on the side of the road with a gentle plop. When she was safe, he turned back to watch the procession.

"Thanks…" The breathless word brushed her lips. She turned her eyes to the sky, but the swarm was nowhere to be found. Nor, for that matter, was the fox. She was exhausted and lost, but at least she was no longer alone.

She cleared her throat. The ogre's drooping eyes swiveled to meet hers. "Um, excuse me. Do you know where this path leads? I'm trying to go back to the human world…"

The ogre shook his matted hair sadly. He held out his clawed hands. Dark stains, like the ones that had crawled all over the dead log, wriggled on his hands and burrowed along his skin. Saki lowered her eyes.

"Ah, so that's why you're not joining the rest. You're not pure either, huh?" A little beggar's bowl sat at his feet, chipped and empty. "Are you just going to wait here? What if you never get in?"

The old ogre looked out toward the crowd. None of the passing spirits paid him any heed. His smell was somewhere between a wet dog and an old shoe, but Saki scrunched up her face and patted his wrinkled arm. Then, after a moment staring at the spirit procession, she took one of the flat marbles from her pouch and held it out.

"Here," she said. "I don't know if you can use this, but I think it's valuable, so you might be able to trade it for something."

The ogre blinked and sniffed at the glass piece. He gave her a sidelong glance, as if she were tricking him.

"I've got lots. You can have this one, I promise."

The ogre held out his two calloused hands. His eyes followed Saki's fingers as she dropped the marble into his palms. The glass liquefied the instant it touched the ogre's red skin. Instead of absorbing him, as it had the mountain witch, the little beads of glass-water sped across his hand and sucked out bits of the wiggling stains. When each bit of darkness had been sucked clean up, the glass hardened until it shattered, leaving the dust to blow away into the night. The ogre's hands were still wrinkled and worn, but perfectly clean.

His rubbery lips twisted up in a smile. His eyes danced, and he held Saki's hand to shake it. The force of the handshake rattled up her arm and shook her all the way to the brain. The ringing in her ears slowly quieted, only to be replaced by a low, sinister buzz. Up in the sky, the swarm blotted out the stars above the Pilgrim's Road. Spirits stopped in their tracks to glance up, and Saki froze, unable to breathe, until the old ogre shook her from her fear. Their eyes met for only half a moment.

The ogre hoisted Saki over his head and set her on the road downhill. He bowed once in a gesture of farewell, then took up his battered club to face the swarm with a mighty battle roar.

Saki summoned all her strength to make her legs move again. The road was smooth, but the curves were tight, and half a dozen smaller paths branched out along the way. There was no way to tell which way would lead her home, if any of them would. Tears gushed from her eyes, but there was no time to stop and feel sorry for herself.

Just before she passed another turnoff, her shadow-strapped geta gave a lurch and ran her off the main road.

The little dirt path was narrower than she remembered, but the daruma lanterns in the trees shone brighter.

In the time it took to blink, Saki found herself thundering down the hill toward her grandmother's house. The door to her room was ajar by only a few inches. For a moment, she thought she could make out her pillow. The buzzing behind her grew louder. The fear rose like bile in her throat, and Saki turned her head. A set of thrashing pincers tore the tree spirit's flowers from her hair and dashed them against the path.

A horde of bug soldiers the size of humans pressed down on her. With every flick of their wings, they moved closer. Their noses stretched out in long, pointed daggers, their limbs sharper than the spider spirit's legs, and their compound eyes burned with a singular flame. Saki tried to scream, but terror took her voice.

No time to think. No time to cry. She ran headlong into the wooden walkway around the house. The force knocked the wind out of her lungs and the wooden geta right off her feet. Saki clawed at the polished wood of the walkway. She pulled herself into the room and slammed her weight against the sliding paper door. It stuck in its frame, and the shadows of the swarm fell across the paper. With all of her strength, she leaned. The door gave a shudder, then snapped shut. The paper on the frame shook with a sound like hundreds of wet

leaves slapping against the side of the house, but nothing got through. No sound filtered inside except for the
buzz of cicadas.

Saki fell back into the covers strewn around her futon.
Her brother let out a long snore. Her head was buzzing
with exhaustion, and her heart was thundering with fear.
In a dizzy instant, her eyes drooped, and she sank her
head into the musty depths of Grandma's guest pillow.

CHAPTER 9

Saki's brother shook her awake to the smell of a hot breakfast.

"Get out of bed, lazy!" he called, already halfway through the door. A grin spread across his face. "You're in so much trouble. They're still trying to figure out what to do with you."

Saki tried to kick off her covers, but the muscles in her legs stung like they'd been set on fire. She picked herself up slowly, bracing against the wall for support. Now that she was home, she couldn't accept the night as anything more than a dream. But she felt as though she'd climbed a mountain, and the skin between her toes was rough and raw where the strap of her geta had rubbed. She could feel a thin layer of grime coating her face and legs. She scrubbed herself with soap and water in Grandma's bathroom yet couldn't quite rid herself of the dirt.

As she moved her old clothes off the futon, tiny pieces of glass clicked together beneath her nightshirt. Saki held the pouch of marbles in her hands for a moment, her heartbeat in her ears, and then stuffed the pouch into the pile of clothes beneath her underwear, where Jun would never find it.

If the night wasn't a dream, then neither was the curse.

Saki hesitated by the main room door, slid it open, and poked her nose inside. Her father, mother, and brother sat around a table of half-empty dishes, skillfully ignoring one another as usual. Grandma was nowhere to be found.

Her father spotted her over his newspaper. "Ah, you're up. Get in and have something to eat."

Saki slunk in, her shoulders hunched. As she lowered herself to the table, Jun kicked her from underneath. She opened her mouth to snap at him, but one glance at her mother's drawn lips made her close it again. Saki swished around the lukewarm soup in her bowl and picked at the floating leeks with her chopsticks.

"If she's in trouble, can I have her spending money?"

"No one's getting any spending money," their mother said. "We're driving Grandma to the valley supermarket this afternoon. Then we're taking her to lunch in Ota."

"Can we get ice cream?"

"The shopping is for Grandma, not for you. I don't want you two arguing either. Especially you." Saki's mother didn't have to point. The sharp look said everything. "And before we leave, you're going out to scrub those gravestones one more time."

"But—" Saki snapped her mouth shut the moment Grandma opened the door, a piece of paper crumpled in her hands.

"Oh, I don't see why they can't have a little treat for helping."

"After last night, they don't need any more coddling." Saki's father eyed her warily. "I still don't think we should have let her keep that blasted phone."

"Hush, both of you." Grandma tucked the slip of paper into her obi belt and bent to pick up a tray of picked-over breakfast dishes. "She's shown she's very sorry. I don't doubt she's learned her lesson. Let's spend our time on better things."

As she leaned forward, the slip of paper fell out. Saki plucked it off the tatami, but before she could summon the courage to speak up, Grandma had taken the tray of dishes back to the kitchen.

Saki's father turned the page of his newspaper. Her brother had dragged their mother into another room to argue his case for a new video game. Saki stuffed the slip of paper into her pants pocket and took her own tray off the table. She took it to the kitchen and set it by the sink as Grandma piled the dishes into different pools of soapy water. Saki took the piece of paper from her pocket. "Here, you dropped this."

Her grandmother looked up from her washing. "Ah,

that's my shopping list. I'll just…" Grandma puzzled at her wet hands. "Oh, dear. Could you put it somewhere dry, dear? I'll finish it when I'm through with these dishes."

"Maybe I could help you? Just tell me what else you need to write down."

"That's very sweet of you, dear, but the trouble is I've forgotten most of what I have in the house already…"

Saki found a pencil and tried to hold in a sigh. This would take a while.

True to her words, Grandma couldn't recall much off the top of her head, and some of what she did remember turned out to be wrong or too far out of date to be fit for human consumption. One bag of wakame seaweed crumbled into a dusty powder as soon as Saki picked it up to check the expiration date.

With grim determination, Saki bent to inspect each package label in the cabinets and strained on her tiptoes to check the recesses of the top cupboards. By the time they'd compiled a thorough shopping list, she wanted nothing more than to collapse in front of a fan, but one last question weighed on her mind. She set the list down on her way out and stopped halfway through door.

"Grandma, are you mad at me?"

Her grandmother stopped the water and turned from the sink, where the breakfast dishes gleamed on the drying rack. "I was sad for a little while, but I believe you're very sorry and your apology is enough. Like I told your father, I don't want to dwell on what's past. Now, do you need any of your laundry done? I want to put out some washing to dry before we go out this afternoon."

Saki shook her head. Grandma gave a wobbly nod and turned the faucet on again. Saki lingered by the door frame, then she remembered the marbles.

"Wait. There's something I need to show you."

Saki hurried back to the room she shared with her brother. Jun was slumped on the floor, pouting. She rummaged through her pile of laundry under the ruse of folding it, setting the pouch of flat marbles by her feet. When she tried to smuggle them out to the kitchen, the glass clicked together, and Jun turned.

"What're those?" he asked, craning his neck for a better view.

"Nothing," Saki said. "Girl stuff."

Jun flopped back down on the floor. "Ew…"

When Saki returned, Grandma wiped off her hands on her apron and took the bag with care. She opened the top and squeezed a piece of glass between her fingers. Her brow furrowed.

"Wherever did you find these? I used to play with toys like these when I was a little girl." She spread half a dozen marbles out on her hand.

Saki shrugged. "I just found them around."

Grandma looked her in the eye. The warm mist of nostalgia turned into sharp and urgent words. "Were you playing in the woods?"

"I wasn't playing," Saki said, averting her eyes. "I was just taking a walk."

"You must be very careful in the woods. Do you understand me?" Saki's grandmother held her shoulder with an iron grip. "The mountain can be very dangerous, especially at night. If you see something strange, you should run away as fast as you can."

"Grandma…have you seen things on the mountain at night?"

Before she could get an answer, Saki's father poked his head into the kitchen. "Mom, Saki, are you ready? We'll need to get going if we want to be back in time for the dance tonight."

Grandma handed the marbles back to Saki. "Keep these in a safe place," she said as she closed Saki's fingers over the pouch.

Saki hurried back to her room for her purse. With a glance over her shoulder at Jun, she stashed the marbles in the folds of her futon. Her mother called from the front door, and her brother dragged himself up with a groan. Before Saki closed the door behind them, she cast one last glance at the doors that opened to the mountain. A gentle breeze rustled the leaves, but no outline of a path appeared.

❦ ❦ ❦

During the hour it took to reach the town in the valley, Grandma sat in the passenger seat talking to Saki's father. Saki never got a proper answer to the question she'd asked in the kitchen. By the time they reached the bottom of the hill, Grandma seemed to have forgotten the conversation entirely.

As soon as she was close enough for a phone signal, Saki delved into her messages. As expected, Hana was angry with her for taking too long between replies. Saki scanned the messages she'd been accused of snubbing, but they were no different than the last dozen. Hana was still mad at Kaori, though the boy who'd started the mess didn't seem to matter anymore, and her new purpose in life was to make Kaori miserable.

There were a bunch of messages about a trip to the karaoke parlor. Hana wanted another girl to tell Kaori about the party, so it would seem like they were inviting her back into the group. After a few hours in the karaoke parlor, some of the girls would leave for the bathroom and the rest would go out to get a "surprise" for Kaori, as an apology for the way they'd treated her. Of course, Hana made it clear that no one was to come back. The real surprise would be when Kaori had to pay for everyone's time at the karaoke parlor out of her own pocket. Part of Hana's scheme was to have Saki message Kaori about how jealous she was to be missing all the fun. The plan was set for tomorrow night.

Saki closed the messages without another thought. She would blame the bad reception for her silence. She'd spent years playing Hana's games, and now it was time for a break. It was disturbing how much pleasure Hana took in trying to break another person's spirit.

The more she thought, the angrier she felt. She was angry at Hana for being a bully, she was angry at Yuko for being the same, and she was angry at Maeda for being right about everything. But more than all of them, Saki was angry at herself.

When they returned to Grandma's house, Saki and her brother carried packs of toilet paper from the car while their mother and father handled the heavier groceries. As Saki and her brother stuffed the rolls of toilet paper into every square centimeter of Grandma's bathroom cabinets, their mother called out from the main room.

"When you kids are finished in there, come out so that Grandma can help you put on your yukata for the dance!"

Jun made a face, and Saki bit back a groan. Grandma had set all of her dressing tools out on the floor and laid out each of the stiff cotton yukata on the tatami.

"Out of those clothes," Saki's mother ordered, thrusting a set of plain white underclothes into Saki's hands. "Jun, your shirt and shorts are in the bedroom."

Jun wasted no time disappearing, covering his snicker as he ducked past his sister. Saki was stuck, nothing else to do but wait patiently as Grandma wrapped her with the yukata and tied sash after sash to adjust the fit. Grandma was diligent but worked so slowly that Saki's legs ached from standing in one place so long.

Grandma finished the knot in the obi, then moved to the front to inspect the fit. Saki struggled to breathe through the tight knot around her waist. She hadn't tried to take any steps yet, but she suspected her knees would have their own troubles.

"How lovely. You remind me of myself when I was a little girl."

"Show us a little smile." Her father came out from the front porch and aimed his camera at her face.

The light from the flash left little spots in Saki's vision. They drifted in front of her like fireflies as she tried to escape to her room, but her mother caught her by the shoulders and turned her around.

"Not so fast. We'll fix up your brother, and then we're all going down to the dance. Stay out here until we leave."

"Aren't you going to wear a yukata too?" Saki asked, eyes narrowing to inspect the flowery blouse and the khaki pants her mother wore.

Her mother pushed her toward the door. "Your father and I are going to trade off with the camera."

"How convenient."

"I'll go get your brother." Her mother's frown was as humorless as her tone. To Saki's delight, her brother had to be dragged out by the scruff of his neck before Grandma could fit him.

The discomfort of the yukata grew tenfold when they were stuffed into the backseat of the car. If Saki leaned back too far, the bow of her obi dug into her spine, so she spent the whole trip down the winding road tilted forward like a queasy teapot. She usually handled motion sickness well, but by the time they reached the foot of the hill, she was blue with nausea.

Everyone at the community center had dressed up for the Bon dance. The dance was part of the Obon Festival celebrations, another way to welcome the spirits of the dead, though each region had its unique songs and steps. The Bon dance popular in the area around the village was a lively performance with lots of movement, though it was easy enough once the dancer had memorized the steps.

A platform for the musicians was raised in the middle of the space, surrounded by strings of lanterns. The order of the food stalls had shuffled, but their menus of fried, battered, and grease-laden snacks remained the same. A few dancers were already circling the platform, moving to the beat of the taiko drums.

Saki's father set up the camera tripod as her mother herded the rest of the family over to pose for a shot.

"Right there. Hold it. Hold it," her father said. The camera stalled and beeped out an error message. "What? Wait right there. I know exactly what's wrong. This blasted thing…"

"Why couldn't we have done this before we left Grandma's house?" Saki shrank from the attention and glared back pointedly at the villagers who'd looked over to size up the out-of-towners. "They're staring like we're zoo animals…"

"She's right, you know," Grandma said before Saki's parents could object. "Tonight is for dancing, not standing around."

"Actually, Grandma, I wanted to watch for a while…" Saki tried to cushion the words as best she could, but the only thing worse than being gawked at while posing for photos was being gawked at while doing a stupid dance. Everyone dancing around the platform was either very young or very old, not a single person even close to her age.

"You two go with your grandmother." Saki's mother turned her attention to the camera. "Did you take the other photos off the memory card before we came? Here, let me take a look…"

Saki would have given just about anything to dissolve

into the ground. All out of excuses, Saki and Jun exchanged pained glances as Grandma led them toward the dancers.

"I'll run if you run," Jun whispered.

Saki rolled her eyes. "Just do it for Grandma, okay? It won't last forever."

Saki went through the motions of the dance. She stepped to the side and clapped. As each one of her feet moved, she held up the arm that matched. The dance was simple and repetitive, and the steps kept the dancers revolving around the drum platform, creating an endless circle of moving and clapping. After only a few minutes, Saki was bored out of her skull. Only when Grandma looked her way did she make any attempt to smile.

After their third revolution, Grandma's cheeks were tinged red. The rest of her skin had turned white, and there was a slight catch in her breath after every turn. Saki remembered her father's warning about the "condition."

"Hey, Grandma, why don't we take a break for some ice cream?"

"What a wonderful idea." There was a slight wheeze in the words that hadn't been in her voice earlier in the day. "Oh my. Where did Junnosuke run off to?"

"Nowhere good, I'm sure. I'll find him." Saki sighed and glanced around the community center lot. He never listened. "Let's meet at the food stalls."

After Grandma left to catch her breath, Saki caught

a glimpse of a familiar yukata pattern on the other side of the lot. Jun had his back to the dance. He leaned up against a bicycle rack as he talked to a group of taller kids in plain clothes.

Yuko's blond highlight shone under the glow of the festival's electric lanterns. After pushing away the flutter of embarrassment at being caught tied up in a stiff yukata, Saki squared her shoulders and marched straight ahead.

The village kids saw her approach and pulled their attention away from Jun.

"Hey, if it isn't Tokyo!" called Yuko. "We were just talking to your little brother."

Saki yanked on Jun's sleeve. "Come on. We're going to get ice cream."

"I'll be there in a second." Jun pulled his arm away with a scowl.

"Yeah, let the kid stay a while," said Yuko.

"I'm not a kid!"

Saki gave her brother a shove. "Go, or I'll tell Mom that you skipped the dance."

Jun stuck out his tongue as he passed, but he trudged off toward the food stalls, the sleeves of his yukata inflating like windsocks when he burst into a run. Saki turned, crossed her arms, and glared at Yuko.

"I thought you guys were supposed to be in the city tonight."

Yuko shrugged. "Change of plans. Besides, now we get to see how cute you look in your little yukata."

"Don't make fun of me. It took more time to put on than whatever you fell into this morning."

"Wow, you sure are cranky. Do you have your obi tied too tight or what?"

"You guys left me to take the fall. How am I supposed to feel?"

Yuko exchanged looks with her group. "Are you mad about that? Jeez, get over it. What did you think would happen when you rang that bell? We didn't want to get caught."

"But you were okay running off without me so that I could take the blame."

Yuko closed her eyes and shook her head. "Well, you're still here, so I'm guessing they didn't kill you or anything. And you didn't rat us out either, which means you're cool in our book. So if nothing happened, what's the big deal?"

"You certainly didn't stick around to make sure."

"Look, I said I was sorry—"

"No, you didn't, actually," Saki cut in.

Yuko put on a fake smile. She seemed to be losing patience. "Well, I'm saying it now. Happy?"

Saki sighed. "Not really, no…"

"Great." Yuko put her hands together. "Because I have

the best plan for tonight. I saw this thing in the graveyard last time, these really old stones…"

Saki couldn't believe what she was hearing. Did they think she was stupid? She bit the inside of her cheek and took a moment to calm down. When she gave her answer, she locked eyes with Yuko. "I'm not interested."

Yuko blinked. "What do you mean 'not interested'? What else are you gonna do?"

"Whatever it is, I'll be doing it by myself."

"Fine. We were just being nice, seeing as you don't know anyone else here. But we'll go without you. Your loss."

Saki smiled. Watching Yuko try to play cool made her next move all the more satisfying. "No, I don't think you understand me. You're not going back to that graveyard."

The rest of the group went still. One of the boys leaned forward. "What, did something happen?"

Saki kept her eyes on Yuko. "You won't be going."

"You can't tell us what to do," the other girl sneered.

"No," Saki replied. "But I can tell my dad who made all that noise last night."

"You won't. You wouldn't dare. Not with what we could do to you."

Saki shrugged a shoulder. "I'm already stuck here in the middle of nowhere, aren't I? How much worse can it get?"

Yuko made an ugly face and a sound as though she might reply, but then turned and stormed off. The other village kids followed in her wake, a rather sad procession. They cast glances back to Saki, as if still trying to understand what had just happened.

Now, if only she could talk to Hana like that. But something like that, where she'd have to stay and live with what she'd done, took more courage than she thought she had. As Saki turned to look back at the dance, another pair of eyes stared back at her. Maeda.

Instead of averting eye contact and pretending that she hadn't been staring, Maeda broke out of her dance formation and headed toward her.

Saki looked away and crossed her arms again, though the long sleeves of her yukata made the gesture difficult. Maeda jogged up, the lines of her yellow yukata perfectly straight and her hair done up in a bun with ribbons.

"I saw you dancing with your grandmother," she said. "I was helping one of the kindergarteners learn the steps. Otherwise, I would have said hello. Are you having a good time?"

Saki snorted. "Are you for real?"

Maeda blinked. "I don't understand what you mean."

"I mean, I can't tell if you're being honest or not." Saki bit her tongue. She hadn't meant to say it like that.

Or at least she hadn't meant it to sound so mean. She didn't know why being around the other girl made her act this way.

The rumor about Saki being a stuck-up Tokyo girl had supposedly started with Maeda, though Yuko had been the one to actually say the words. But at least Yuko had been more obviously untrustworthy. She still couldn't tell with Maeda.

"And I can never tell if you're making fun of me or if you're just insecure." Maeda's face remained impassive. "Or maybe you're just bored. City girls are probably used to more excitement. Did you end up having fun at the graveyard last night?"

Saki shuffled her feet. "I never wanted to go. It was Yuko's lame idea."

"They tried to scare you, didn't they?" Maeda was now looking straight at her. Saki couldn't read her eyes.

Saki kicked a rock on the pavement. "Look, I told you last night that I could handle them. If you want something from me, just say so."

"What do you mean?"

Saki sighed. "Isn't that what you came over here for, to say 'I told you so'? Well, don't bother asking for a bribe or anything. I'm in big trouble already, so there's not much you could do to make it worse."

Color rose to Maeda's cheeks. She frowned and took a

half step backward. "I wasn't going to tattle on you. I just wanted to make sure you were okay."

She seemed upset, and Saki didn't know what to say next. "Sorry, I just thought—"

"That I was like Yuko or whoever else you're friends with in Tokyo? Not everyone is that selfish."

"Hey," said Saki. "Thinking that way is just normal. Everyone has to look out for themselves."

"No," Maeda told her. "It's not normal, especially if you can't even trust the people you call friends. You shouldn't have to try so hard to impress someone just to make them like you."

"Come on, you're so naïve." Saki was starting to lose patience. Sure, it would be nice to act without being judged by other people, but life didn't work that way. "Weren't you trying to impress me at the grave cleaning? Isn't that why you kept 'helping' me like I was too dumb to figure it out on my own?"

Maeda looked as though she was about to cry. "I was just trying to be nice. You came from a big city and didn't know anyone, so I thought I would talk to you. But you don't care about meeting people or making friends. You just want to get out of here as fast as you can. This might be a small village, but we've got more than you think. If you can't even bother to look around and see it, then maybe you really are stuck-up."

The tirade stunned Saki into silence. She couldn't meet the other girl's eyes. As words hung unanswered in the air between them, Maeda turned back to the dancers and wiped her yukata sleeve under her eyes. She spoke again without looking at Saki.

"Well, if you think you know so much, I guess you don't need naïve people around to weigh you down. I won't bother you anymore. To tell you the truth, I was only trying to be nice because your grandmother asked me to. So there. I hope you can get back to your city soon."

Maeda walked back to the dance, leaving Saki completely alone. Anger and guilt twisted her stomach into knots. Lately, none of Saki's relationships were turning out right. First Yuko, then the fox, then Maeda… Saki was so caught up in feeling sorry for herself that she didn't notice a voice calling out her name. Her mother waved through the crowd.

"There you are. Grandma's been waiting for you. You can't just keep running off without telling anyone. I thought we talked about this last night!"

Saki resigned herself to the scolding. All of her fighting spirit had gone with Maeda's confession. "I know. I'm sorry."

❧ ❧ ❧

In the car on the way home, the color had returned to Grandma's face. She reached over and patted Saki on the knee.

"I think I had more fun tonight than I've had in a very long time."

Saki did her best to return the smile despite the squirming guilt in her stomach. She didn't really deserve Grandma's forgiveness, but she was glad for it. At least she could make one person happy, even if she was making a mess of almost everything else.

As the house came into view, Saki turned her eyes to the woods. The night obscured everything but the vague shapes of the trees. After all of the problems she'd been having in the real world, an encounter with a hungry spirit from the Night Parade might actually be a nice break. But with the fox long gone, would she be able to cross over at all? The fox had mentioned two other guides, but Saki knew nothing about what they would look like, act like, or—most important of all—what they would want from her.

Maeda had been wrong about one thing, at least. Saki had seen part of the village that no other living person would ever believe.

CHAPTER 10

The floorboards whined and jarred Saki out of her uneasy slumber. The old house creaked and cracked. Her grandfather used to say that the house was simply "settling" into the earth and the complaints of a few wooden beams were no cause for alarm. Still, sweat collected on Saki's skin underneath the covers.

The thatched roof shifted against the attic. The paper in the shoji doors rustled as the frames rattled in their tracks. The woven reeds in the tatami mats shifted against one another. Saki stared wide-eyed at the dark ceiling. She tossed sideways, turned her back on the door to the woods, and kept the pouch of flat marbles tied to one wrist.

The rhythmic creak of the wooden planks from the walkway outside her room sounded like footsteps. The dust that moved through the air felt like breath against her cheek. Her mind made hands out of the shadows, and she heard scraping in the frames, like the slow opening of a door. Saki shot up, clutching her phone, the metal charm, and the glass marbles close to her heart.

Her brother was still asleep, and she was sure that her parents couldn't sneak around half so well. Grandma's old body would have creaked louder than the house... The moonlight cast silhouettes of the forest trees against the paper doors. The hands clawed at her again.

"Who's there?" she whispered into the dark.

The creaking noises ceased abruptly, leaving her brother's snores as the only sound in the room. Saki waited, her heart pumping in time with the cicadas' cries outside. After a few long breaths, she lowered herself back down to her futon, but she kept her eyes trained on the shoji panels of the door. As her head brushed the pillow, the door to the forest wiggled open a finger's width.

Saki slid her legs out from under her blankets. She tried to muffle the sound as best she could, slowly peeling back each layer of her sheets. She pressed the charm and the phone into her pocket and tugged the string tied to her wrist. As she reached out for the door, the dark silhouettes blew across the paper panels and turned the shadows into great black wings.

"Hello?" she called in a voice smaller than a whisper. "Are you a friend of the fox?"

Saki opened the door wide enough to peek through. She pressed one eye to the opening and peered out onto the empty walkway. There was no fox, nor any other living creature out beyond the perimeter of the house, and she was too far back to see if the shadow-strapped geta had been laid out beneath the walkway.

The anticipation was maddening. Every rustle or flicker of shadow seemed like a spirit crouching to snatch at her. She pushed the door open wide enough to slide through sideways and kept her hands against the walls of the house as she peered over the edge. She thought she saw two bumps in the darkness. She took a half step closer.

A pair of wooden geta sat underneath the walkway overhang, perpendicular with the shadow. Saki glanced around, but there were no spirits to be found. Her brother's snores echoed from the house, and the cicadas cried against the bark of the tree trunks. The shoes might have been an old pair of Grandma's misplaced during the day. Perhaps they'd been there all along. The most logical possibility, despite the dull ache still creeping through her legs, was that she had dreamt the entire story up, from the fox to the whole procession of spirits. The pain in her legs could have been from kicking off her covers during a vivid nightmare, and the marbles might have been stuck between the futon covers from the start.

A simple test would do the trick, and then she could sleep without interruption. Saki sat on the edge of the walkway and eased her feet into the wooden geta. From the shadow straps down to the way her feet fit into the wood, they were undoubtedly the same.

The moment her heels settled, the trees surrounding the house began to quiver. Their leaves rustled, and from the depths of their branches, hundreds of black wings burst forth. The wings circled overhead, blotting out the moon and pressing down onto the house. Saki dangled over the edge of the walkway. There was no time to rush back inside. She threw her hands over her head to shield her face as the mass of feathers bore down.

❦ ❦ ❦

Dust tickled the inside of her nose, and Saki woke with a violent sneeze. She was curled up on a stone floor in a dark room. She blinked, shifting the dust particles that had wedged themselves above her eyelids. Slowly she sat up in the dark and held out a hand. The walls around her were made from old wood riddled with holes. Moonbeams peeked through and swam across the dusty air before settling in blurry patches on the floor. She sniffed and sneezed again. The dust was drifting down from somewhere up in the vaulted ceiling. She tilted her chin up. Crouched among the rafters, a feathered spirit stared down at her over its blood-colored nose.

Saki screamed and reached for the pouch of marbles, but the ties tangled on her wrist.

The spirit craned its neck and clicked its claws. With a single motion, it dropped from its perch and landed before her on a pair of clawed feet. It stood upright, like a man, and wore a battered metal shoulder guard over one arm of its dark robe. Across the red skin of its face, inky feathers shone in the dusty moonlight. The smell of pipe smoke and carrion clogged Saki's nose along with the dust, and the orange glint in the creature's eyes silenced her scream.

The spirit cocked its head and poked its long nose into her face. "Is that your battle cry?" he asked, his sonorous voice somewhere between the firm pluck of a bowstring and the sharp whistle of an arrow cutting the sky.

Saki trembled as the spirit waited expectantly for an answer. She started twice before she could push out a word. "Are you…are you going to eat me?"

The spirit's nose brushed past her hair and sniffed. "Not today, humanchild. I prefer my meal flavored with glorious death on the battlefield. Also, insects."

Saki scooted herself away from the feathered spirit until her back hit the wooden wall. "If you don't mind, I'll be leaving now. I have to lift a curse…" She rose on shaky legs and felt the wall behind her for an opening until her fingers curled around the edges of a swinging door.

The spirit took a bobbing step toward her, the feathers on his crown rising in anger. "What insubordination! I took great care to recruit you, yet you cannot be bothered to await my briefing. Perhaps the fox is such an indulgent escort, but I will not allow my command to be disrespected." The spirit flared all of his feathers until he was at least twice his original size. His orange eyes stared down his beak nose as he loomed over her.

Saki held up her hands. "I'm sorry! I didn't mean to offend you! I'm just really confused. You did sort of kidnap me, you know." The spirit shrank down a little at the apology. Saki narrowed her eyes. "So the fox sent you to help, huh?"

The feathered spirit jerked his head to and fro as though he were shaking off beads of water. "That swindler has no authority over me! Her trickery is an insult to her office, and her kind are a blemish upon the Night Parade. I deign to succeed her role only because it is my duty, not my choice."

"At first, I thought she was pretty nice…" Saki brushed the dust from her face as her panic began to retreat. "But I guess she tricks everyone, doesn't she?"

"In some ways," the feathered spirit explained, "she cannot help it. We are all bound by our nature."

"So what kind of spirit are you?" Saki asked.

The feathered spirit straightened his arms at his sides and bent into a stiff bow. "I am a tengu, bound to defend this shrine from impurity and malevolence. What is your rank, humanchild?"

"Um, thirteen? I'm in my second year of junior high…" Saki didn't think this was what the tengu meant, but he seemed to consider the answer.

"Ah," he said. "You are moving up, I see. But be cautious; the further a soldier rises in rank, the less he can see his feet."

Saki nodded without understanding. "If you're my guide, where should I go first?"

The tengu swept his arm up and pointed past her to the door set into the wall.

Saki turned her back to the tengu and set her hands against the wood. The hinges creaked as the door eased open and wind rushed against her face. The wooden room she'd woken up in was one of many watchtowers set atop a high stone wall. None of the holes in the walls were visible from the outside, nor had she felt a single gust of wind. Saki didn't spend much time worrying over this. She was focused on the high stone wall they stood atop and the alarming knowledge that if she fell from the edge, she would have a long time to scream before reaching the ground. Saki bit her tongue and stepped back from the drop-off.

Inside the confines of the wall, overgrown gardens choked dozens of half-finished roads and long, low buildings. The haphazard arrangement of the complex made a labyrinth of paths that wound through the grounds in dizzying curls. At the far end of everything rose a towering castle that shone as bright as the moon. Steep stone repelling walls jutted up to form the base, and the golden tiled roof rose even higher than where Saki and the tengu stood. Settled atop the stone walls, the castle blazed white, gold, and green.

Saki stood in awe. "What is that place?"

The tengu bobbed to her side and poked his great nose over the edge of the wall. "That is the seat of the great spirits, the palace where the Midlight Prince dwells. There are ancient forces in that house that few have ever held audience with. Do you sincerely wish to break this curse?"

"I don't really have much of a choice, do I?"

"The desire toward life is a choice in itself," said the tengu.

Saki sighed. "Then yes. Of course I want to break the curse. Just show me the way."

"The only way up is through the Path of the Gods," the tengu told her. "But it is not so easy to find."

Saki untangled the pouch of marbles around her wrist as she eyed the tengu. "Well, can't we just use your wings? You can fly, right?"

"Look carefully." The tengu raised his head and pointed his nose to the sky.

Flickers of shadow and reflections in the moonlight became more distinct. The air was thick with giant insect wings. Saki shrank back against the watchtower door.

The tengu raised his own feathered wings. "Do not be so quick to retreat, humanchild. You may thank your first escort, the nefarious fox, for this inconvenience. The insect soldiers are on their guard now for any suspicious happenings, including a humanchild who has wandered into the Night Parade."

Saki counted the marbles still left in her pouch, but even by looking at them, she knew there wouldn't be nearly enough for every member of the swarm. "What do we do?"

"We must stay out of sight." He surveyed the landscape with a sweep of his nose. "The gardens below are full of their spies. Do you see the buildings between the paths?"

"Those paths are like a maze. We'll never get through if we don't think of some way to mark where we've been."

"So we will not take the paths," the tengu told her. "If we advance under the protection of a roof, the horde will not be able to spot us."

"But none of those buildings are connected!" Saki protested. "Some look only half-finished. We'll get caught for sure."

The tengu blew air from his beak of a nose. "Just because you cannot see the connections does not mean they do not exist. The buildings will keep us from being detected from the air, but in other ways, they will be more treacherous than the paths or gardens. What weapons are you trained with?"

"I have these." Saki shook the pouch of flat marbles.

The tengu nodded vigorously, a gleam in his orange eyes. "Those are powerful, indeed. Keep them close to you at all times. The shrine complex teems with spirits, not all of whom are kindhearted."

"I also have this, if you think it might help." Saki felt for the phone in her pocket.

The moment the tengu saw it, he recoiled as if he'd been struck. Saki immediately shoved the phone back in the folds of her clothes. He let out a breath and lowered the feathers he'd splayed in alarm.

"Never, ever display such a thing without the direst of need. Only if your very life is in danger, do you understand? That object has no place in our world. You will surely lose your way if you use it flippantly."

Saki pushed the phone down deeper into her pocket. The tengu took a moment to compose himself as they stood staring out into the maze of disjointed buildings.

He inhaled with a sharp sound. "There is no time to waste. We must make the first plunge and position ourselves to infiltrate the compound."

"So…that means we're sneaking in?"

The tengu hesitated. "We are infiltrating the compound."

Saki tried not to snort. "Yeah, that still counts."

"Now, look alive. We must remain vigilant. There is a ladder no more than a dozen paces in front of you. Do you see it?"

Saki took a few steps toward the outline of an old bamboo ladder. "Uh, that doesn't look very safe. I don't think it's going to hold one of us, let alone two."

"Of course," the tengu explained, "I shall not be climbing. I shall track your progress from the air and descend to meet you. Is this agreeable?"

"Why don't you just take me down with you?"

The tengu cleared his throat. "The laws of aerodynamics dictate that with the addition of your considerable weight—"

"Excuse me?"

"Your considerable weight," the tengu repeated, unfazed. "As I was saying, to allow for the angle of descent—"

"Stop. I get it. I'm climbing, all right?" Saki gritted her teeth, knelt near the edge of the wall, and tried to convince herself she wasn't scared. She frowned at the bamboo and pressed the top rung with the toe of her wooden geta. The ladder whined and bent but didn't break.

The tengu clicked his clawed feet against the stone wall. "Are you just going to sit there, looking at it?"

"Hey, don't nag me! Not all of us have wings to catch us if we fall," Saki muttered. She scooted closer to the edge and turned around to get a good foothold on the next rung. She tried to fix her attention on the cracks in the wall as she moved one foot after the other down the rickety bamboo ladder.

When all she could see overhead was the long shape of the tengu's nose poking over the wall, he called down to her. "Excellent work. Continue like this and you should be able to descend without detection."

Saki missed a step and nearly stopped her own heart. "Detection?" she called back. "You said we would be fine going this way!"

"I said"—the tengu cleared his throat again—"that once inside the compound, we should have less conventional troubles."

Saki's mouth went bone dry, but she forced down a heavy swallow. "So those giant bugs can get me up here?"

"The swarm will not pay attention to you here," the tengu replied, his voice much closer.

Saki breathed a sigh of relief and turned her head to see the spirit circling the air next to her.

"Of course, they will ignore you because they expect other spirits to finish you off before you reach the ground... But do not let that discourage you!"

"Don't you think you should have told me that before I started?"

The tengu sailed lower and ignored the question. If

she wasn't clutching the bamboo so hard, Saki would have reached out and plucked one of those inky feathers right off his back.

Every step down was a gamble against a sudden snap of bamboo. Every second wasted in hesitation was a gamble against being detected by terrifying spirits. She dug her nails into the ladder's rungs and tried to keep a steady pace.

With the squeaking and creaking of the bamboo, the howling of the wind, and the beating wings of the tengu, Saki didn't hear the clicking until the sound shook the sides of the ladder. Above her, packs of flat-shelled spirits descended in droves. They thrashed their front pincers and raked their barbed legs down the old bamboo as they came. They scuttled sideways, and their eyes poked out of their shells atop twig-like antennae. The crab spirits were not deterred by the creaking of the bamboo ladder. They swarmed over every surface until the structure sagged with their weight.

Against all the good advice she'd ever heard, Saki looked down. Another half of the ladder's length stretched out below her. There was no way she would make it to the bottom before the crabs caught up. Her hands were slick with sweat, and she lost her grip on the bamboo for a brief, breath-locking second. With all of her strength, she pushed her weight against the wall to keep her body from falling backward. As her fingers knotted together to secure her grip, she steadied herself.

"A little advice would be nice," Saki called to the tengu, her voice shaking with panic.

"Move faster," the tengu suggested. "Or face them in combat."

"Oh, right." Saki began to move again, clutching the rungs harder than she ever had before. "Since I have both hands free and all."

Her sarcasm didn't impress the tengu, if he understood the concept at all. He flew lower and lower until Saki lost sight of him completely.

"A lot of help you've been," she growled to empty air.

The tide of crabs was close enough for Saki to see the spikes protruding from their legs. They'd probably go for the hands first, then the face, then the rest of her… Saki shuddered and skipped a rung as the ladder whined and sagged closer to the wall.

The mass of darkened shapes on the ground were now distinct trees and garden paths. Just her luck. At the first sign that solid ground was near, Saki was out of time.

She closed her eyes as the first wave of crabs scuttled down the bamboo rails by her fingers. Their legs poked her skin and left prickles of pain down her arms, but none of them lingered, not even to tear at her with their pincers. When Saki opened her eyes, the crabs were already a dozen rungs below her.

She let go of the breath she'd been holding and tried to rein in the wild beating of her heart. With a thrust of his wings, the tengu flew up to meet her. She gave a shaky smile and leaned against the bamboo.

"Have you surrendered so easily, humanchild?"

"They didn't want to fight," Saki said with a sigh of relief. "I guess my luck is catching up to me."

The tengu's bloodred skin was livid. "Relaxation is the surest path to a swift defeat. You were not confronted because there are easier means of disposing of you. You have allowed the enemy a great tactical advantage by your negligence!"

Saki's puzzlement was interrupted by vibrations along the bamboo. The supporting poles buzzed as the ladder gently swayed from side to side.

Near the ground, the crabs had all gathered at one point. With their claws and their pincer jaws, they sawed at the bamboo. If they cut away enough of the ladder supports, the whole structure—and Saki along with it—would go tumbling down in a mess of splinters and shattered bones.

Saki bit back a curse. Working the muscles in her arms and legs furiously, she propelled herself down. She didn't need to get to the bottom, just close enough to jump to the ground without harm.

The ladder moved away from the wall, pitching her back. The bamboo fibers beneath her strained and cracked under the shifting weight. The sawing of the crab spirits stopped.

Every one of Saki's movements stopped too. Even if she commanded her arms and legs to work, there was no place to run.

The tengu dove past her. "Release the ladder before it falls and crushes you!"

With no option left but to follow orders, Saki released her grip on the bamboo. The tengu wheeled in the air and dove for another pass. He stretched out his claws to grab at her. In a single moment of clarity through her thundering panic, Saki reached out to him. Her fingers grasped at his clawed foot as he curled his toes around her wrist.

The tengu slowed her fall, but the sudden new weight on his wings spun them out of control. With a snap of feathers, they dropped a full three stories. Right before they hurtled to the ground, the tengu ceased flapping and extended his wings to their full length.

Tree branches rushed at Saki's face. The leaves and the supple branches spared her from the crushing force of the impact, but they didn't save her from a barrage of stinging welts and cuts. Once they tumbled to a halt, Saki held fast to a thick branch as the tengu struggled to free his wings from a tangle of twigs. Her feet dangled beneath her, the weight dragging her down. She dug deeper for the will to cling on, but her drained muscles spasmed in betrayal.

From within the canopy of tree branches, a multitude of beady eyes stared out at her. A sudden spike of energy rushed back into Saki's limbs. She half turned her head to look for the tengu without letting her sight stray from the shapes moving in the tree.

"How close are we to the ground?" she whispered.

The tengu swiveled his head to look at the same sea of eyes. "Falling would be unadvisable."

Saki crawled backward along the branch, away from the center of the tree. The wood sagged, and she held on with all of her might. With one hand, Saki dug into her pouch for a marble.

With the black eyes came another horde of crabs. They moved in from every angle, up the base of the trunk and through the leaves at the end of the branches, until Saki and the tengu had no other exit. She pinched the marble between her fingers but hesitated to throw it. If she attacked the crabs, getting down the tree would still be a problem. If she used the marble to get down, the crabs might follow and attack anyway.

The flat piece of glass began to shift underneath her fingers. The marble inflated until her hand could no longer contain it.

"What are you doing?" demanded the tengu.

"I-I don't know!"

The marble popped out of Saki's grip, rolled onto the branch, and exploded.

She found herself falling for the second time. Dozens of crab claws snapped open and shut as Saki and the tengu, squawking out a battle cry, tumbled past them. She thrust out her hands and shut her eyes to brace for the impact of the ground, but her body gave a jerk upward.

She was covered with tiny, pearlescent bubbles. A few of the bubbles on her back had inflated like balloons to slow her fall. On the tree, crabs were falling from the branches, covered in the same foam of bubbles. These ones appeared to have stiffened, locking the crab joints in place.

As Saki floated closer to the ground, the bubbles inflated to cushion the landing. She hung on top of them for a split second before they popped, dropping her into the dirt next to a litter of immobilized crabs.

The tengu landed next to her and shook his feathers free from his own share of bubbles, which seemed to serve no function other than to annoy him. The rest of Saki's bubbles fell off when she stood, dissolving into thin air the moment they touched the earth. From her position on the ground, the tree and the wall both loomed impossibly high. A few paces behind her was the first of many disconnected shrine buildings.

"Let's not do that again," Saki said.

"This was only the first obstacle," the tengu warned her. "The paths through the shrine will present many challenges. Steel yourself for the trials ahead. We may be able to fool the less powerful spirits for a while, but we must each adopt a fitting disguise."

The tengu's figure rippled. His robes and his armor softened into fuzzy black down. Each feather shook as his red nose hardened and shrank. He jumped into the air with a flip. When he returned, the barbaric figure was a small black bird. His red nose had transformed into a beak and a train of black feathers burst out at his tail, though his orange eyes remained as piercing as ever. He flapped in the air before resting his clawed feet on Saki's shoulder. She stared for a moment, then recalled that of the strange occurrences she'd witnessed in the last two days, this was one of the milder ones.

"Not bad. Unfortunately, they don't teach us that trick in junior high. We'll have to find my disguise in there somewhere." She began to circle the small building. "Where's the door on this thing?"

"You shall not find a door here."

"Of course not. That would be too easy."

"We'll have to crawl beneath." The tengu bobbed his head at the dark gap beneath the raised floor. "There is a hidden way that will deliver us to the compound's interior."

"I was afraid you were going to say something like that." Saki grimaced at the thought of crawling around in the dirt, but compared to dangling in the air at the mercy of a swarm of angry crabs, any form of solid ground was more than welcome. She rolled up her sleeves and bit her tongue.

CHAPTER 11

After Saki pushed up a loosened tatami mat and let her eyes adjust to the light, she found herself in a storeroom piled high with chests and large pieces of covered furniture. She propped the mat against a wall and pulled herself up onto the floor. The tengu dug his bird claws into her shoulder and flapped his wings for balance, kicking up clouds of dust. Saki sneezed and coughed to clear her nose and throat, but her eyes itched fiercely, and she held her hand up to her mouth to filter the air as she breathed. When the clouds of dust settled, she took off her wooden geta and tucked them under one arm. She stood up and brushed the dirt off her knees as she took stock of the room.

The storeroom was lined with ceremonial weapons that had rusted all the way through. Stacks of chests were piled across the floor, with only a small path carved out as a walkway among the boxes. Saki sneezed again as the tengu appraised the items. He hopped off her shoulder and onto the top of a chest.

"We can use this room to outfit you properly. Everyone passing through the compound must display their rank and title through their dress. We must select something that will keep the inhabitants from asking too many questions. Open that chest there, on your right."

Saki cracked the lid open and saw nothing but silk shoes. "There're some sandals in here. Should I pick out some slippers to wear inside?"

"Why not use the pair underneath your arm?"

"But these are—" Saki grabbed the wooden geta to show him, but they had changed their shape and become two thin house slippers. The shadow straps still arched from the base, which was now soft and pliable.

"Quickly," the tengu said. "We do not have time to dawdle. Put those on and open the next chest."

Saki dropped the shadow-strapped slippers to the floor and slid her feet back inside. She opened the next chest along the wall and pulled the tip of a glistening feather robe from the top of the pile. The material was opaque, lighter than anything Saki had ever worn. The tengu hopped closer and clicked his beak.

"No, those are far too flamboyant. Such fine robes surely belong to spirits of very high standing. If you are mistaken for one of them or accused of stealing, you will have quite a deal of trouble. Try another chest," the tengu said. "We want not to be seen. You need something to make you invisible."

Saki replaced the feathered robe with a sigh. Her fingers lingered on the softness even as she began to close the lid. To quell her disappointment, she flipped open the next chest.

"Oh yes, these will do!" The tengu perched on the mouth of the chest and peered down at the stack of straw cloaks packed inside. Saki pulled out the top cloak, and the woven straw rustled and scratched against her skin.

She raised an eyebrow. "This? They'll hear me coming before they even see me. This is hardly invisible."

"Just wait and see for yourself. Wrap the cloak around your shoulders and pull it over your head," the tengu instructed.

"If you say so…" Saki put on the cloak but didn't feel any stealthier. "Like this?"

"Excellent." He hopped onto her shoulder and nestled himself into the straw until he was nothing more than the tip of a red beak poking out from her shoulder. "Now you are ready to proceed."

Saki found the storeroom door, pulled the sliding screen, and poked her head into the corridor beyond. It stretched out both ways, without an end in sight. The halls seemed to be deserted, and a number of doors dotted the walls on each side. At the tengu's urging, Saki stepped out onto the wooden floor of the compound.

"This part of the compound is very far from the main

shrine, so the security will not be as stringent. Only lower officials frequent these areas. You can relax for the moment, but do not allow yourself to become careless."

Saki set off in the direction of the great castle she'd seen far at the end of the walls. As she walked, she passed identical doors, hallways, and courtyard openings. Everything looked the same, and there was no way to tell how far or how long they'd been walking. Saki's legs began to tire, and even with the cushioning of the shadow slippers, her feet were getting sore. She tried to move faster, but the hurry only earned her labored breaths and a roll of sweat down her back where the straw cloak scratched at her skin. When she couldn't take the endless monotony anymore, Saki slowed down to catch her breath.

The tengu poked at her shoulder with his beak. "What are you doing? We've not even begun to breach the middle compound."

"How long does this hallway go on? I feel like I've been walking for hours." Saki took a seat on the floor. "I need a little break, okay?"

"This is completely out of line!" the tengu protested. "You cannot linger in the middle of the corridor. What if someone were to catch you idling about?"

A few dozen paces down the hallway, one of the identical doors flung open. A pair of dogs wearing court clothes stood at the doorway, propped up on their hind legs like courtiers, with tall, square hats perched between their ears.

"Aha!" one dog spirit cried. "We heard someone making noise out here while Her Ladyship was trying to sleep!"

Saki stood up with a start. Their billowing scholars' robes blocked the path deeper into the complex, and from the way their jaws were set, it looked as though they had no intention of moving. Saki bowed and tried to appear apologetic. This was the last thing she needed.

"I-I'm sorry, I thought these rooms were empty," she said. "I didn't know anyone was trying to sleep. If you just let me pass, I promise it won't happen again."

The dog spirits glanced at one another. One with crooked ears stroked his shaggy beard. They both leaned in to examine her.

"Unacceptable. Her Ladyship is deeply upset. Losing sleep will surely irritate her beyond measure," said the crooked-eared spirit.

The other, a pointy-eared spirit, nodded along in agreement. "If you truly wish to repent, you must pay Her Ladyship the courtesy of a visit."

They both hurried to Saki's side and took her arms in their paws. "Her Ladyship will be pleased to invite you to tea!"

"Tea?" Saki tried to struggle, but the dog spirits were

too strong. "I'd really prefer to just write a note or something. I'm sure a court lady doesn't want to see someone as boring as me…"

The tengu hissed in her ear: "You should have listened. I told you there were dangers along these halls. Now attend to your obligations." He burrowed back into her straw cloak without another word.

As annoying as the delay was, the dog spirits didn't look like they were any danger to her. The lady of theirs, however, was another matter. As the spirits pushed her into the room off the corridor, Saki braced herself for the worst.

Far from the dusty storeroom, Her Ladyship's living chambers spoke to the elegance of her station. An extensive collection of folding screens in many colorful designs littered the room. After closing the door and barring Saki's escape, the two dog spirits hurried to the corner and began to prepare a pot of tea.

Behind one of the folding screens, Her Ladyship yawned and shuffled. She poked her head out from the top and turned a pair of dark, human-like eyes on Saki.

"Oh my…I haven't had company in such a long time."

Her Ladyship's skin was pale white and her hair as dark as the night sky, the glossy locks arranged in a simple style on top of her head, though a few stray hairs had escaped their bonds and floated just above the chignon's sleek curve. The lady smiled with lips as red as camellia blossoms.

"Come in, child," she said. "You hide under that dreadful straw mat, but I can see you are truly a very pretty child. Come behind the screen and join me. Though I'm afraid I'm still a little disarrayed from my nap."

Saki bowed and walked around the lady's screen to meet her. She stopped so suddenly that she nearly toppled forward to the floor. Her Ladyship's head continued to smile, but her body lay several screens away, connected to the head by a long, curving neck that twisted like a snake across the room.

Behind Saki, one of the dog spirits gave a little cough. Her Ladyship's smile faltered. The floating head turned and began to wail.

"Oh, she can't stand the sight of me! Am I such a pitiful creature? What a wretch I have become!" The head cried and cried, but the hands on her faraway body were unable to wipe her tears.

"Oh no, Your Ladyship! Do not weep! It is only a wretched child we found huddled on the doorstep. We thought it might bring you some amusement." One of the dog spirits jumped up with a silk handkerchief to dab at the water flowing down Her Ladyship's cheeks. "How is it to understand your lamentable circumstance?"

Her Ladyship sniffled and composed herself. Her

lower lip still quivered, but she looked down over her high cheekbones at Saki. "Yes, of course. I forgive you for your ignorance, dear child. If you do not find my appearance too revolting, please sit and speak with me over a cup of tea."

Saki bowed again, but she kept her gaze fixed on the tatami mat floors as she replied, lest she spark another round of tears from staring too long at the lady's unnatural neck. "Thank you very much, my lady. I'm very sorry if I offended you."

"Not at all," Her Ladyship replied, though her strained smile told a different story. "Please, take a seat on one of my cushions."

Saki pulled a little round cushion from the corner and sat as demurely as she could. The tengu rustled under her straw cloak.

"My dear, what is that under your hood?" Her Ladyship asked.

Saki fidgeted, unsure of what to say. The tengu, in his bird guise, popped his head out of the straw and surveyed the room.

"He's my friend," Saki answered, wringing the hem of her shirt underneath her cloak.

Her Ladyship smiled. "How lovely. I do enjoy a tune from a songbird. Sing for us, sweet songbird. I would be delighted to listen to your beautiful voice."

The tengu pulled himself all the way out of Saki's cloak. He dropped to the floor and gave Saki a glare of annoyance.

"He…uh, he can't sing," Saki replied. "He lost his voice."

Her Ladyship frowned. "Oh, how unfortunate. I do hope he finds it again soon. I lose so many things, with my hands down there and my eyes up here. It surely is a great inconvenience."

The lady's two dog spirit attendants brought out teacups and a plate of bean paste sweets.

"One cup for the little bird as well," Her Ladyship called, and another cup was brought out for the tengu.

Saki touched the cup to her lips with care, but instead of the fresh, piping hot tea she'd expected, the liquid was lukewarm and flavorless. She tried to smile, so as not to offend the lady, and choked a mouthful down.

Her Ladyship inhaled the scent of the tea with the greatest anticipation. She was unable to pick up the cup with her hands, her body being three screens down, but she sipped against the edges the way a giraffe might drink from a pond.

"Delicious!" Her Ladyship licked her lips. "Simply exquisite. I can't believe the others complain about these bountiful gifts we have received." She leaned close to Saki to share her gossip. "They say that on the first night of the Parade, a she-fox sneaked into the shrine and stole the granary key. Everyone is so upset, claiming there's an offering shortage or some such nonsense. I taste this tea and simply cannot believe a word. How much do you like it?"

Saki nodded and took another sip. The tea slid down her throat and left an oily residue in her mouth. "It's good," she lied. "You, um, said there was a fox last night? Did anything else happen? I mean, she must be in a lot of trouble."

"Oh, certainly!" Her Ladyship's eyes lit up. "That fox has been lurking around for years. She tramps through the forest with those tree spirits from outside the walls. Of course, we are all unique in our own ways, but those kinds of spirits are simply not refined enough to mix with proper shrine spirits. You understand, I'm sure. There are boundaries that one must adhere to. I cannot thank the New Lord enough for strengthening the wall to keep our way of life pure. Ever since he took over, everything has been so easy."

"Do you mean the Midlight Prince?" Saki asked, readjusting her legs on the cushion. She wanted to know more about the great castle at the center of the shrine.

Her Ladyship screeched with laugher. "Not at all! The prince has never involved himself with the business down below. He has a much higher vocation. The New Lord has told us many times to allow him peace."

"Would it be difficult to ask for an audience? With the prince, I mean."

"An audience? My dear, no one sees the prince. As I said, he is far too busy."

"What if it was something really important? Like life or death."

Her Ladyship frowned. "My dear, you must learn to snuff out such fantasies. You should put your energies into becoming a more refined courtier. Daydreams and idleness will not be rewarded in the least."

Saki abandoned the topic and picked up one of the bean paste sweets. The insides of the crushed beans had turned green, and the paste stank like overripe fruit. Saki waited until Her Ladyship was distracted with her tea to slip the sweet under the billowing curves of a nearby cushion.

"Now," Her Ladyship began, savoring every word. "I suppose you are dying to hear of my tragic life." She continued before Saki had a chance to respond. "It began when I was but a young spirit, during one of my first Night Parades…"

Saki learned very little from Her Ladyship's tale, except for the fact that Her Ladyship was an insufferable gossip whose neck had grown long from her habit of eavesdropping on conversations that did not concern her.

"Yes, it is shocking, I know. Life takes one down so many unexpected roads."

Saki blinked desperately in an effort to stay awake

when a knock shook the door that led out to the great hallway.

Her Ladyship lifted her head above a folding screen to call out to the guests. "Yes? How may I be of assistance?"

The door rattled in its frame, and dozens of footsteps soon filled the room. A squad of human-sized grasshoppers dressed in heavy armor waited around the door with their long pointed spears at attention.

"Lady Longneck," said the husky voice of the most decorated grasshopper. "The lieutenant's wife has requested your presence to attend to a serious matter."

"Oh, I do detest that name…" Her Ladyship chided. "Why must I go? My condition is hardly fit for travel. I am afraid I'll be of no use at all."

The grasshopper replied, "You owe the lieutenant's wife many favors. She has supplied you with servants and comfortable living, despite your shortcomings within the court."

Her Ladyship's head slunk back, and her camellia-red lips formed a thin line. "Here, take my little servant girl in my place. She is very efficient and much more skilled at labor than I."

Saki's jaw dropped in disbelief. First she had been a simple child, and now she was a servant? For spirits who thought themselves too refined to mingle with the nature spirits outside the walls, neither the lady nor her attendants had any manners.

"Very well," the grasshopper soldier said. "We shall take her into our custody. Come with us."

The lady's dog attendants pulled Saki to her feet, then thrust her into the care of the soldiers. In the commotion, the tengu had hopped up and burrowed back under her straw cloak, while Saki's voice of protest retreated after one close-up look at the point of the grasshoppers' spears.

The grasshopper soldiers dragged her down the hallway. They were twice her height, and their long legs took the strides with ease, but Saki had to run just to keep up. Their spears hit their armored shoulder pads as they walked, while the short knives at their belts swayed. Saki tore her eyes away from the weapons and focused on the hallway ahead. At the very least, every step she took was a step closer to the center of the compound.

The decorations in the long hallway slowly filled out, becoming more and more elaborate with each stretch. The carved detail in the wood that ran along the tops of the doors twisted and grew, like vines coming into flower. Smaller corridors branched off the main path, and the way became just as twisted as the labyrinth of roads and gardens outside.

The grasshopper soldiers stopped in front of a series of gold-accented sliding doors. The squad commander pushed back a heavy panel, and each soldier filed in to prostrate himself on the floor inside the room.

Saki, too, was rushed in and pushed into a low bow on the floor. She was already panting from the run, and her head swam as a rush of blood flooded to her face.

A deep voice croaked at them to stand. A frog, wrapped up in baggy lord's robes, squatted on a pedestal in the middle of the room. Seated below him, the frog's slug wife shifted her thick body and left a trail of slime on the tatami mats.

"Sir," the grasshopper leader announced, "Lady Longneck humbly sends her servant to do your honorable bidding."

"I don't really think I'm the person you—" Saki began.

"Hush," the frog said. "Come here and receive instruction from your new mistress. If you can perform your duties to my lady wife's satisfaction, you will be graciously rewarded. I work directly under the New Lord himself."

Saki shuffled forward and bowed again when she reached the pedestal.

The slug spirit dabbed at her eyes with a fancy handkerchief, but she had to stretch the handkerchief above her head to reach the feelers that held them out from her body. Her skirt fell around the platform, oozing slime across the floor. She cried out with sticky sobs for a few moments before turning her optical feelers on Saki.

"Little girl, I can hardly stand to speak for all the misfortune I have suffered!" Though it seemed, as the slug spirit went on, she had quite a lot to say on the subject of her suffering. "The horrors began months ago, though only now have they become unbearable. Every evening, my ladies and I journey to the bathhouse to cleanse our bodies. On the way, we use the courtyard outhouse to relieve ourselves, but…"

Saki snorted but quickly bit down on the inside of her cheek. What in the world was a slug trying to accomplish by taking a bath? Oblivious, the lieutenant's wife continued.

"I had begun to notice that every day the outhouse was becoming dirtier. When I sent in servants to clean, they would come back with wild stories, telling me there was no way to remove all of the filth, that some manner of wicked spirit was willing it so. However, given the choice between using a dirty outhouse and not using one at all, of course I would try to do my best with what I had.

"The other day, as I was beginning to prepare for the Parade, I stopped by alone to freshen up. I took off my prized shell, so I would not get it dirty, but when I came out, my precious heirloom had disappeared!"

A murmur cascaded through the assembly. The frog lieutenant patted his slug wife on the back as she wept.

"As you can see," the frog said, "my wife's shell must have gotten lost in all of the filth. Because of the stench, none of my other servants dare go near. You must clean the outhouse until you find the shell or a hint of where it may have gone."

Saki stood up to protest. If spirits couldn't endure the smell, there was no way a human would be able to hold their stomach. Before she could say a word, the grasshopper guards thrust a bucket full of brushes and cleaning rags into her arms as the rest of the courtiers rose to escort her out to the courtyard outhouse.

The lieutenant blinked his wet eyes. "If you cannot succeed, we will have no choice but to stamp you out."

Saki wasn't certain what he meant, but a peck from the tengu under her cloak assured her that the outcome was not at all desirable.

CHAPTER 12

The smell hit Saki before she even saw the outhouse. If the ice cream she'd eaten at the Bon dance hadn't been so long ago, she would have gagged it all up again. She carried the bucket of cleaning supplies with one hand and pinched her nose with the other, clamping down until the pain was as bad as the stench. The grasshopper guards would only take her so far before retreating to the shelter of the shrine walls. Saki stood alone in front of the squat little building, wondering whether she would be in more danger if she ran or if she stayed. Light from the braziers along the edge of the courtyard caught the garden flora and cast undulating shadows on the walls of the outhouse as the fetid smell seeped into Saki's pores.

The tengu poked his head out from under her cloak. Although his gigantic nose had been turned into a beak, the smell still seemed to affect him powerfully.

"Your marbles," he choked. "Get out the marbles."

Saki dropped the bucket and dug around in her pouch. She took one out, then held it up for the tengu.

"What should I—?"

The tengu thrust his beak into the glass, which became a mask over his face.

"Ooh, I see…" Saki fished out a second marble and did the same.

The odor was still powerfully rank, but the marble masks let them breathe without retching. The glass felt secure enough, but Saki took no chances. She clamped her hand over it and moved to push open the outhouse door.

Not even the moonlight that filtered through the vents could soften the sight of such squalor. Slime slicked the floors and oozed up the walls. The water basins were yellow and cracked, the mirrors fogged and splattered with crusty specks. Grime covered every inch of the walls. The toilet stalls were walled off with crooked doors, but Saki didn't want to imagine what was hiding behind the wood.

A stream of hot saliva dripped onto her shoulder.

Crouched on the ceiling, a ghoulish spirit with a long tongue looked down at her with bugging black eyes. The stench rolled off the spirit in waves, and Saki held her breath through her mask, too disgusted to be scared.

"Have you come to tidy up?" the spirit asked. Its tongue was too long to fit into its mouth, so the words sloshed around its lips.

Saki couldn't hold her breath. She sucked in just

enough air to reply, "Are you the one making this place so dirty?"

"Not dirty, filthy!" the spirit exclaimed. "I couldn't have done it without all of that glorious slug slime. I'm so grateful to that precious lady for making this place so deliciously filthy." The spirit's tongue licked a long trail of slime on the wall. It smacked its lips as if the slime were the most delicious treat in the world.

Saki craned her neck to get a better look at the Filth Licker. "Do you know if the lady ever left anything behind?"

"Of course," the Filth Licker replied. It scurried off the ceiling and down into a toilet stall. The Filth Licker's tongue pushed open the door, and it stood holding a wide display of trinkets in its bony hands. "I keep everything she leaves. I love clutter almost as much as I love filth."

The Filth Licker held wadded-up handkerchiefs, used ear picks, and small pieces of jewelry that were covered in a layer of brown tarnish.

"Have you ever seen something that looks like a shell?"

The Filth Licker narrowed its gaze and turned to hide its trinkets. "You'll never have it. It's the best part of my collection. She'll never come back if I give it away."

"Are you sure? I can trade you something good." Saki reached for the pouch of marbles but couldn't risk dropping them all over the dirty floor.

"No, that won't do at all. I *need* it. She won't come back, and I need her slime. Don't you understand?"

Saki blinked. "You want her to make the outhouse...dirtier?"

"Filthier!"

"Right." Saki paused for a moment. If she got the shell back, the frog would let her go. But cleaning the outhouse might mean fighting the Filth Licker, and that was hardly fair. Past its putrid smell, its horrid slime, and its odious habits, it wasn't really hurting anyone. If this outhouse was the only place where it could make its home, what gave her the right to oust it? There were other places that the slug and her ladies could go. Saki looked back to the Filth Licker, her hands on her hips. "Let's make a deal."

The spirit waited for her to continue with a nervous jerk of its tongue.

"I need to bring back that shell so I can get out of here. What if I helped you make your home dirtier—I mean filthier—right now? We'll make it even worse than slime on the walls. Or better, I guess? What do you say?"

The Filth Licker considered her proposal. It scurried back up the ceiling and gave her a sidelong glance. "What will you do?" it asked. "I want it really, really filthy."

"First of all..." Saki looked around. Only the enchantment of her geta kept the floor from sticking to her feet. "Mud! It's some of the filthiest stuff around. You can only get what other spirits track in here, but I could bring you a heap of mud. Whole buckets, even."

The Filth Licker nodded. "Yes, yes. Mud is sticky, like slime. Oh, I would love to have some nice mud. What else?"

"Where there's dirt, there should be bugs," Saki continued. "You might get lonely in here by yourself, so we'll find all sorts of bugs to keep you company."

"Yes, yes, yes!" The Filth Licker was slobbering everywhere. Its black eyes gleamed, and the corners of its mouth curled up in a smile. "I want lots of friends. You do all this, and I'll give you the shell."

"You have to promise," Saki told the spirit. The spirit world seemed like a place where a promise could come to life. She wouldn't take chances like she had with the fox. Leaving intentions unsaid could only lead to trouble.

"Yes, yes, I promise. Please do what you said. I'll give you any treasure you want."

The tengu shifted underneath her cloak as they returned to the clearer air of the courtyard. "Good. Appease both the creature and the lord. Now we'll see if you can carry out this plan."

"Thanks for all your help," Saki mumbled. "I hope you're better at your usual job than you are at this guide thing…no offense."

"If you do not wish to give offense, you ought to better curb your tongue." The tengu dug his claws into the flesh on her shoulder. "And I was a soldier once, in this very compound."

"Once? What happened?"

The tengu ignored her question and pointed with his beak. "Go fetch your tools. Make quick use of them, and let us return to our journey."

Saki emptied the bucket of tools and ran it down the well in the corner of the courtyard. When the water came up, she poured half of it back down the well, then filled the other half with handfuls of dirt. The earth stuck underneath her fingernails and wedged into the cracks of her skin.

"Well, it's not like I can get any dirtier." Saki wrinkled her nose and thrust her hands into the bucket to mix the mud.

The mud was thick and extremely heavy, and Saki's arms were slicked from fingertips to elbows. The moment she started to pull the bucket away from the well, her grip slid off the handle.

"You've got to be kidding me…" Saki wiped her hands on her cloak. When the bucket still wouldn't budge, she began to reach into her pocket for the flat marbles.

The tengu squawked at her and flapped his wings. "If you rely on those to solve every problem, you'll end up solving nothing."

"But you told me to use them earlier!"

"Discipline is one of a soldier's greatest assets," said the tengu.

Saki grumbled and put the pouch away.

The water had slopped over the side as she mixed, and the bucket now sat stuck, unable to budge. If she could just think of a way to keep the bottom of the bucket from dragging on the ground…

Saki left the bucket where it stood and went to the edge of the verdant courtyard.

"What are you doing now?" the tengu asked.

"Solving problems."

She pulled half a dozen long, flat leaves from the ornamental plants in the courtyard garden. Placing four of the leaves on the ground in front of the bucket, Saki wrapped the last two leaves around the handle. She was able to lift the bucket high enough to drop it onto the mat of leaves as a dollop of mud sloshed over the edge. With the leaves underneath, Saki slid the bucket across the courtyard to the entrance of the outhouse.

The bucket overturned, spilling mud all over the floor. Saki grabbed a mop from the cleaning tools and pushed the mud around, into the corners and underneath the stall doors. The Filth Licker cackled and clapped its hands. Saki thanked her ancestors and every spirit she could think of for the marble mask across her face. When the muggy odor of the outhouse became too much, Saki escaped outside for a second bucketful.

Soon the outhouse was coated in another layer of thick mud. A few dead leaves had fallen into the well water and mixed into the mud, sticking out in clumps across the floor. Saki admired the disaster for a moment. But how in the world would she deliver on her second promise?

She paced outside, away from the Filth Licker's stench and lolling tongue.

"Bugs," she said. "I need to find a bunch of bugs." Her brother would have been perfect for this job, but he was snoring away at Grandma's house and would be no help to Saki in the spirit world.

"If you had the capabilities of an insect, where would be the best place to fortify your holdings?" the tengu asked.

"A riddle, huh?" Saki turned toward the flower bed in the courtyard. "If I'm a bug, then I usually crawl around on the ground. I'd have to find something to eat, so there would have to be plants nearby, but...I don't like to be seen, so I would have to hide out where nothing could get me."

"Excellent deduction," said the tengu. "So where will you look?"

Saki trudged over to a flat rock that was only a frog's hop from a flower bush. "Right under here."

She flipped over the rock. The soil beneath teemed

with dozens of squirming insects. At the first hint of moonlight, each creature began to crawl on whatever legs would carry it back into the quiet darkness. Saki scooped up handfuls of the insect-laden earth and dumped them into her empty bucket. She winced with each touch, trying not to imagine the hundreds of creepy, crawling bugs squirming beneath her fingers.

With one final scoop, the bucket held more than enough friends to appease the Filth Licker. Saki raised a hand to wipe the sweat off her brow but froze as a tiny worm wriggled out from the dirt caked between her fingers. On second thought, a little sweat had never hurt anyone.

Saki deposited the bucket of bugs into one of the outhouse washing basins. The insects made themselves right at home, venturing out to explore the muddy refuse on the walls and floor. The Filth Licker squealed with glee.

"Oh, this is the most wonderfully filthy sight I have seen in ages!" The Filth Licker hurried over to check on the progress of the bugs in the basin. "My abode will be the envy of all my kind."

"You should open your windows too. The flies will catch wind of your smell, and this place will be full in no time." With that suggestion, Saki crossed her arms. After all the work she'd done, she was collecting on the promise they'd made, one way or another. "Now, I did this for you because you promised to return the lady's shell."

"Of course, of course. My promise is as strong as my odor, I assure you. This favor will not be forgotten, not as long as spirits walk this earth."

Saki began to blush. "Um, that's great. I'm glad you like it. There is one more thing you can do for me though. I was supposed to come here and get rid of you, but I think that as long as you agree to stay here and not muck up anyplace else in the shrine, all the other spirits should let you be."

The Filth Licker nodded vigorously. "They can't take my wonderful home away. They can't."

"Trust me, I don't think you'll have much competition for a place like this…but if you want to make sure that no one bothers you, you have to swear not to leave the outhouse."

"Why would I ever want to leave? This is the perfect place for me."

"Good. You should tell that to anyone who comes around here. They might be looking for trouble, but they might just be ignorant. If they think you've tricked them, they probably won't be happy."

"I will, I swear. I'll warn everyone that to stay here, they must bring filth to share with me and my friends. We'll stay here, together, in the dark."

"That's probably for the best." Saki sidestepped to make way for a dung beetle scurrying down from the basin.

The Filth Licker descended into the stalls of the out-house and returned with a spiral shell bigger than Saki's torso. The surface of the shell, which might have once been beautiful, was covered in the Filth Licker's spindly handprints. The spirit handed the shell to Saki the way a parent might part with a newborn baby.

Saki heaved, unable to hold the weight of the shell, and the edges slipped from her hand. The shell made a wet thump on the muddy floor. Saki winced, and the Filth Licker looked to be on the verge of tears. Despite the noise, nothing appeared to be broken. Saki wheeled the shell down the stairs and out of the outhouse, gave the spirit a brief smile, and shut the door.

"Fine work, humanchild," said the tengu. "Now deliver the shell to the slug, and we must be on our way. The night has slipped past us as we've dallied among the shrine spirits."

"I know. I'm going as fast as I can. But we can't just give the shell back covered in muck. The guards will never let us through the door."

She rolled the shell to the well and grabbed the pulley. Saki heaved up bucket after bucket of water. Each time the shell was doused, a little more of its pearlescent shine returned. With a scrub brush from the cleaning tools, Saki polished the surface until she could see her face reflected back.

"There, that should do it."

As soon as the words were spoken, a troop of grasshopper guards filed into the courtyard and swarmed toward Saki and the gleaming shell.

"She's retrieved the lady's shell from the monster."

"Take her to the lieutenant at once."

CHAPTER 13

The grasshoppers picked Saki and the shell up with their bristled legs. As they passed the threshold back into the compound, the glass masks on her face and the tengu's beak fell away. The soldiers deposited them in the frog's audience chamber as all of the court attendants fell to their knees and bowed low, their clothes brushing the floor. Saki did the same, leaving an outline of dirt on the clean tatami mats.

The slug lady received her shell with a titter of glee.

"So you have vanquished the horrid beast," said the frog. "We owe you a great debt."

Saki cleared her throat and sneaked a glance at the frog lieutenant. "I was able to find the shell, sir, but the spirit is still there in the outhouse."

"Pardon me?" The frog's eyes narrowed. "Are you telling me that the monster remains to torment my poor wife?"

"Not at all." Saki looked up properly. She'd been putting together a speech in her head to explain the compromise she'd reached with the Filth Licker. "The spirit agreed not to bother any of the court spirits as long as it can be left alone. It just wants a place to live, like anyone else. Even though it looks terrible and smells even worse, I think—"

"Silence!" the frog demanded. "I do not care about what you think. My poor lady wife will continue to be tortured by that monster. Your failure has kept us from our peace!"

The slug began to cry into her shell. The frog's throat inflated to three times its original size as he let out a thundering croak.

Saki scrambled to her feet. After all the work she'd done, they were still ungrateful. None of them had risked their noses to go in and fix the problem, yet they saw no fault in criticizing her. She hadn't even been allowed to finish explaining. Disgusting as the spirit was, at least the Filth Licker had listened to her and treated her like an equal. The anger bubbled over until Saki could no longer contain herself. "I found your shell. Isn't that what you wanted? You stupid frogs never bother to think about where you're going! Why don't you just ooze around someplace else and leave that courtyard alone?"

A scandalized gasp from the courtiers shook the audience chamber. The slug lady froze in shock, and the frog drew his sword. Saki's toes curled as the hair on the back of her neck stood up. She shut her mouth as fast as she could, but the damage to the spirit's pride was beyond repair.

"How dare you insult your lord and master!" the frog croaked.

Saki slipped a hand into the pouch in her pocket and pulled a marble free. "You're not my master. You're just some warty old toad."

The flat marble hit the tatami and unfurled every straw in the mat. The fibers wrapped around the frog and his sword and immobilized the grasshopper guards reaching for the hilts of their spears. Quick as a whip, Saki turned to the gilded doors and heaved them open.

Her feet pounded on the hard wood of the corridor. Behind her, the sound of the guards slicing through the binding straw carried through the complex.

"What do I do?" she asked the tengu between gasps for breath.

The bird spirit looked down the hall behind her and ruffled his feathers. "This is your battle plan. You must be three steps ahead in your strategy."

The shadow-strapped slippers gave her feet a gentle tug at an intersection, guiding her down the left path. Saki followed the tugs left, then left again, then right. After a while, she lost track of how many turns they'd taken. The halls grew bigger and darker. No sound of the grasshopper guards came from behind them, but Saki didn't stop to make sure. The ceiling vaulted upward, letting beams of moonlight stream across the top of the corridors. She took a sharp turn, and they came to an area where all of the branched corridors converged.

"Stop!" the tengu cried.

Saki halted on the first beam of the floor. A loud bird-call sounded through the complex.

"What just happened?" Saki asked in a whisper.

The tengu pulled himself out from under her cloak. "This is the last path before the gates to the palace. The way is guarded by the nightingale floor. Its cries will alert the entire complex to your presence here."

"But there's nowhere else to run!" Saki snapped her head back to check the halls behind them.

"A true soldier remains calm in the face of danger," said the tengu. "Because of the Night Parade and the fox's intrusion, the soldiers are spread out all through the complex. One call from the floor isn't likely to alert too much suspicion, but we must ensure that we make no more sound."

Saki took a breath of relief, but they weren't safe yet. In the world of the spirits, she was discovering that no place was ever truly safe.

"Of course, the lieutenant's guards are still in pursuit," the tengu continued. "And I doubt they would forgive an insult so easily. We must be cautious but hasty."

Saki gulped and shook her head to clear it. "So how do I get across a floor that cries out every time I touch it? We could fly. Or *you* could. Last time we tried going together, it didn't work out so well. Maybe if…" She pulled out her pouch of marbles.

"Be careful with those," the tengu warned. "You may end up hurting more than helping."

"I'm just going to try something out." Saki held a single marble in the palm of her hand. "I need some seeds, please."

For a moment, nothing happened. Then the surface of the marble began to tremble. The glass stretched out, drooping below Saki's palm. The form inflated and sagged with a newfound weight and the clear object turned opaque. Saki held a melon-sized sack between her hands. She reached inside and pulled out a handful of tiny seeds.

"Perfect!" She grinned at the tengu, then looked to the floor. "I hope these work."

"What is your strategy, humanchild?" the tengu asked.

Saki dropped a pinch of seeds on the floorboard before her feet. The seeds wedged their way in between the boards, where they were soon snapped up by a creature just out of sight.

"Ah, a clever tactical maneuver!" said the tengu. "You shall defeat the nightingale floor by keeping its mouths full."

Saki's grin grew wider as she threw a handful of seeds in a line straight ahead. While the nightingale floor feasted, she tiptoed along, throwing more handfuls as she kept on walking.

The corridor stretched on as far as her eyes could see, but thankfully the bag of seeds replenished itself with every step. Saki kept tossing the seeds and following her tracks. The only sounds in the corridor were from her muffled footsteps and the greedy munching of the spirits beneath. Though the work wasn't hard, she couldn't advance until the floor ahead was covered, keeping her pace to a painfully slow walk.

In the distance, Saki caught sight of a towering gate.

"I think I see the end of the hall," she told the tengu. "Maybe that way leads to the palace?"

He held up his head and flew farther down the corridor. After a short turn, he landed back on her shoulder.

"Affirmative. That marks the entrance to the Path of the Gods."

She was almost there. She'd ask the Midlight Prince to lift her curse and then she could go home.

The thought was bittersweet. The Night Parade had been strange, terrifying, and completely unpredictable, but she'd seen more wonderful things in the past two nights than she'd seen in all of her thirteen years. Saki couldn't live with the weight of a death curse looming over her, but there would be no reason for a guide to take her through the Night Parade when the curse was gone. This was the end.

With a sharp snap, the tengu swiveled his head back the way they'd come. "Our enemies may intercept us earlier than I predicted. Quickly, spread the seeds!"

The buzz of the grasshopper guards filled the air, edging closer and closer. Picking up her pace, Saki threw the seeds on the floor and jammed her hand back into the bag for more. Her legs were restless. The adrenaline in her body told her to run, but a fistful of seeds would only let her move so far.

"Stop looking behind you, humanchild! You're wasting time!" the tengu screeched. He launched himself from her shoulder. His wings beat around her as she pulled seeds from the bag. The gates were so close.

A glint of armor and the blur of wings appeared down the corridor behind her.

"Faster!" called the tengu.

Perhaps she wouldn't make it. What if she was caught? There had always been a way out before, both in the shrine and on the Pilgrim's Road with the fox. But with every small step she took, Saki's time was running out.

The grasshopper guards had been joined by the black insect soldiers from the air patrols. In a din of buzzing wings, they glided over the floor as their dark shadows sped toward her.

Saki dropped the bag and ran.

Without the seeds, the nightingale floor shrieked and trilled with each of her footfalls. A cacophony of birdcalls echoed through the corridor, but there was no reason for caution now. The entire compound was after her, and the gate towered just ahead. She leaned all of her weight into her steps.

The tengu was shouting at her for breaking formation, but his orders faded into the sea of sounds.

In another instant, black shapes swarmed around the entrance of the gate. The insect soldiers glared out at her from both sides. Their multifaceted eyes burned. Their pincers flexed.

Saki couldn't stop running. The momentum carried her forward, straight for the gate. Her chest burned with the fluttering of her heart.

Claws pulled at her back. Her straw cloak split in two and scattered its fibers across the floor. The tengu hovered above her in his true form, the midnight-colored feathers of his massive wings wrapped around her body. He held his bright red nose high in the air.

"Who dares to interfere with my sacred office? Let us pass, at once!"

A ripple went through the soldier's lines. They paused

for only a moment, then continued to advance. There were too many to flee from and too many to fight off with the marbles. Saki thrust one hand into her pocket and clenched her shaking fingers around her grandfather's charm. Tears in her eyes blurred her vision. It was the end, but not at all the end she'd hoped for.

A bright spot shone between the gates. The piercing light forced the insects to halt and shield themselves. Their armor and weapons clattered on the floor as they shrank back to make way for the figure that approached. Saki lifted her head.

At first she thought another human had wandered into the Night Parade, but her face was far too beautiful to belong to any living being. The woman wore a silver kimono, and her long obi sash was tied simply in the back. Her hair was pale white and her eyes as dark as steel. She held up her hand and halted the insects at Saki's back.

Her voice was sharp but calm. The soldiers gnashed their jaws as she addressed them.

"Have you all been upset by such a small human girl? This disturbance ends at once."

The frog lieutenant battled his way to the front of the group.

"My lady," he croaked, "This wretched servant insulted the honor of my dear wife. Please have her punished severely!" There were dark spots squirming on his skin, like the stains Saki had seen on the begging ogre's hands.

By the gate, the silver spirit shook her head. "This girl is not a servant. Even if she were, your grievance must be addressed through the tribunals. Have we devolved so far in these years that we have forgotten our traditions?"

"The New Lord would have her executed at once!" the frog exclaimed. The dark stains grew to cover his face.

A chorus of grating voices from the insect soldiers answered in agreement as they took up their weapons once more.

The silver spirit threw out her arm. The soldiers around her recoiled. Her eyes were bright and terrible.

"I am the commander of this army. As long as the Midlight Prince reigns, I am honor-bound to protect the pilgrims of the Night Parade."

"She is a human," called the grasshoppers. "Take out her heart to feed us!"

"The New Lord commands her death! Slay her!" called another.

"Silence!" The silver spirit illuminated the room with a pale fire that gave no heat, only an intense, throbbing light. The fire flared throughout the room and gathered at her feet, encircling Saki and the tengu in a protective barrier. The silver spirit stepped toward them and spoke in quiet tones. "These creatures are past reason. Darkness has twisted their spirits. You must flee at once."

"But I need to speak with the prince!"

"I am very sorry, but the night is nearly through and you will find no quarter here. You must seek another way. One night still remains before the Parade is done. Now go! I will hold them here."

The tengu nodded his head. Through the open rafters of the corridor, hundreds of blackbirds dove into the fray. They circled Saki and the tengu until she saw nothing but a hurricane of black feathers.

Only the voice of the silver spirit cut through the darkness.

"You must hold close to courage. Do not fear the night."

CHAPTER 14

Morning came. The sunlight behind the paper doors shone between Saki's eyelids, and she woke sprawled across her futon, the cries of the nightingale floor still echoing in her ears.

In the other room, her father called her name. "Come out and eat your breakfast! We're all waiting on you."

Only Grandma looked up when Saki entered. Her father read the newspaper as her mother scribbled down a list of chores for the day. Her brother was picking at his rice in between levels on his video game.

"I've finished the list," said her mother. "We'll start in the inner rooms and work out, then finish on the walkways and the yard work."

"How long is that gonna take?" Jun paused his game and shoved another bite of food into his mouth.

"That depends," their father said from behind his newspaper. "If you spend every minute complaining, I'm sure it'll take longer."

Saki sat down and began to tune out the breakfast

conversation. There was only one night left before the spirit world was closed off for good. Before that she had to…

Saki's mother snapped her out of her reverie by passing a pair of cleaning gloves across the table. "You'll be in charge of the washing. You'll need rags and a brush. I'm sure I saw a bucket outside somewhere…"

"Washing?" Saki straightened, her eyes wide. Her thoughts strayed to the Filth Licker the night before. "No way. Anything but that."

Her brother snickered. "Why not? Looks like you could use a good scrub yourself." His gaze flitted down to her hands.

Crescents of dirt were caked under her fingernails. Saki made a face and snapped her hands under the table, but her mother was already giving her a frown of impatience.

"Saki, you have to do something," her mother said. "If you don't want to wash, then go help Grandma sort out the storage room. But wash your hands before you start touching anything. What were you doing, digging in the dirt?"

Saki's cheeks flushed red, and she excused herself to the bathroom. The dirt hid underneath her nails, but she scrubbed until her skin turned pink. Her clothes, when she went to inspect them a second time, suffered from nothing more than a few wrinkles.

"Weird…"

"You're weird." Her brother barged in and dropped his game in a pile with his dirty laundry. "They told me to come get you. Ugh. Since when did the word *vacation* mean more work? This is the worst."

In the main room, Saki struggled to roll up the pants of an old set of work clothes over her shorts. The clothes were spotted and snagged from years of use cleaning the temple, but at least they'd keep her own clothes from ending up in the same sorry state.

Wielding rags and dustpans, Grandma led her to a little room piled high with old apple boxes. They overflowed with old records, odd knickknacks, and souvenirs, even a few moth-bitten pennants from the 1964 Tokyo Olympics. One box was filled entirely with broken straw sandals.

"Grandpa always wanted to mend those, but he never had the time," Grandma sighed. "I'd mend them myself, but I wouldn't have any use for them afterward."

Saki placed the box firmly in the trash section with a broken radio. For all the hidden treasures, there was three times as much trash. Saki threw out books of coupons that had expired before she was born, dozens of gardening supply catalogues, and three boxes full of Grandpa's lifetime subscription to *Fish Frenzy* magazine.

Saki would have bet money that she'd hauled at least a hundred boxes off the shelves, but by noon, more than half the storage room was still piled high. She collapsed near a box of special occasion dishes that hadn't been used since her brother was born and wiped the sweat off her face with the back of her hand. She loosened the straps of her work clothes to let more air flow through, fanning her face with a rag.

Grandma chuckled as she stepped out to get rid of a bag full of burnable trash. She came back with two cups of cold barley tea and a broad smile.

"We need to get something in you before you shrivel up and start looking like me!" she said. Yet in spite of the hard work, Grandma seemed to have no trouble keeping up with Saki.

At the Bon dance the night before, Saki had been worried, but Grandma was in fine spirits now. When Saki had found a shoebox full of letters and old photos tucked away behind a jumble of sports equipment, Grandma's cheeks had gone rosy as she showed some of the old letters that Grandpa had written her when they were young.

"You're not shriveled, Grandma. You're just…experienced." Saki sipped her tea. The barley tasted earthy and smooth, and the flavor brought the energy back to her movements.

Grandma chuckled and took a sip from her own cup. "You're right. I could have it a lot worse. The mountain air is good for your blood, they say. What do you think?"

"Well, it certainly gets the blood moving."

Saki drained the rest of her tea and set the cup on the floor by her feet. With all that had happened, she'd forgotten all about showing Grandma the pouch of marbles and the answer that had never come. Now they were alone, without her parents or brother to overhear. Saki cleared her throat.

"Did you used to walk around the mountain a lot when you were younger?"

"Oh yes," Grandma said. "I was up and down every day as a girl. I would go with my sisters to collect mushrooms. Back then, no one ever got mushrooms from the supermarket. Even if we had a supermarket—which we didn't—our family didn't have a lot of money. My father died in the war, you know."

"Oh. I...I didn't, actually." Whenever her father or her grandmother started telling stories from the good old days, Saki had always tuned them out. She used to think that the past had nothing to do with her. Though she'd been born in Tokyo, her father's family had been living in this village for as long as the family had existed. Her family name was written on the torii gates over and over, from a time stretching back hundreds of years, in both this world and on the Night Parade. Now that she had finally started paying attention, she realized the stories had everything to do with her. Saki dragged her fingers along the edge of another box. Her grandmother must have endured a lot of pain over the years. She'd lost so many people in her life: her father to the war, her husband to illness, and her son to the city.

"You must miss him a lot."

"I did, for a while. But it was such a long time ago. Anyway, I don't have to go far to find him if I get lonely. The same goes for your grandfather," she said.

"You mean they're always with you in your heart?"

Grandma tilted her head and chuckled. "I mean their graves are in the cemetery across the road, dear. But I suppose you could say, in some way, they're with us. That's why every year we invite them to come back. That's what this time of year is all about, our past being the road to our future."

Saki's fingers played with the metal charm hanging from her pocket. Somehow, the charm and the bell in the temple were connected. Everything led back to the beginning of Obon. Grandma bent down to collect their cups. She paused for a moment to look at Saki.

"Are you feeling well?"

Saki shook her head. "Yeah, I'm okay. Just thinking. I've been thinking a lot the last few days."

"Yes, I hear that your exams are coming up. Young people today have so much more pressure on them than when I was a girl."

"You didn't have to worry about any of that?"

"No, not the tests. I also didn't have the same opportunities that you do now. Though I do understand a few of the troubles."

Grandma glanced toward the door. She held the dirty cups in her hand, half turned toward the kitchen. With one more look outside, she slid the door closed, put the cups back down on the floor, and took a seat on the box next to Saki.

"Were those children from the village bothering you last night?"

Saki fidgeted. Guilt gnawed at her conscience. She'd been careful to keep the details of the graveyard game a secret. Her family knew she'd been messing around in the temple, but they didn't know about Yuko and the village kids. As far as she knew, Maeda had also kept her word and said nothing.

"I guess we had a disagreement," Saki answered neutrally.

"I see." Grandma folded her hands in her lap. "Although it's nice to have friends, you don't seem like you'd fit in well with those kids. I know all of their grandmothers, so I've heard what kind of trouble they get into."

Despite having just drunk her tea, Saki's mouth ran dry. Grandma kept talking.

"You're a smart girl, so I know you don't want to be around those kinds of people. But I did see you talking to the Maeda girl, Tomo. Now, she's a nice friend for you."

"Grandma, I need to tell you something." The weight on Saki's chest kept down the words, but Grandma didn't press her for more. They sat together in the storage room for a long moment until Saki spoke again.

"I met them on the first night we were here, those kids... I told Mom that I was going to get my jacket from the car, but I really went to the convenience store. I saw them there, and they told me they wanted to hang out. That girl, Maeda, was there too. She told me not to go. I knew they were just trying to get a laugh out of me, but I agreed anyway."

Saki tucked her chin into her chest. She couldn't meet Grandma's eyes. The weight bore down until it was a throbbing pain in her chest.

"I'm really sorry."

Grandma put a hand over hers and smiled. Like a dam had given way, the pain in her chest lightened.

"I forgive you. Even if you made a mistake, you had the good sense not to repeat it. Is that what you were fighting about at the dance?"

"Yeah. They asked if we could meet again at the graveyard. They just wanted to see if they could scare me again. But I told them that I'd tell the truth and get them all in trouble. That's really what I should have done from the start."

"You should have told them I was a witch and that I'd punish them with my magic," Grandma said with a cackle.

"You're definitely not a witch," Saki said with certainty.

"But I can use a little magic. I'll call their parents this afternoon."

Saki cracked a smile and shook her head. "I don't think they'll come again."

"You're probably right. And I wouldn't want to get you into any trouble with them, even though you'll be leaving tomorrow. I know you didn't have much fun here, but you might decide to come back one day."

"I haven't had a bad time," Saki confessed. Despite the fact that she still hadn't lifted her curse, she'd had more adventures this week than in all of her years in Tokyo combined.

Saki flipped a stray bit of hair out of her eyes. The only part she really regretted was messing up with Maeda. Maeda was probably the only person in the village who had tried to be a real friend to her. But even if Saki wanted to, there was nothing she could do now. Tomorrow her family would leave, and she wouldn't see the other girl for at least two more years. Two whole years was much too long to wait for an apology.

The storage room door rattled open, and Saki's mother wandered in with a fist full of old shoji paper from the windows and doors. "Oh, there you are. I tried calling, but these walls must be thicker than I thought."

"All the boxes keep the sound out," Grandma said. She braced one hand on the shelf behind her and slowly rose to her feet. "Do you need help with the screens?"

"If you could spare Saki for a little while, I just need someone to smooth out the wrinkles as I glue."

Saki stood but stayed put. "Grandma can't move these boxes by herself. What if something falls?"

"Don't worry," Grandma said. "This room is clean enough for now. I should really start fixing lunch."

"But…"

"No buts. Go and help your poor mother."

As Grandma cooked lunch, Saki glued shoji paper screens outside in the burning hot sun. After lunch came even more chores. By dinnertime, no one wanted to do anything but take a bath and collapse on the tatami in the front room. However, there was one last thing Saki needed to do.

The talk about Yuko had her thinking about Hana, and thoughts of Hana reminded her of the horrible trick Hana had planned for Kaori at the karaoke parlor. Saki fished her phone out of her bag. Reception hovered at next to nothing, but she held her breath and forwarded all the messages that Hana had sent her about the plan to Kaori. When the screen flashed that the message had gotten through, Saki breathed in deep, turned the phone off, and shoved it under her pillow.

After all she had survived on the Night Parade, Hana no longer seemed so frightening.

While Saki and her family drank tea after dinner, Grandma went back to the storage room for the shoebox full of photos to show the others. Her father took his time sorting through the pile, and her mother smiled fondly as her father talked about his life before he'd left home. Saki also sat to listen, but her brother retreated into their room to amuse himself while their father and grandmother took turns telling the tale of an old fox that used to sneak into the kitchen and steal eggs.

Grandma handed Saki a photograph. "He chased it out with incense from the temple while the boys banged on pots and pans. It never came back, poor ragged thing."

"This is Grandpa?"

"Can you believe it? He still has his hair," she said.

Saki ran her fingers over the edges of the photo. Grandpa was standing next to one of the torii gates on the path up the mountain. He wasn't smiling, but she recognized the welcoming curves of his face and the softness in his eyes. She wondered if, in all of the years he'd taken care of the shrine on the mountain, he'd ever seen the phantom path through the woods that appeared for the Night Parade. A pang of sadness closed up her throat when she realized that she could never ask him.

At home, her father never talked about his life before he'd moved to Tokyo, but in the old house, he came alive with stories. The crickets began to chirp, and Saki pulled her attention away. Had they really been talking for so long? In Tokyo, everyone's schedules were so different. Between her school, cram school in the evenings so she wouldn't fail her high school entrance exam next year, and her father's working hours, Saki could go for days without seeing him at home.

In spite of the warm atmosphere at the table, Saki's anxiety built as the night wore on. There was only one night left to navigate the Night Parade. If she couldn't rid herself of the curse by morning… She didn't know what would happen, and that was the scariest part.

Soon, all four of them were yawning. Grandma packed up the letters and the photos and ordered them all to bed. As the night came, Saki waited under her covers with the bag of marbles hugged tightly against her chest.

CHAPTER 15

Saki lined up her futon on the floor and cracked open the door to the woods. She set her head on the pillow to watch the wind brush against the trees. The leaves whispered softly in the night. After a while, the sound lulled her eyes closed.

Something hit the side of the house so hard that it shook the walls of the room. Saki's eyes snapped open with a start. She pushed her hair back and blinked through the veil of sleep as a second noise thumped and clattered on the walkway outside. Her brother slept through it without even a hitch in his snores.

She sat up and pressed her eye to the crack in the door. The wooden geta, with their translucent shadow straps, lay strewn upon the walkway. Not a single figure, footprint, or silhouette appeared among the trees to show what might have thrown them.

Her vision went dark. A third object hurtled toward her face and hit the crack between the door and the wall. Saki recoiled, her heart in her throat. The object outside rolled around on the walkway for a moment before coming to a rest. With careful shuffles, Saki approached the crack in the door again.

A fat brown teakettle rested sideways against the house. Saki waited a few moments, and when she was sure that nothing else would lob itself at her head, she crept out onto the walkway and gathered up the shadow-strapped geta.

She scanned the line of trees, but there was still no sign of any spirit out in the woods. She looked up. No spirits waited in the sky. The path from the first night, where she had followed the fox, appeared and disappeared through the leaves.

"Hello?" she called out to the darkness. "Isn't a guide supposed to, I don't know, guide me somewhere?"

The third spirit, whatever it was, was taking its sweet time. With a scowl, Saki sat down on the walkway and kept her eyes on the trees.

"I don't have time to wait around all night, you know. I have to get to the Midlight Prince before the Night Parade ends."

No answer came but the whisper of the wind as it shifted an object behind her. The teakettle that had hit the house was still overturned. Saki hoisted it upright and noticed a strange crinkling sound from the spout. She dug a finger inside and, with a little effort, drew out a rolled-up slip of paper.

Saki unfurled the paper and squinted in the dark. The childish characters scribbled on the paper were blotted with globs of dark ink.

"*Careful of the hole in the bottom...*" she read aloud. "What's that supposed to mean?"

Saki turned the kettle over and tapped on the metal. If there was supposed to be anything that looked like a hole, Saki couldn't find it.

The teakettle's handle flicked up and became a furry tail. The spout morphed into an animal's head and looked up at her. The spot where Saki had just tapped was the creature's rump. Giggling with delight, the animal passed a load of gas.

Saki dropped the creature face-first in the dirt. She jumped up and swatted the air, trying to get rid of the horrible smell.

"Ugh! Gross! Why would you do that? What kind of spirit are you?"

"The brilliant kind," the furry creature replied. "Bet you've never seen anyone do that trick before."

The stripes on his narrow face ended in a wet, black nose. The spirit was a tanuki, a raccoon dog. His potbelly swayed as he came forward, sitting his round rump below the walkway with his paws splayed out. His mischievous eyes were fixed on Saki.

She restrained herself from jumping down and giving

him a good smack. She crossed her arms and looked down her nose at the creature. "Are you my guide or what?"

"Whoa, whoa, whoa. Hold up, sweetheart. Can't a fella take a stroll alone?" He polished his front paw on the fur of his belly. "But I guess I am kind of irresistible. I can't blame you for wanting a piece of this action. Doesn't everybody?"

Saki made a face.

"Hey, what was that for?" the tanuki demanded. "You've got a bad attitude, sweetheart."

"Look, I don't have time to play games," Saki said. "I have to find the Midlight Prince to lift my curse before the Night Parade is over. And I have to get all the way back through the shrine before morning. If you're not going to take this seriously, tell me now before you waste any more of my time. I'll go by myself if I have to."

The tanuki scratched his head. "Wow, that's a lotta stuff to do. But you'll never make it back there. I heard they got all sorts of creepies and crawlies trolling around lookin' for some human girl."

Saki bit her lip.

"Huh. I guess that's you, sweetheart."

Saki leaned back against the wall of the house and tried not to cry. It was her last night to lift the curse, she couldn't get through the shrine without being picked apart by insect soldiers, and the one spirit who was supposed to be helping her was sitting around cracking jokes.

She'd have been better off going back inside and pulling the blankets over her head.

"Hey, why the long face?" The tanuki paraded around her ankles, trying to catch her gaze. "Since you're in a real pinch, lemme help you out. I got some friends who might be able to sneak you up to this prince-y fella."

Saki brushed back her tears. "You do?"

"This prince guy ain't as handsome as me, but who is, really? I even know a secret shortcut. No way those shrine drones are gonna find you there. We got a deal?"

Saki opened her mouth to reply then stopped. She tilted her head as the tanuki fidgeted with his paws. "Why didn't you just tell me that from the start? What's the catch?"

"Catch? Sweetheart, why you gotta do this to me? Don't I look like a spirit you can trust?"

Saki blinked once. "No."

The fox's betrayal was still fresh in her memory. She crossed her arms and stared down the tanuki.

"All right, all right, I'll fess up. Truth is I heard what you did for the fox. I know she tricked you and all that, but you gotta understand that the lady hauled in some major goods. You know what I mean? I just want one of them little magic marbles for myself, that's all."

"Thanks anyway," said Saki. She slid on her geta as she hopped off the edge of the walkway and trudged down the path to the Pilgrim's Road.

The tanuki called after her. "Wait! Hold up, sweetheart!"

"I'm not your sweetheart."

"Yeah, okay, that's fair. Just let me finish. She told me not to lose you!"

Saki pivoted. The tanuki almost ran into her leg.

"She? You're working for someone else?"

"I wouldn't say 'working for'… She asked me for a favor is all. And when a spirit like that asks you for a favor, you ain't saying no. Now she ain't like Mr. High-and-Mighty in his super-shiny tower, but she's the next closest thing. They call her the Lady of Bells, and she guards the shrine. I heard you met her last night. Sharp, nice curves. A real prize."

The silver spirit had stopped the insect soldiers on the nightingale floor. *You must hold close to courage*, she'd said.

"She's a close, personal friend. I don't want to disappoint her."

"I'd rather she take me to the Midlight Prince," said Saki.

"You're stuck with me, sweetheart. You called me."

"Aha!" Saki turned on him with an accusatory finger. "So you *are* my guide."

The tanuki slid away from the main path and winced. "I hate that name. I'm not like those other stiffs, the fox and that terrible tengu. He gives me the skeevies."

Saki snorted. No other spirit quite inspired that same

squirming feeling in her guts, and while he had spent too much time barking out cryptic orders, he'd had discipline. She shrugged one shoulder. "He was a bit stern, but at least he had a plan. Wait, where are you going?"

"I told you, sweetheart. There's more than one way to climb a mountain. Especially on the Night Parade. Follow me."

The tanuki waddled along the line of trees, and Saki followed behind. She glanced back at the fox's path one last time before it disappeared into the forest. The tanuki made a sharp turn. He zigzagged between the trees, following no particular route. Saki almost tripped over a tree root as she hurried to keep up.

"Wait!" she called after the spirit. "The path's too narrow. I can't see where we're going."

"Can't see? Sweetheart, you need to take a better look around."

Saki passed another tree. With just one step, the path became a winding road. She and the tanuki were the only beings in sight, and the road sloped up so gradually that the landscape looked more like rolling hills than a steep mountain face.

"Are you sure this goes to the right place?" Saki asked. "I can't even see the top of the mountain."

"Sure I'm sure. As long as you know where you wanna go, just about any road will do."

"Tonight is all that's left. We've got to hurry."

"Whatever you say, sweetheart. Say, you wouldn't mind giving an old tanuki a lift, would ya?"

"I only have two legs. You have four. Therefore, you should only get half as tired."

"You sure are a strict one, aren't you?" he grumbled. "The tengu musta rubbed off…"

A crop of posted signs emerged as Saki and the tanuki continued down the back road, written in an old style with characters so strange that they were nearly impossible to read. The most peculiar part by far was the height of each one. Even the biggest sign only reached Saki's hip, and some were even shorter.

"Are you sure you know where you're going?"

"I know this road like the back of my tail. Relax, sweetheart. Enjoy the scenery."

The road curved to and fro, as if it hadn't decided where exactly it wanted to end up. Around the next bend, lanterns of all shapes and sizes began to appear in the trees. Some were fat, some were tall, some were red, and some had faded far too much to tell what color they might have been. Much of the paper covering the lanterns was ripped and riddled with holes.

The roadside lanterns were not at all like the kindly daruma lanterns from the Pilgrim's Road. Their lights flickered and cast long, dancing shadows in the forest.

Sometimes it looked as if someone were there, watching from behind the trees. Saki picked up her pace, and the tanuki waddled to keep up.

"Hey, where's the fire?" he asked.

"I think it's nothing," said Saki with a glance over her shoulder. "But we should keep moving anyway."

When she turned her eyes back, Saki ran headfirst into an old umbrella sticking up in the road.

"Ouch!" She staggered back and rubbed her forehead. "You could have told me I was about to run into something," she hissed at the tanuki.

The furry spirit was too busy rolling on the ground with laughter to hear her reprimand. Saki scowled. How hard would he laugh with his tail stomped beneath her foot?

"This isn't funny."

"Eheheh… Sweetheart, you need to lighten up. Maybe another bonk on the head will knock that frown off your face."

Saki didn't understand why she hadn't seen the umbrella before. The road was wide and clear. There hadn't been any sharp turns or blind corners. Also, it wasn't nearly tall enough to have hit her in the face. Planted straight up in the road, the umbrella only reached Saki's stomach.

"What in the world…" she wondered aloud.

As Saki stepped closer to examine the umbrella, a rip pulled apart in the center of its battered paper. The movement was slow, like an eyelid opening. The darkness inside the umbrella folds stared back at her.

The ribs of the umbrella pitched up and smacked Saki on the chin.

The tanuki howled with laughter. "Oh, it got you good!"

Saki grabbed her smarting chin and recoiled from the strange umbrella. It flexed its joints, its paper folding up and down in a silent fit of giggles.

The lanterns all around them had pulled apart as well. Their candle flames danced in the center of the rips like pupils. They rattled their paper and rolled out long, wet tongues of melted candle wax.

"They're all alive." Saki fell back onto the dirt in wonder. "Have they been watching us this whole time?"

The tanuki scratched his nose with a back paw. "I don't see why they wouldn't be. We're heading straight into their village, after all."

There was a tug at Saki's pocket. She turned her head as the umbrella hopped down the road, her bag of flat marbles caught on a splinter on its handle. Saki scrambled to her feet and took off after it.

"Hey! Give those back! They're mine!"

The tanuki lagged behind, wheezing as his potbelly swayed from side to side. As Saki ran, the flickering gazes of the lanterns followed her down the winding road.

CHAPTER 16

In the span of a few steps, the dirt road became a tiny village. The umbrella dove behind a building, and Saki lost sight of the thief. The houses around the village were small and very old. Some had reed thatching, like her grandmother's house, but some were nothing more than wooden shacks.

On the tips of her wooden geta, Saki crept around the building the umbrella had darted behind. She leaned her ear to the wall for the telltale thumps of the umbrella's handle on the ground. The village was eerily quiet. Saki sneaked along the side of the house, edging toward the corner. Every muscle in her body tensed as she leapt out to grab the strange creature.

Her hands caught nothing but air. The umbrella had vanished. There was a tap on her shoulder.

Saki turned her head into a face full of umbrella paper. The umbrella leapt back, flexing its joints and shaking the pouch of marbles in a silent taunt.

"You little…I'll take you apart!"

Saki swiped, but the umbrella jumped out of reach. It bounced through the village as she gave chase around curves and between houses. When she couldn't run anymore, her knees hit the ground and she collapsed in the middle of the road. After a few seconds of silence, the umbrella leaned out from behind a house to peer at her.

Saki sat in the dirt, sniffled, and wiped her nose on her collar. The umbrella took a small hop forward. Saki turned her eyes downward and heaved a heavy sigh.

"If I don't get my curse lifted, something really bad will happen…" She dropped her head between her knees. "I guess there's…there's nothing I can do now."

She started to wail. The umbrella came closer. It fanned out its paper half-heartedly, and Saki raised her head, tears in her eyes.

"What do you care? Just take them."

It dipped down and swayed, as if suddenly full of remorse, then ruffled its paper again.

"What do you want now?" She stood up and brushed the dirt off her nightclothes, giving another thick sniff for good measure. "You made me cry. You can't just mope around and expect me to forgive you."

The umbrella trembled.

Saki narrowed her eyes. "Well, maybe if I can have a hug…"

The umbrella snapped to attention. It waddled to Saki like an eager puppy.

With a carefully timed quiver in her lip, Saki wrapped one arm around the paper. With her other hand, she reached around and plucked the bag of marbles off the umbrella's handle. The umbrella tried to open in protest, but Saki tightened her grip, and its folds stayed firmly shut.

"Aha!" A wicked grin spread across her face. "Gotcha."

She pushed the umbrella away but kept a tight grip on her pouch. It hopped back in shock as its paper began to shake.

"Hey, don't be mad that you fell for it. I have a lot of experience with crocodile tears. I do have a younger brother, after all."

The umbrella's shaking carried all the way down to its tip, as though it would spring after her at any moment. Then the object toppled to the dirt, rolling in a flurry of giggles. For the first time, a real sound reached Saki's ear. The umbrella spirit's laugh was like a wheezy cough.

All around her, different laughs poured out from the village houses. Sandals came out and laughed scratchy, dry laughs. Wooden pots laughed with deep voices that echoed through their chambers. The lanterns in the trees sounded like hot wax sizzling in a cool breeze. Old, battered objects collected in the road to laugh at the trick she'd played on the umbrella.

The tanuki slid up to her side. His fur tickled the skin on her leg as he shook the sweat off his brow.

"Looks like you don't need me to make introductions. I see you've met the locals."

"What is this place?" Saki asked as a battered abacus clacked out of a nearby hut.

A low desk trotted through the crowd of objects. On its back rode a string of prayer beads, the same kind that Saki's grandfather used to use in his temple services. Parts of the painted surface had rubbed away, leaving a pair of beads that looked like gray-pupiled eyes.

In a clicking voice, the string of beads declared, "This is Tsukumogami Village, the Village of the Object Spirits. So you are the breather that the rumors have spoken about."

Saki looked down to the ground and flushed. After her confrontation with the shrine's army, she doubted the gossip was anything good.

"I didn't mean to cause trouble," she mumbled.

The object spirits laughed as if she'd told another funny joke.

"Why not?" strummed a broken biwa. A few of its strings had snapped, but its voice was still a jumble of music. "Without a little mischief, this world would be way too boring."

"We love a little excitement," chorused a group of sandals.

"Even from a breather," added a squat wood stove.

The tanuki spun around in a circle. "Then you'll love what we've got planned next. We're gonna crash the prince's palace!"

A wave of awe washed over the crowd. The umbrella popped its joints all the way up in surprise.

"Impossible," muttered the prayer beads.

"We don't exactly have time on our side," said Saki, "so if it's all right with you, we really should be moving on."

"We must caution you against your errand. Beyond our village, the road is far too dangerous. One of our companions has already been taken by the foul beasts that wander the forest beyond," said the beads.

Turning back was no longer an option. Saki patted the pouch of marbles in her pocket. "I have a few tricks of my own. I appreciate the warning, but I don't have the option of taking my time."

"Wait a moment," said the prayer beads. "Those are the mountain witch's gems, are they not? It's said they can defeat even the most vicious of beasts."

The object spirits stared at her with rapt attention. Saki shrugged in a vain effort to push their gaze away.

"I'd rather not find out. My first plan is to sneak past without getting caught."

"If you have no intention of using the gems for yourself, perhaps it would not trouble you to grant us a favor?"

The object spirits pressed closer. The umbrella hopped near enough to brush its paper against her arm. She clutched the pouch of marbles with both hands, just in case. The prayer beads paused for a breath, or whatever else object spirits did to calm themselves, before continuing.

"Our village has been plagued by a group of ogres who dwell in the forest off the road. They rarely pass into the village, but they have intercepted many of our kind who stray beyond the village boundaries. Their interference is typically limited to harassment and mischief making, but now they've added abduction to their list of crimes against us. Our good friend, the cotton shroud, has not been seen for days. We searched high and low but found no trace."

"Are you sure your friend isn't playing a trick on you?" Saki asked. This particular village seemed like a place where that explanation was the rule rather than the exception.

The prayer beads rattled. "We are absolutely certain. If you continue down the road, you will see for yourself where the ogres have wreaked their havoc. Please, you must help us."

"Hold on a second. I'm not saying I don't feel for you, but I'm in a big hurry. I can't just stop everything to go on a rescue mission."

"Yes, a rescue mission!" the other object spirits exclaimed, completely oblivious to the protest. The straw sandals stomped on the ground, the biwa plucked its strings in a jaunty tune, and all of the other spirits joined in with an impromptu dance.

"Rescue the shroud!"

"Protect the village!"

"Show those ogres who's boss!" yipped the tanuki, swept up in the excitement of the moment. His perky ears withered under Saki's glare. "Uh, I mean, whatever you decide, sweetheart."

"We will not waste your time," said the prayer beads. "There are many shortcuts along the road that will lead one to the mountain summit. After the shroud is rescued, we shall escort you there ourselves."

The tanuki tugged on her clothes for attention.

"I know you're on a pretty strict deadline, but these folks could really use your help. They ain't got a lot of options out here in the sticks."

"Tonight is my last chance. What's going to happen if I don't make it in time?"

"That I can't tell you, kid. Your guess is as good as mine." The tanuki slid away to avoid her gaze. "All's I'm saying is that if you're gonna make the call, better make it quick."

Though the object spirits had no real eyes, all of their

attention was focused on Saki. Their only hope of saving their friend rested with her. But as she looked to the horizon and saw the even forest, without even the barest hint of a mountain slope, her fear dug in deep.

"Look, I can't fight an ogre. I'm just a kid."

"You said yourself that your best skill was sneaking around without being caught," said the prayer beads. "If we can return the cotton shroud without any confrontation, it would spare the village from the ogre's retribution."

"I'm sorry. There's nothing I can do." Guilt twisted in her stomach like a greasy eel, but she bit her tongue and let the matter rest.

The tanuki butted between Saki and the object spirits.

"Arright, you guys. Girl says she can't do it. We all best be moving along."

The object spirits lingered for a moment. An old mosquito net was the first to turn its back and slink back into one of the houses. The energy in the crowd fizzled and died. One by one, the object spirits began to disperse. Soon, only the umbrella and the prayer beads stood with Saki in the village square.

She groaned and held up her hands in surrender. The eel had won.

"Wait. Just...wait. I'll help you, okay?"

In a flash, the object spirits returned and descended upon her. Saki was almost knocked over by a joyful charge from the umbrella. A small army of sandals flopped at her feet as an old wood stove tried to give her a hug.

The prayer beads were quick to put together the expedition party. For a village full of jokesters, the object spirits were surprisingly organized. Saki and the tanuki were joined by three mismatched straw sandals, a wooden rice pot, and a painted cup-and-ball toy. The umbrella and the prayer beads both agreed to lead the group to the ogres' den.

As they set off down the road, the biwa tagged along behind Saki. It strummed a three-note song and used the end of its broken string to conduct the march.

"When we have finished with the ogres, you must tell me your tales," said the biwa. "I am a composer, you see. I will perform a glorious opus to commemorate your victories."

"Wow, that sounds pretty amazing. Could you play one?" she asked.

The biwa's notes pitched up, and its melody turned fast and frantic.

"Uh, well, they're not ready yet. I'm still, uh, working on some of the arrangements."

The rice pot let out a hearty laugh. "You've been singing that same tune for the last hundred years. Don't expect much from that one, little breather."

The tanuki was having a grand time with the object

spirits. They shared a love for pranks and childish humor that quickly devolved into a contest of slapstick routines. The tanuki emerged as the clear victor, as none of the object spirits could match his violent explosions of gas. The procession was interrupted and forced to a halt more than once by objects rolling along the ground in fits of laughter. The merriment was enough to break the biwa out of its embarrassment, and it struck up some tunes to orchestrate the silliness.

Every second they stood idle, Saki looked again to the horizon. There was still no sign of the mountain. During one of the many delays, she told the prayer beads all about the curse and the previous nights she'd walked the Night Parade.

"Your predicament sounds dire indeed," the beads said when the tale was through. "But I would not lose hope. You are a resourceful human girl, and you have learned to navigate our world quicker than I would have expected of a breather."

"Thanks," Saki said. "But I'm having a little trouble figuring out this road we're on. And your village too, for that matter. Why don't you live with the other spirits in the shrine?"

The prayer beads drooped. "We're not welcome among many of the natural spirits. They see our origins as an embarrassment."

"Why would they think that?"

"You breathers have everything so easy, both humans and regular spirits. You get a soul just by being born, without ever having to work for one. But we object spirits have to exist for a hundred years before we can gain a soul. Most of us don't make it that far, and the ones that do... Well, you know what happens. Unless we're expensive or rare, we just get tossed out with the rubbish."

"Do you remember what it was like before you gained your souls?" Saki asked. If they had all been objects in the real world, it explained why the spirits were so comfortable being around a human.

"It's not really a memory," explained the beads. "It's a lack of memory, like a hole that we can't fill. But we can tell whether or not we were cared for. We get our souls from the energy that people put into us. If that energy was good, the spirit will be good. If that energy was bad or neglectful..."

Saki thoughts drifted back to all of the boxes that she'd sorted for trash with Grandma. She hadn't been able to tell the exact ages of all the things in the storage room, though it was possible a few of them were nearing their hundredth birthday. Saki swallowed a pang of remorse as the prayer beads continued.

"An object that was crafted with great care is more likely to have a strong soul. I suppose in that way, we have parents, just like you breathers."

"So are you saying that every object I touch absorbs my energy?"

"There's not a lot made these days that follows the old rules. They get thrown away or replaced in just a few years. Besides, there's too much interference. That stuff that runs through the black cords, it's all over now. We can't stand it. It pulls our energy right out."

It wasn't until her eyes wandered upward in thought that the image hit her.

"Black cords... Do you mean power cords?"

"Whatever the breathers call them, we hate them. That's why there are so few of us left. Those cords cover so much of the land. We have a hard time crossing over, so the few of us who still remain are all separated. Our village is lucky that the mountain has stayed untouched for so long."

The object spirits were like nothing else Saki had encountered on the Night Parade. Like herself, they shared a connection to the human world. She opened her mouth to ask more, but their conversation was interrupted by the frenzied jumping of the other spirits in the party.

"Look!" called the biwa. "The path to the cave is over here!"

The group collected around a footpath that ran off the main road. The trees in the forest leaned over the path, blocking out the light of the moon. It was a long, dark tunnel to nowhere. The object spirits clustered behind Saki and peered out warily. The dirt on the path had been packed down, but Saki found a few outlines of footprints as long as her arms and as wide as her shoulders.

"We must be cautious," the prayer beads warned.

"You don't have to tell me twice," Saki agreed. Any creature heavy enough to leave an impression deep enough to lose a shoe in was not the kind of beast Saki wanted to stumble into unprepared. Or stumble into at all, for that matter.

The object spirits had grown quiet. All jokes were forgotten by the time the three straw sandals volunteered to scout the footpath. Once they returned, unnerved but unharmed, Saki and the others followed them back into the dark.

Branches whipped Saki in the face, and she lifted her knees high to keep from tripping over roots that jutted up from the ground. When she stumbled, the umbrella caught her from behind.

"How long does this go on?" she asked.

"Looks like just a smidge more," the tanuki said from a few paces ahead. "There's something bright a little ways away. You need some help, sweetheart?"

"No, I'm fine," she grumbled as another tree branch slapped her across the cheek. They didn't have time to waste nursing all of her scrapes.

She could see the light now too. The path curved to the left, where a handful of moonbeams poked through at the edge of the forest. Saki and the spirits stepped out into a clearing in front of a steep rock face. The entrance to the cave was a good twenty paces away, but the shouts of the ogres came echoing all the way to the edge of the footpath.

Trying to make as little noise as possible, Saki herded the tanuki and the object spirits to a patch of bushes.

"They must be keeping the cotton shroud somewhere in the cave," the prayer beads explained. "When they go out, they roll a boulder in front of the entrance to keep other spirits out. Otherwise we would have gone to look ourselves back when all of this began."

Saki nodded. "So we need to sneak in and grab the shroud before they see us." She paused for a moment and counted the group. "We can't all go. We'll get caught for sure if we're all moving around at once. Someone has to slip inside."

The object spirits pretended to go mute. Once again, their attention rested on Saki. Even the tanuki looked at her with an expectant gaze. Saki slapped a hand to her forehead and groaned. She should have known better.

"Fine. I'll go. Everyone else wait here."

The prayer beads hopped toward her. As they jumped, she caught them between her fingers.

"Let me accompany you," the beads said. "Slip me around your wrist, and I can help you assess the situation."

At least one of the spirits supported her. As the beads slid over her wrist, they tightened so that they wouldn't fall off. For a string of clackity beads, they made surprisingly little noise as she crawled out from behind the bush.

"Good luck!" called the tanuki.

"We'll be right here!" sang the biwa.

She shushed all their guilty encouragements with a violent gesture to the air.

CHAPTER 17

Saki crept up to the entrance of the cave. Firelight flickered across the walls, and the ogres inside started up a drinking song, stomping their feet against the floor with the beat. They belched and whooped with laughter. Saki crouched low, waiting for a lull in the festivities to make her move.

In the bushes behind her, the tanuki had fled from sight. The object spirits were well hidden in the leaves, all except for the umbrella. Its tip poked out of their hiding place by a full hand's length. All she could do was hope that ogres had poor eyesight.

She leaned forward to catch a glimpse of the cave's layout. Three ogres lazed around the fire, holding jugs of rice wine in their gnarled hands. The blue ogre had the largest jug of wine, the yellow ogre was the fattest, and the green ogre had a balding head. They pounded their bellies with their hands and pounded the floor with their feet for music. The ground trembled like an earthquake and rattled Saki's teeth.

Behind the blue ogre was a rock wide enough for Saki to crouch behind. The ogre leaned against it like a chair, but she could cover the distance in a few seconds if she kept low along the wall.

The green ogre sneezed and let loose a trail of snot. The yellow ogre bashed the green one on the head as all three of them devolved into uproarious laughter. As their eyes were closed in fits of belly laughs, Saki seized her chance. She dashed out to the rock, stopped in its shadow, and stood very still as she waited for her heartbeat to slow down. None of them had spotted her.

A tug on her wrist from the prayer beads made her look up. The beads pointed with a battered tassel toward a pile of huge iron clubs. Four of them were stacked messily in the corner, and around the handle of one in the middle was a wriggling piece of cloth pinned together with a giant thorn. The cotton shroud looked dirty but not beyond rescue.

Saki considered her next move. The clubs were in the farthest corner of the cave. Even with their drinking and their mindless games, the ogres would certainly notice if she went over and started to tug at their weapons. She would need a plan.

The green ogre picked his nose, and the fat yellow ogre tried to lick up a bit of rice wine that he'd spilled on his chest. The blue ogre seemed to be nodding off. He snapped opened his eyes and took another swig of his drink, only to droop again a few seconds later.

Saki grinned and cupped a hand over her wrist to whisper to the prayer beads.

"I think I've figured out how to distract them, but we'll need to get help from the biwa."

"Understood," said the beads. "Relay the instructions to me and then throw me across the gap. I'll tell the biwa what to do."

"Won't that hurt you?"

"I don't have flesh to feel the pain. Do not worry about me."

Saki kept her whispers short and low. While the ogres were preoccupied with a belching contest, Saki slid the beads off her wrist and tossed them over to the mouth of the cave. The prayer beads landed in a patch of soft grass. After a few beats, the beads slinked across the ground into the bushes.

There was nothing left to do but sit and wait until the biwa came to her aid.

The ogres were chugging entire jugs of the rice wine when a soft piece of music filtered through the air. With only three notes, the biwa's song was simple, but effective. The tempo was slow, and the pitch was clear. Before long, the ogres were exchanging yawns. The yellow ogre blinked to stay awake while the blue ogre gave in and curled himself into a mountainous ball on the ground.

Saki tiptoed out from her hiding place. She rolled her feet from heel to toe in order to keep her footsteps as quiet as possible. When she came to the clubs, she knelt down and reached for the cotton shroud. The ogres had lodged a thorn through the layers of cotton around the handle. She yanked the thorn up, down, and sideways to dislodge it, but the obstruction refused to budge. Rolling back her shoulders, Saki leaned in closer to get both hands on the club.

The ogres had started to snore. The biwa's lullaby stopped, but the music had done its job. With both hands, she pulled at the thorn until it popped free of the club handle. The sudden release sent her flying onto her back.

She bit her lip to keep from crying out, then sat up slowly. The shroud had unfurled itself from the club handle and began to shake out its wrinkles. Saki offered her hand so that they could escape together, but the shroud froze just short of her fingers. It began to tremble as the tips of its tail pointed over Saki's shoulder. A shadow fell over them both.

Saki looked up to see a red ogre's face staring down at her. His teeth were sharp and bright white. His lips slowly twisted into a hideous grin. In one hand, he clutched the biwa spirit by the neck. As Saki took a terrified step back, he let out a mighty roar.

The other ogres in the cave stirred out of their slumber, rubbed their eyes, and scratched themselves. The red ogre began to laugh.

"Look here," he grunted, his voice as thick and as deep as the darkest cavern. "Found tasty bite."

The other ogres licked their lips and leered at Saki. The shroud tried to slip past the red ogre's guard, but he pinned it to the floor with his foot.

"Where you go, soft white? Found new friend."

The ogre rattled the biwa and poked at its strings with a thick finger.

"Sing pretty now."

Too terrified to move, the biwa did nothing. The red ogre's face contorted, and he tossed the biwa to the ground. The yellow ogre picked it up and plucked at the strings, giggling.

The red ogre grinned again and reached for Saki. "We eat now."

"Wait!" She scrambled to the back of the cave and held a hand up in front of her. "You can't eat me!"

The red ogre stuck out his lip in a pout. "Why no eat?"

"Because," Saki said. She reached behind her back and pulled a flat marble out from her pocket. The light of the fire glinted off the glass, and specks of light like fireflies danced on the roof of the cave. "You wouldn't want me to use this."

The ogres jumped back in surprise. As the shock faded, huge grins spread across each of their faces. The yellow ogre gave up bullying the biwa, and the red ogre took a step forward, freeing the cotton shroud. Both of the object spirits wriggled away toward the cave entrance while the ogres were distracted with Saki. So much for loyalty.

Saki tried to keep her voice from shaking as she brandished the marble again. "See? It's very frightening, so you should let me go at once."

The red ogre grabbed her with one hand. Her feet dangled above the ground as he brought her to his face.

"Not go. Have shiny!"

"Shiny!" the other ogres repeated. Firelight glinted in their eyes.

Saki bit her tongue before she could say one more stupid word. The marbles were very valuable to the spirits, and she'd flaunted one right in their faces. Now the ogres wouldn't let her go until she'd handed over her entire pouch, then they'd probably go right back to the original plan of eating her.

"Put me down! If you don't put me down right now, you'll regret it."

The red ogre placed her down next to the fire. The

cave entrance was too far away to make a run for it, and the height of the flames blocked her view to the outside. All of the ogres had their eyes on Saki's marble, but none of them moved to take it.

"You nice," said the red ogre. "You help ogre."

"Uh…" Her mind was blank. The only image in her head was an old story of a boy who'd climbed a beansprout and a giant who'd made bread out of bones. "I'm sorry. What?"

The red ogre shook his head. "You help ogre. You help go to shrine. Give magic water." The ogre held out his hands and mimed washing them.

Saki's jaw dropped. She remembered the first night on the Pilgrim's Road and the sad, old ogre she'd given one of her marbles so he could pass through the torii gates.

"You knew the ogre from the other night?"

"Yes, know ogre! Uncle ogre. Nice girl help ogre. We like nice girl."

The other three nodded. Their floppy smiles slowly began to look much less frightening.

"Um, thank you. Your uncle helped me too. I would probably have gotten skewered by those bugs if it weren't for him."

"Yes, help. Nice girl ogre's friend. Nice friend."

"You…want to be friends?" Maybe being a friend would mean she wouldn't get eaten.

"Friend! Friend! Be friend?" The red ogre held out his huge hand.

Saki touched the tips of her fingers to his palm. Alone and under threat of being dinner, she had nothing left to lose. "Okay, friends."

The ogre swept her up into a hug. Saki was afraid she might be crushed, but his arms were so big that he couldn't pull her in too tightly. The ogre spun her around with such force that when he set her back on the ground, Saki swiveled on one foot and lost her balance. The other ogres laughed and stomped their feet in mirth.

When Saki could see straight, she staggered up. "I'm really glad we could be friends, but I can't stay."

The red ogre shook his head. "Not go. Stay ogre's friend."

"Look, I'm really sorry, but this is the third night of the Parade and I have to get to the palace at the top of the mountain before dawn."

The ogres cocked their heads. "Friend go up mountain?" the red ogre asked.

"Yes, I have to go and lift my curse."

"Ogre come with friend. All go up mountain."

The mouth of the cave was quiet. Unless the tanuki and the object spirits had cast off their cowardice since she'd left them, none of them were coming to her rescue anytime soon. Saki scratched her head and shifted her feet.

"I don't know…I don't even know where this road is supposed to take me."

The red ogre wagged his hands with encouragement. "All go together. Not get lost."

Saki took a deep breath. It was better than wandering around the woods on her own. "Okay. Let's go."

The ogres celebrated with a series of ground-shaking roars. The red ogre hoisted Saki on his shoulders and spun her around again as he and the others danced through the cave. When the excitement died down and Saki staggered back to her feet, the ogres grabbed their clubs and marched outside. The blue and green ogres rolled the boulder over the entrance to the cave as Saki scanned the clearing for signs of the object spirits.

The bush next to the entrance was empty. With a heavy heart, she followed behind the four ogres, across the clearing to the beginning of the footpath back to the road.

Above them, the leaves in the trees rustled. A split second later, the object spirits tumbled down onto the heads of the ogres, the air thick with made-up battle cries.

The rice pot landed the most effective hit, dropping right over the yellow ogre's head. The three straw sandals took turns slapping the blue ogre's face. He swung his club out in front of him to push the attackers away but only succeeded in hitting the green ogre on the back of the skull.

The red ogre braced himself in front of Saki. He brandished his club and stared down the umbrella, which popped its joints up and down in a frenzy. Near the red ogre's foot, a rock shifted and transformed back into the shape of the tanuki. Before the ogre realized what was going on, the tanuki sank his fangs into the ogre's big red foot. The red ogre unleashed a howl.

"Stop!" Saki jumped out in front of the raging umbrella, her arms splayed wide. "I said stop! Everyone, stop it right now! Stop fighting and listen to me!"

The straw sandals gave the blue ogre one last slap before obeying. The rest of the object spirits drew back and hovered by the edge of the clearing while the ogres nursed their wounds.

Saki took a look at the mess. The sandals, the pot, the umbrella, the cup-and-ball toy…some of the spirits were missing. "Where are the prayer beads?"

The shroud and biwa shifted out of their hiding place among the treetops, with the prayer beads crammed between them. The beads shimmied across the branch and dropped into Saki's hands.

"Were you harmed, Saki? We staged an ambush to rescue you from these monsters. I heard them talk about eating you!"

The red ogre came up behind her. "Friend okay? Friend hurt?"

"Both of you—I'm fine. Nobody's getting eaten. Can we please stop and talk about this?"

"What can we possibly talk about with these creatures?" scoffed the beads. "They kidnapped our fellow spirit. They come to wreak havoc on our village. They can't be reasoned with by any civilized peoples."

Saki turned to the red ogre and pointed up through the trees at the cotton shroud.

"Why did you take their friend from the village?" she asked, not unkindly.

"Not take soft white. Just borrow. Club hurt ogre hands. Soft white feel nice on ogre hands." The red ogre grunted at the blue ogre. "Show hands."

The blue ogre held out his hands, which were blistered and cracked. The skin was swollen, and the ogre yelped when Saki touched it.

"But taking their friend wasn't very nice," she said. "You can't have fun if one of your friends is gone, can you?"

"No." The red ogre looked at the ground. "No fun."

"Right, so you should say you're sorry to the object spirits."

"Not say sorry!" the ogre shouted. "Not friends!"

"Why not?" Saki pleaded. "They're my friends, and I'm your friend. Why can't we all be friends together?"

The prayer beads turned away. "Please, Saki. This is ridiculous. We're wasting everyone's time."

249

Saki held the beads with a hard grip. "Have you ever even tried talking to the ogres before?"

"Well, no, but—"

"Then you just stay here and listen." Saki bent her head to catch the red ogre's gaze. "Tell me why you won't be friends with the village."

The red ogre sniffed. Tears welled up in his eyes. "Not nice to ogre. Not friends. Call ogre mean name. Say stupid. Say bad things. Ogre not like."

"Is this true?" Saki asked the object spirits.

"Look around at all the trees that have been snapped," said the prayer beads. "They destroy everything they touch. They can't help themselves."

"Ogre not bad. Just heavy!" The red ogre brandished his fists as if he was ready to restart the fight.

Saki held up her hands before the ogre could raise his club too high. "Look, I think there's been a mistake. But if you give me a chance, I think I know how we can fix it. Will everyone listen to me for a minute?"

Slowly, each spirit nodded in turn. None of them seemed particularly happy about standing next to one another, but at least they'd stopped fighting.

"Okay, I want you all to come out so that you face one another."

The red ogre opened his mouth, but Saki raised a finger and cut him off before he could say a single word.

"No, no arguments! You said you'd listen. You can't back out now."

"I hope you know what you're doing, sweetheart," the tanuki told her. "We don't got a lotta time to waste, you know."

Saki shushed him. "Trust me." Despite the confidence in her voice, her stomach did a flip. She could hardly keep from fighting with her own brother, and they were related. Still, it was worth a try. "Could everyone who likes to have fun please raise their hand? Or their strings, or whatever."

Slowly but surely, each one of the ogres and the object spirits held some appendage in the air. The tanuki had his paw up behind her. Saki raised her own hand as well.

"Who likes to sing songs?" None of the spirits dropped their hand. "Who likes to dance? Who likes to tell jokes?"

Saki paced between them.

"Don't you see now? You all like to do the same things. But just because you're different, you think that you can't be friends."

The prayer beads shifted. "Be that as it may, we cannot forget what they've done to us all these years."

"Ogres? Do you have anything to say?" Saki asked.

"If click-clack not sorry, ogre not sorry too!"

Saki heaved a sigh and buried her face in her hands. Through the lattice of her fingers, she thought of her own battles with her brother and his favorite way to finish them. Maybe Jun had the right idea all along. She swiveled on her heel. "All right, fine. If you can't settle this with words, we'll use our fists instead."

"Uh, sweetheart." The tanuki tugged on her clothes. "I thought the whole idea was to get 'em to stop bashing each other on the head?"

"Not that kind of battle." Saki raised her fist in front of her. "One game of janken. The loser apologizes first."

A light glimmered in each of the spirits' eyes. Even the ones without eyes bounced in excitement. None of them were very good with words, but they all loved games. The red ogre raised his fist on behalf of his group, but the object spirits stopped to look at one another. Saki's face fell.

"Oh, right. You don't have hands."

The cotton shroud floated down from the tree branches. It did a loop around Saki's head and contorted itself into a ball, relaxed and folded itself in half like a pair of scissors, then went rigid and flat once more. The object spirits cheered.

Saki grinned. "Perfect! All right, one representative for each group. Are you ready? On my mark… Go!"

The red ogre clenched his hand in a tight fist as the cotton shroud curled into a ball.

"Two rocks. It's a tie!" Saki declared. "Try one more time."

The tension in the air was as thick, but the wind had

shifted. Each spirit was alive with anticipation and excitement, but their anger was fading. As the cotton shroud went rigid and the ogre drew out two thick fingers, a cheer burst from the other three ogres at the victory. But they weren't the only spirits excited by the game. Though the object spirits shared a groan, the impassable wall of resentment had melted away.

At Saki's urging, the prayer beads bowed and wiggled forward. "I do suppose we were a little quick to judge… Our apologies."

Saki turned. "What about the ogres?"

The red ogre slumped out of his celebration and twiddled his thumbs. "Ogre sorry take soft white from friend. Ogre not mean bad."

Saki held out her hands to the beads and the red ogre. The prayer beads hopped into one of her palms as the ogre touched a massive fingertip to the other.

The object spirits had broken out of their tight group and edged closer with slow, careful hops. The three sandals took the initiative. They hid a leaf underneath one of their bodies and shuffled the others around, then wiggled to prompt the nearest ogre to guess which sandal had hidden the leaf. The green ogre pointed his finger, and the sandal rose up to reveal the ground beneath. No leaf. With a scratchy giggle, the chosen sandal jumped up and smacked the green ogre in the face.

Saki stiffened. The green ogre gave a stunned blink as the yellow and blue ogres looked down at the object spirits.

Opening their great, wide jaws, both ogres burst into laughter. The green ogre, catching on to the joke, started to laugh as well, and the rest of the object spirits joined them. Halfway through another round of chuckles, the green ogre sneezed all over the sandals, which only made everyone laugh harder.

The red ogre and the prayer beads exchanged knowing glances and turned to Saki.

"Ogre find new friend. Nice girl make friend. Ogre much happy."

"Yes, thank you, Saki. We'll try our best to be more hospitable to our neighbors."

Saki blushed. "I'm just glad you didn't go smashing each other up. Or me. And I really hate to run out like this, but…" Her relief had turned to cold, creeping dread. The trees blocked out most of the sky, but there was still no sign of a mountain anywhere.

"Yes, I almost forgot. You're headed up the mountain to see the Midlight Prince. After the help you've given us, we'll gladly show you the shortcut," said the beads. "But we must move right away. The road is very long for small spirits like ourselves."

"Not problem!" The red ogre pounded a fist to his chest and flexed his muscles. "Ogre take friend. Ogre run fast."

Before Saki could open her mouth, the red ogre swept her onto his shoulders. The prayer beads shimmied up to join her atop the ogre's head, then looped around one horn. Saki curled her fingers around the other.

"Hey, wait for me!" The tanuki wiggled his rump and launched himself up. He caught Saki's shirt with his claws and scrambled up between the ogre's horns. "Ladies and gentlefolk, strap your strings, lock your hinges, and clench your lids on tight. We're going for a ride!"

When the rest of the ogres had picked up the last of the object spirits, the ogres ambled down the footpath to the main road. With their sweeping strides, they emerged from the forest after only a few paces.

"This doesn't seem to be much faster than walking." Saki frowned and gripped the red ogre's horn tighter.

"Just you wait, sweetheart." From his perch, the tanuki winked.

When the last ogre emerged from the trees, all four of them stopped. The red ogre let loose a howl, his voice shaking the leaves of the trees. Three more howls joined his, rising into the night until the stars themselves gave a shudder. At the end of the howl, the ogres bent and launched themselves into a wild sprint.

CHAPTER 18

The ogres bounded down the road, their feet slamming the earth with enough force to shake the trees. Saki bounced up and down with each stride as her teeth clattered in her skull. The experience was halfway between a horseback ride and sticking her head out the car window. The air rushed into her nose and stifled her breath.

The landscape sped by like watercolors in a rainstorm. Only the moon hung steady in the sky. Above the canopy of trees, the gilded walls of the palace appeared in the distance. The building that had seemed as big as a mountain the night before was now little more than a fleck against the horizon. Saki's heart dipped, and she pried her eyes away from the skyline.

The road opened into a flat plain, and the ogres slowed to a jog. The plain was nothing more than a wide expanse of rocks and shrubs, except for a series of high wooden poles that stretched to the sky. Shapes moved at the top of each pole, but Saki couldn't get a steady look until the ogres stopped moving. When the red ogre swung her down to the ground, Saki's jaw dropped.

"Are those...are those *fish* on top of those poles?"

The tanuki tumbled over her head before landing with his four paws on the ground. He shook the dirt off his fur and scratched his nose. "Yup. Those are air koi. Don't see much of them where you come from, do you, sweetheart?"

"How do they survive out of the water?"

The red ogre untangled the prayer beads from his horns and handed them to Saki. "Can't eat. Too high." The ogre pouted.

The prayer beads rearranged themselves in Saki's hand. "The air koi are spirits, like the rest of us. Air is like water to them. They capture the wind with their mouths and store it in their bellies. The more they store, the higher they float. When the air koi are at the highest point on the poles, the wind is ready to harvest. After their air is taken, the koi start right back at the bottom of the pole, and the whole process begins again."

Saki squinted and stood on the tiptoes of her geta. The closest koi swam around its pole and flapped open its mouth with every shift in the breeze. "They look like they're pretty high up already."

"Lucky for you," said the tanuki. "We can use the wind to take us all the way up to the palace. No gates, no guards, no problems. All's we gotta do is wrangle one down."

The tanuki waddled over to the closest pole, made from single tree trunks like the smooth, unblemished wood of the torii gates on the Pilgrim's Road. The grain of the wood was soft under Saki's fingers.

"How are we supposed to get one down?"

"The mechanism is quite simple, really," said the prayer beads. "One takes hold of the pulley at the bottom and—oh. Oh dear…"

The umbrella held up a line of cord from the pulley. Its end was sawed off. A whole section had been removed, so it was impossible to even tie it back together.

"Not to worry," the beads assured her. "We'll just have to move on to the next one."

The next pole's pulley was cut as well. A murmur of worry spread from one ogre to another as the object spirits fanned out to check different poles. Each reported the same news: none of the pulleys were working.

Saki sank down to her knees next to the red ogre's gnarled foot. Though each of the ogres expressed some concern with grunts and awkward pats to her shoulder, none of them had much of an idea what to do. They fanned out around her and picked their noses as the object spirits hopped around in a desperate search for a working pulley. Saki drew her legs to her chest as a sickening despair crept up behind her. This had been her last chance, and she wasn't even close to where she needed to be. They'd hit a dead end. After tomorrow, she would have no way to remove the curse. Saki sniffed and wiped a tear from her cheek.

"Look." The blue ogre pointed up at the sky. "Floaty."

Saki ignored the ogre's nonsense and buried her face in her knees.

The other ogres were transfixed. The tanuki scraped Saki's arm with his paw.

"Sweetheart, you might want to take a look at this."

Saki lifted her head and pushed her hair away from her face. Above them, a butterfly flapped a pair of delicate, incandescent wings. The creature fluttered down slowly until it landed on Saki's knee.

The ogres huddled around to look, and their eager breaths blew the creature's wings from side to side. Saki cupped the butterfly like a sputtering candle to keep it from blowing away.

The butterfly's soft light bathed the air around it in warmth. When it spoke to her, Saki felt the words in her heart rather than her ears.

"You are the human girl who has come to walk the Night Parade."

The object spirits hurried back from their searches to stop and stare at the mysterious butterfly. With all the spirits gathered around, the butterfly's light glowed even brighter.

"I am sent by the Guardian of the Shrine," the butter-fly told her. "I am to help you reach the Palace of Souls."

"Is this true?" asked the prayer beads. "I had no idea you were a personal friend of the guardian."

"Uh, neither did I," said Saki.

The tanuki nudged her. "The guardian is the Lady of Bells, remember? The one I was telling you about? Sheesh, she must like you a lot to keep sticking her hilt out like this."

"For the Lady of Bells herself to send an envoy…" The beads were stunned into silence. The rest of the object spirits drew back in reverence.

"The silver spirit sent you?" Saki asked the butterfly. "We tried getting there on our own, but all of the pulleys are broken. Can you fly us up to the palace instead?"

"Alas, I cannot hold any soul but my own," the but-terfly said. "This obstacle, however, was no accident. The one called the New Lord had ordered that all spirits of the Night Parade should halt your progress before you reach the Midlight Prince. The lesser known roads, such as this one, are not as traveled, but this is most certainly the work of his followers."

"I don't know what I've done to upset him. I just want to lift my curse!" Saki pleaded. "What the fox did wasn't my fault.

"He doesn't sound like a lord at all. He sounds

more like a bully. How can we get past him to see the prince?"

"Once you are on the Path of the Gods, he cannot follow you. It is a secret road beyond the shrine, open only to the sure of heart. He has not yet polluted the innermost sanctum."

"But he'll know that I'm coming." Saki touched her grandfather's metal charm as a slip of fear wriggled into her chest.

"Yes. If that is so, then you must be stronger than the darkness," the butterfly said.

The silver spirit had told her to hold close to courage. As far as she'd come, she couldn't let herself turn back now. The ogres and the object spirits edged closer. The honest concern on their faces lit a beacon of hope in Saki's heart.

"Okay. I'll try. Just tell me how to get to the palace." She would figure out the rest later.

The butterfly flapped its wings. "Outside of riding the wind, I know of no other way. This road goes everywhere and nowhere. In the time you have left, you may never reach the Palace of Souls."

Saki dug in her pocket for the marbles. There was no other choice. A weight settled on her shoulder as the red ogre patted her with two huge fingers.

"No worry. Friends help."

"But there's nothing we can do. None of us can reach that high," Saki told him. Whether the marbles would work or not was another story.

Before she could undo the pouch, the prayer beads hopped into her lap. "He's right, Saki. We might need a little coordination, but we should be able to reach the rope if we work together. Trust us. If we didn't figure out how to work together, nothing in the village would ever get done. Have you ever seen a sandal or a jug build a hut by themselves?"

Saki let go of the marble pouch and cracked a tiny smile. "I've never seen a sandal or a jug build a hut at all."

"Here," said the red ogre. "Look at ogre."

He grunted instructions to the blue and yellow ogres. They stood by the closest pole and crouched down. The red ogre climbed their backs like steps and braced his feet on their shoulders. With the extra height, the dangling rope was much closer.

The green ogre took his turn. He climbed to the top of the ogre pile and took a seat on the red ogre's shoulders. He reached up to grasp the rope, but the tip swung just out of his reach.

The two ogres on the bottom began to growl from the strain. Their feet slipped in the dirt, and both the red and green ogres swayed.

"Be careful!" Saki jumped to her feet and rushed to

help support the weight before all four of them would topple over. She bent her knees and pushed up. Her meager strength wouldn't keep the yellow and blue ogres from collapsing, but maybe it would buy them a few more seconds. Straw brushed against her leg. The object spirits clustered around either side of the ogres' feet and added their own strength to the tower.

The tanuki hurried over, wiggled his rump, and jumped up to catch his claws in Saki's shirt once more. With careful footsteps, he climbed up to perch on her head.

"Ouch! Hey, that hurts! What are you doing? This isn't the time for messing around."

"I got that, sweetheart." He jumped from the top of her head to the arms of the ogres, one leg dangling over the ground until he heaved himself up. "But your buddy in green needs at least a tail-length more. He's never gonna catch that rope on his own. Be back before you can say 'banzai'!"

The bulk of the two ogres on the ground blocked Saki's view of the top. The only measure of the tanuki's progress was his huffing and puffing as he scaled the tower of ogres. The weight pressed heavier and heavier with every breath. Just when Saki thought she was about to be crushed, the ogres relaxed, and the object spirits fell over one another on the ground.

"Hey," called the tanuki. "Can I get a little help here?"

Saki stepped back and craned her neck to see the top of the pile. The tanuki held the rope between his paws as half a dozen air koi wriggled on the line. The wind caught in their bellies was so light that the tanuki might have floated away had the green ogre not kept a tight grip on his furry tail.

"Coming down! Everyone who doesn't wanna get stepped on, get outta the way!" the tanuki cried.

The ogres tumbled from their pile one by one. The ground shook as their feet hit the earth, rattling Saki's teeth. With the line in firm ogre hands, the tanuki perched between the red ogre's horns and waved his tail back and forth like a drill sergeant.

"Heave, ho! Heave, ho!"

The ogres tugged the air koi all the way down the pole to the ground. The koi were three times bigger than Saki and about thirty times bigger than their water-bound relatives, but their scales were the same white, orange, and black. Their mouths opened and closed as they tried to suck up any stray veins of wind along the ground. Strands of whiskers floated around their faces, tickling Saki's cheeks when they swam past her head.

With the weight of the four ogres underneath them, the air koi were anchored to the ground. The silver spirit's butterfly messenger darted between the giant koi and landed on Saki's arm.

"Excellent work," said the butterfly. "Now you can follow me to the Palace of Souls where the prince and my mistress await."

"There's still one minor problem…" Saki turned to the object spirits. "Any suggestions for how to get the wind out of these fish?"

"Not to worry," said the prayer beads. "Ogres, could you hold down a koi for us?"

The three sandals helped the ogres tie the pulley line to the ground as the air koi wriggled. The ogres caught one of the koi between their big arms and wrestled it to the ground. Two ogres pinned the fins down while a third held the tail. The red ogre gripped the air koi's floating whiskers until all it could do was flap its mouth in distress.

The prayer beads clicked against Saki's wooden geta. "We will be sad to see you go. If you ever have need of our help, you know where to find us. Those of our kind who have not yet awakened may also aid you, if you ask them. But you already have a powerful ally in the guardian."

The tanuki pulled her over to the air koi's flapping mouth, and the red ogre stepped aside with a bow of his head. "You'll need something to keep you up there," said the tanuki.

The umbrella poked its way through the group. It lifted its paper up and down to mimic a bird flapping its wings.

The tanuki scratched his ear and tilted his head. After a moment, he nodded. "Yeah, I s'pose you'll do. Saki, hold tight to that handle."

Saki took the umbrella with both hands as the cotton shroud wrapped around her waist and twisted into a knot, tying her to the wood of the handle. The tanuki climbed up her back one last time and settled into the loose space between Saki and the shroud.

"All right, sweetheart. You ready to fly?"

The butterfly flapped past the string of koi and drifted up into the night.

"Wait." Saki swallowed hard. Her palms began to sweat. "You mean, like, right this very second?"

The tanuki waved his tail and hollered back to the red ogre. "Let's go!"

Saki took one look over her shoulder. The red ogre made a running jump, hurtled into the air, and landed with a heavy thump on the bloated body of the air koi.

A gust of wind hit Saki's back. The burst filled the umbrella, and the strength of the push launched them into the air. Saki's scream was lost in the rush of the air, and she clutched the umbrella handle so hard that her knuckles turned white. Her feet dangled below her, the only solid ground one long, perilous fall away.

CHAPTER 19

Saki shut her eyes tight. When the wind slowed and she could breathe again, she found herself floating past the tall poles of the wind fields. The ogres were becoming colored blurs on the ground, and the object spirits were already too small to see.

She twisted her neck, but she didn't dare take a hand off the umbrella to wave. "I didn't even get to say good-bye!" she shouted. The wind took her words the moment they came off her lips.

The tanuki held his muzzle by her ear. "It's okay. Those rascals have a knack for showing up in unexpected places."

The mountain peak loomed closer, but they were still a long way off. The butterfly messenger beat its wings against the night sky, faster than any real butterfly could. When a bank of heavy clouds rolled in and stifled the light of the moon, the spirit glowed and led them through the dark.

Saki couldn't tell how far up they had climbed. The ground was nothing more than a vague shape beneath them, as if they were floating through a land of shadows. The shroud held her tight to the umbrella, and her fear of falling was soon overwhelmed by wonder.

The wind carried them up, up, up until they nearly brushed the clouds. The mountain in the spirit world was ten times the size of the mountain she'd seen in the daylight. Tiny flecks of light wandered through the dark woods and collected into one long procession. The Pilgrim's Road teemed with the spirits of the Night Parade making one last journey before the sun came. Their path glowed like the Milky Way beneath Saki's feet, each fleck of light another guiding star.

Saki tugged on the tanuki's tail. "Can I ask you a question?"

"Yikes, careful with the merchandise, sweetheart!" he yipped. "What's eating ya?"

"Well, I've spent so long worrying about how to lift the curse, I hadn't really thought about what happens after."

"That's easy. You go home, no curse and no worries."

"And when the Night Parade ends, the barrier between the worlds is restored."

"Hey, why so glum? I thought you didn't want anything to do with any more spirits."

"I thought that, but…" Saki frowned. The pang of disappointment was unexpected and illogical, but no more illogical than believing her adventures the last three nights had been anything more than wild dreams. Yet with each step along the spirit roads, she'd stopped doubting, not only her eyes but herself. It would all be over in moments, and she might never be able to come back.

The umbrella swerved, and Saki's stomach did a flip. The tanuki pressed himself closer. Ahead of them, the butterfly messenger was struggling against the currents of the wind.

They neared the high walls of the palace. The white stones with their gold and green trim stood pristine against the darkness of the night, but a moat of black liquid writhed and tossed at their base. The rising tide surrounded the palace and made the wind tremble with each undulating movement.

Frantic gusts tossed them back and forth. The air burst like pinpricks on Saki's face. The wind from the air koi kept them going forward, but every other current in the sky tried to push them away. The palace, which had once seemed impossible to reach, towered above them, too tall for even the clouds to cover.

On closer inspection, the moat of black liquid was not liquid at all. Long, slimy tendrils had woven together until they formed a writhing river. They groped along the white walls, leaving stains and refuse in their wake. The tendrils crawled on top of one another at the corners, groping at the towering heights of the sanctuary.

The black moat opened like a festering wound. Tendrils of squirming filth shot up from the ground and grasped at the air, fumbling to catch the intruders in the sky.

The captured wind bucked and reared, tossing Saki and the spirits up and down. Saki's sweat-slicked hands slipped on the umbrella handle. Gust after gust howled past. Her teeth would have chattered from the cold, but her jaw was clenched hard enough to make her head throb.

They rode out the storm while the black tendrils scraped the skies. The palace was within reach. As long as the wind held, they could cover the distance in less than three bursts of air.

A sudden drop made Saki scream. The umbrella flapped to keep them steady, but the wind that had carried them from the fields was failing.

"Only a few more seconds," she called to the umbrella. "We've almost made it!"

Nauseous fear seeped into her mind. If they couldn't reach the palace, every trial she'd passed would be for nothing. If the wind couldn't hold, she would be lost. This was her very last chance.

Something wet and cold brushed Saki's leg. A black tendril wrapped around her ankle and pulled.

Their wind scattered into a burst of loose breezes. The tendril hauled Saki and the spirits down from the walls with force enough to snap the umbrella's joints. It flapped desperately but couldn't slow their plunge.

The butterfly dove down with them. A glow spread from its wings as it latched onto Saki's arm. Soft light eddied around them, and the cold tendril retreated from her leg. Though still in freefall, the butterfly's power nudged them away from the pulsing pit of black sludge.

Saki hit the ground hard. Covered in the butterfly's light, she rolled along the stones until she came to a stop under the empty sky. The Palace of Souls towered above them, its high walls blocking out half of the moon. The wind hadn't lasted long enough to push them inside the courtyard, but they had made it to the inner gate.

On her ankle, a chill prickled where the tendril had touched, as if it had left something of itself behind inside of her. The ghost of the darkness wrapped around Saki's chest and squeezed.

"You okay, sweetheart?" The tanuki pawed at her.

Saki sat up and breathed deep, but the chains of dread only drew tighter. The umbrella and the cotton shroud were scattered only a few paces away. They were battered and broken but alive.

The butterfly lay beside her on the ground. It neither moved nor flapped its wings, and its light sputtered and dimmed like a candle flame. Saki scrambled to her knees and crawled to its side.

"Oh no… Please be all right. Where are you hurt?"

The butterfly's wings twitched. It made no further move to get up. "I am sorry that I could not guide you to the palace. I have failed."

"You didn't. You saved us." Saki picked the messenger up and set its frail body on her lap. "Now you need to rest. Is there anything I can do?"

"Leave me," said the butterfly. "There is no time to waste. You must cross the bridge and enter the palace gates. The enemy has already felt your presence."

"We're not abandoning you. I'll carry you, and you can tell us the way to go."

The light was almost gone. The edges of the butterfly's wings flaked away and dissolved into the air.

"I used my power to get you to this bridge. Forgive me for not seeing your journey through to the end." The butterfly's body lightened and faded. "Remember the words of my mistress. Hold close…to courage…"

Saki cupped her hands to keep the last bit of the spirit from disappearing. Tears fell into her open palms. Every last trace of the spirit was gone.

The inner palace gate stood in front of them. The outer gate to the shrine compound was boarded shut behind. As Saki wept, black tendrils crawled up from beneath the bridge and blocked the way forward. The clouds fled, and the light of the stars grew dim. A row of sharp teeth sunk into Saki's arm.

"There's no time for mourning," the tanuki barked. "Go now or you'll miss your chance forever!"

Saki staggered to her feet, took a step, then hesitated. The umbrella and the shroud were still mangled and strewn across the bridge. The tanuki held his front leg as though it had been broken.

The chill on her ankle was now as cold as ice. Once the tendrils snared them, they'd be finished. The darkness in Saki's chest seized so hard she gasped. The moment the tanuki saw her turn back, he bared his fangs and gave a fierce, rasping growl.

"I said scram! Get out of here, human!"

Saki turned and charged toward the palace. *Hold close to courage. Do not fear the night.* She repeated the words in her head like a mantra, even as the black tendrils wriggled up between the wood at her feet.

Was it courage or was it cowardice, leaving them there to fight alone? Her chest seized again, and her vision flashed. She staggered and gasped for breath as the night pressed all around her.

The tendrils of slime wove together until they formed a net over the palace entrance. More tendrils branched out and followed her. They snapped like vipers on her heels as she ran toward the gate. With voices as dead and hollow as a curl of shed skin, they sang, a chorus of hissing cries to drown out the pounding of her heart.

The end of the bridge came too soon. Saki's knees buckled, and she slid down toward the dark mass. The tendrils groped for her foot. They curled around one of her wooden geta and tore it away when she pulled her leg back.

Her lungs strained for a breath that wasn't there. There was nowhere left to run. The entrance was blocked. It was all over. She was helpless.

The hissed chorus became a roar of triumph. The roar twisted into a voice. A thought, dark and unbidden, leaked into her mind.

This is all your fault.

Saki shook her head. The thought didn't belong to her. Something cold and rotten clawed up through her heart and slipped into her head. She tried to push it away, but the rotten feeling held on. She felt tendrils looping through her mind, the black roots pulling out her fears and the poison feeding on her deepest doubts.

She tried to scream, but she couldn't breathe. With one hand, she clung to the bridge. With the other, she clawed at her frozen throat. The voice in her mind pushed deeper into her head.

You gave us this power. You lit the flame. You opened the

*gates for us to slip in. We've made this world ours, thanks
to you.*

Saki's nails drew blood. The sharp burst of pain loosened something inside of her and she drew in a desperate breath. "Stop it! Leave me alone! I didn't ask for any
of this!"

*You called to us. You set us free. You called the spirits as
well. They took you and showed you the fruits of your labors.*

Saki struggled to keep her breaths under control. The
tendrils were poised, waiting. A predator playing with
its prey. On the back of her tongue, she could taste the
slithering darkness. Her voice shook when she spoke.
"Let me pass."

You have no need of this world.

"I'm going to the palace. I'm going to lift the curse. Get
out of my way." Her hands could barely lift the marble
pouch out of her pocket, and her fingers trembled vio-
lently against the strings.

The tendrils stretched out, and the voice that had
invaded her head seemed to laugh. Each burst felt hollow,
like the tolling of a graveyard bell.

*Those will not touch us. Our roots have dug too deep.
Now this world is ours to take. You left it long ago with
no one else to care for it. The curse you fear is not for
you, selfish child. The curse is for this world. We are the
curse. We are the end of this miserable, forgotten place.*

Return with your pitiful life and leave this broken world to its end.

A mass of twisting darkness rose into the air like a tidal wave of hate and decay.

Leave, wretched human. This world belongs to us.

Her fault. It was all her fault.

The black tendrils covered the bridge and stretched for Saki's legs. She kicked them back with her other wooden geta. Behind her, the tide of darkness washed over the umbrella and the cotton shroud. The tanuki was gone.

"Give them back!" Saki screamed at the writhing mass.

They belong to us.

"They belong to no one! Let them go!"

Saki lunged at the wall. If the death curse was not for her, then she could still fight. She had to fight. She clawed at the black tendrils, but each one she ripped away grew back twofold. The stench was overwhelming. Her skin reeked of wet mold, and sticky fluid ran into her hair.

"I'll tear you apart! Let them go!"

You do not belong here. You cannot stop us.

Saki's scream died in her throat. Her nose flooded with the smell of death and decay. Everywhere, black tendrils closed in as the wave of darkness crested, fell over her, and tore her away from the safety of the ground.

LEAVE. DO NOT COME BACK.

She struggled, her breath once again trapped in her

chest. She twisted upside down and inside out as the tendrils burrowed under her skin, snaked around her insides, and burst through her mind like corpse worms. Around her, nothing remained but the dark. Darkness and the smell of rotten wood.

CHAPTER 20

A cool hand smoothed Saki's forehead. Whispers lingered in the air. Saki forced her eyes to open, but the lights blinded her. She moved her neck, and her head throbbed in reply. The same cool hand brushed the matted hair from her face.

"Saki, dear, can you hear me?"

When Saki tried to sit up, the cool hand pushed her down. Three blankets had been piled on top of her body, yet she shivered.

"Saki, say something."

Her tongue was sluggish in her mouth, but she recognized the voice and the hand. "Grandma?"

"That's right, dear."

Saki's eyes had adjusted to the light. She was stretched out on a bed in a small, clean room. A man with thick glasses stood nearby, clipboard in hand.

Grandma stroked her hair. "Do you know where you are?"

"This isn't your house…" Saki rubbed her eyes, and the room drifted in and out of focus.

"No, dear. We had to take you to Dr. Maeda. You have a bad fever."

She was in Maeda's house? It was bright and spacious, and the floors were made of wood, not tatami. She'd assumed that Maeda was from a farming family, like most of the village. Then again, she'd never bothered to ask… No, there was no time for guilt.

Saki pushed herself into a sitting position. Her vision swam, but she brushed Grandma's hands away. "We have to go home."

"You won't be leaving today. You have to rest, Saki. Maybe tomorrow." Grandma tried to pat her hand, but Saki couldn't keep still.

"No, we have to go to your house," she insisted. "We have to go back now."

The daylight would hide all paths to the spirit world, but she had to do something. Anything. The last she'd seen of the tanuki and the object spirits, they'd been sucked into the darkness on the bridge. And what about all the other spirits in the groves, on the roads, and in the villages?

"I have to go," Saki repeated.

Grandma rose from the bedside chair to hold her back. The doctor, Maeda's father, hurried over and swung her legs back into bed.

Saki's head throbbed, and every quick movement

made her dizzy. Grandma continued to stroke her hair while the doctor rummaged through a collection of bottles. After sorting through the shelf, Dr. Maeda handed her a folded paper filled with powder and pressed a cup of water into her hands.

"Drink this," he said. "You'll be back on your feet in no time."

Saki upended the paper and drank the medicine. The powder stuck in her throat, even after she drained the entire cup of water.

"Your parents will be back soon," said her grandmother. "They took your brother out to get some dinner in town."

Saki's voice cracked in her throat. "I've been asleep all day?"

The fever burned under her skin, as if her body was trying to expel something from her system. The rotten smell of the black tendrils stuck in her nose. Saki snapped to attention, then clutched her forehead as a burst of pain pierced her skull.

"What's the matter? Does it hurt?" Her grandmother set a hand on her back.

"Grandma, are we lighting the Farewell Fire tonight?" The throbbing pain retreated as Saki breathed in deep. That was the last part of the ritual, the final rite of Obon.

Grandma patted her back and gave a sad smile. "I

know you don't care much for old superstitions. We don't have to think about it tonight."

"No, I want to do it, please! We have to get back in time to light it." Saki remembered the smell of wood smoke and her grandfather's strong arms holding her to watch the fire crackle around the sakaki branches. One fire welcomed the dead, one fire laid them to rest…

Grandma held her hand. "You shouldn't trouble yourself, dear. You need to relax and wait for your strength to come back. We'll be keeping you here with Dr. Maeda until he thinks it's safe to take you home to Tokyo."

If her body hadn't been racked with fever, Saki would have jumped to her feet and run the rest of the way to the mountain. Every second she spent in bed was another moment that her friends in the spirit world were in danger. The black mass wasn't a spirit; it was from *her* world. She'd seen it the very first day she'd arrived.

Most importantly, she had an idea of how to stop it.

"Grandma, you have to listen to me. I need to go back up for the Farewell Fire. I have to get another branch and—"

Grandma stood up. "I think I've heard enough. All I'm doing is upsetting you, so I think I'll step out and let the doctor take over."

"Wait, Grandma!" Saki held out her hands, but Dr. Maeda was standing by to hold her down on the bed.

When Grandma left the room, Saki saw another figure

in the doorway. Maeda watched her from the hall as the door swung shut. She offered Saki's grandmother a cup of tea in the living room, their muffled conversation filtering in through the hall.

"Lie back down and try to rest." The doctor tucked Saki's blankets into the bed. "We'll take good care of you, I promise."

When she settled back down, he checked the watch on his wrist and excused himself. Before the door latch clicked shut, Saki pushed the blankets back. The fever still made her head swim, but her energy was returning with every minute. On wobbling legs, she hunted for a way out.

She opened the door a crack, but the hallway was dark, and she didn't know the layout of the house. She gave up on the door and crept to the window near the bed. She pressed her face against the glass and looked down.

She was in a room on the second floor. There was enough roof underneath the window to sneak along and a trellis reaching up the side of the house. She flicked the window latch and pushed up on the frame to see if it would budge.

"Even if you get out, our house isn't even close to the mountain. You'll be walking for half an hour at least." Maeda stood in the doorway, a tray of rice porridge in her hands.

Saki put her back to the window and tucked her hair behind her ear, feigning innocence. "I don't know what you're talking about."

The other girl's mouth twitched into a lopsided smile. "Yes, you do. You've been making that same face ever since I met you, like you're planning some sort of prison break."

"I'm not just playing around this time." Saki dropped the act and turned back to the window frame. "I have to get back to the mountain sometime tonight, with or without your help."

"My help?" Maeda raised her brows.

"No. I mean, of course you wouldn't." Saki grimaced. The fever made it hard to think straight.

"What about Tokyo?" Maeda set the tray of rice porridge on a table near the bed. "You're supposed to eat this, by the way. Doctor's orders."

Saki shook her head and paced around the room. "Tokyo doesn't matter right now. Anyway, I can't explain it, but there's something that I have to do."

Maeda watched Saki turn all around the room. Just when Saki thought the other girl would go fetch her father, Maeda crossed the floor and pushed the door shut. She looked back at Saki with a curious tilt of her head.

"I still haven't forgiven you, but if something can make you forget about your big city, it has to be pretty serious. What exactly do you have to do?"

Saki snorted. "You wouldn't believe me."

"Try me," Maeda replied with a shrug.

Saki took a seat on the bed. "On the first night of Obon, I sort of messed up the Welcome Fire. It summoned some kind of vengeful spirit that's gone and cursed the whole mountain and everything that lives there. Now all of the other spirits are going to be destroyed unless I can get back to light the Farewell Fire and send the darkness away for good."

Maeda scratched the back of her neck and grimaced. "Um, I think you should go back to sleep for a little while..."

Saki scowled. That was the reaction she'd expected. "I'm not crazy. I really saw them. For the last three nights, I've been going to the spirit world. They call it the Night Parade and—oh forget it. You said yourself you haven't forgiven me, so why would you help?"

"I might, if I didn't think you were delirious," Maeda said.

Saki raised her legs onto the bed and tucked her knees under her chin. "You don't have to pretend to be nice to me, after all of the things I did to you. You were right about everything you said at the Bon dance. I was a jerk...and I'm sorry."

"Yeah, you kind of were a jerk," said Maeda. "But I also shouldn't have yelled. I accept your apology."

Saki quirked a brow. "Just like that? Do you even remember what I said to you?"

"I remember. But you apologized, and now I've forgiven you. What good does it do me to hold a grudge?"

Saki gave a grim smile and shook her head. "You know, I thought the goody-goody act was just for show, but you're the real deal, aren't you?" Girls like Yuko, Hana, and her friends from home would have laughed Saki out of the room after a story like that.

In a single movement, Maeda took a step from the door and stood in front of Saki. "Okay, I've decided. I know a way to sneak you out."

"Uh, what? Wait. Didn't you say I was delirious?"

"Yes, I did." Maeda couldn't stay still, and she took up Saki's job of pacing back and forth by the window. "But I've changed my mind. It's too much work to make yourself sick just to mess with me. I don't think you're that desperate, so you're probably telling the truth. So I'll help you." She bound over to the window and scanned the one-lane road outside.

"Thank you." Saki didn't give Maeda time to change her mind. If there was any chance they could reach the shrine before the night ended, Saki would gladly take it. "How can I get out of here?"

Maeda put a finger to her lips and went back to the door. She waved Saki down the hallway while her

288

father and Saki's grandmother talked over tea in the living room downstairs. They tiptoed down the steps, and Maeda stabbed her finger around the corner.

"Take the back door by the kitchen and meet me around the house," she whispered. When Saki nodded, the other girl turned toward the tea party in the living room.

Outside, Saki slipped on a pair of oversized garden shoes and pushed the kitchen door closed behind her. The click came as soft as a sigh. Saki let out the breath she'd been holding and shuffled along the side of the house, trying to keep her feet from slipping out of her stolen shoes. Maeda came around from the front and waved her behind the family's car.

"I told them I was going to borrow a book from a girl on the other side of the village. That should buy us some time. We'll take my bike."

"If we get caught, you're going to get in a lot of trouble, you know. Let me take the bike, and I'll go on my own."

The other girl flashed a grin over her shoulder as she turned a key into the bike lock. "Nope. You're not getting away that easily. You're not well enough to be going all the way up there alone. And besides, if you're telling the truth about the spirits, I want to see them too."

"I don't even know if I can get back to the spirit world now that the Night Parade is over, let alone bring someone else," Saki said. Not to mention the black tendrils…

Maeda kicked up the stand and wheeled the bike out into the street. "We'll see about that when we get there. Come on, get on the carrier."

It wasn't safe for either of them, but it was a chance Saki had to take. She squeezed in behind Maeda. There wasn't a lot of room, but they managed to fit well enough for Maeda to kick off down the road. The summer air was still warm, but Saki's fever left her shivering in the wind. The sun was setting at their backs, and the orange twilight grew darker as Maeda turned the bike onto the main road through the village.

"I sort of have a confession to make!" Maeda called from ahead.

"What?" Saki had to raise her voice to beat the wind.

"I was lying when I told you that your grandmother asked me to talk to you. When I saw you at the graveyard, I thought you looked kind of cool. If you didn't notice, I don't have a lot of friends my age around here…"

Saki blushed. "I thought you were being condescending. But I guess that's because you seemed like one of those girls who's always good at everything, who gets good grades and gets along with her parents. It was intimidating."

"You were intimidated? By me?" Maeda laughed as she turned a corner.

"Yeah, kind of. I guess we were both pretty dumb, weren't we?"

"Some of us more than others."

"You're never going to let me live this down, are you?"

"Nope."

The bike sped past the convenience store and up toward the mountain road. The forest rose through the red dusk. Maeda stood to pedal as beads of sweat streamed down her face. They were halfway up the steep road to the graveyard when the weight of two girls became too much. The bike tipped over on a switchback turn, and Maeda threw out her foot to keep them steady.

She cried out, and the bike fell anyway. Saki tipped back and landed on her side in the dirt. One tire spun idly in the air as Maeda curled up in the middle of the road clutching her leg.

Saki bit back a yelp and scrambled to her feet. "Are you okay?"

"Sorry…I'm just…a little winded…"

Saki pulled the bike off the road as Maeda sat up and rolled back her sock. It hadn't even been a minute, but the ankle already looked pink and swollen.

"Don't worry," Saki said. "We can walk up from here. Give me your arm."

Maeda put an arm around Saki's shoulder and hobbled along with one foot. She frowned down at the dirt on her clothes and cast one last look at the bike before they continued. "I guess slipping back into the house without my dad noticing is out of the question now."

"Do you think your ankle's broken?"

"No, it hurts, but not that bad." In spite of the brave words, Maeda's face was drawn and pale. She winced with every other step. "I bet it's only a sprain."

"I owe you even more now. Whatever you want, just name it."

Maeda laughed through the pain as the shape of the house appeared through the trees. "A glass of water would be nice."

Saki left her on the steps outside and kicked off the garden shoes. The village was so small and the house was so far up the mountain that Grandma never locked her door. Saki hurried to the kitchen to pour a glass of water.

Maeda took the glass with one hand and caught Saki's wrist in the other. "You're still taking me, aren't you?"

Saki opened her mouth, but the lie withered on her tongue. She'd already ruined too many lives in the last few days; she wouldn't let anyone else suffer. Even if Maeda could walk, the spirit world was no longer parades and adventures. The darkness that had taken over was far too dangerous for any mere human.

Saki looked out at the forest, her mouth thin with guilt and worry. Maeda released her with a pained smile.

"That's just my luck. Next time then. Just be careful, okay?"

Saki couldn't think of anything clever to say. If she was wrong, there wouldn't be a next time. But Maeda believed her. She had to start believing in herself, mere human or not. In lieu of words, Saki flashed the other girl a peace sign and disappeared back into the house.

In the corner room, the clothes she'd worn to bed had been washed and stacked in the corner. Her phone, Grandpa's metal charm dangling from the side, sat on top. Saki rifled through each pocket and turned over every piece of bedding, but the pouch of flat marbles was gone. Even a search of her brother's things yielded nothing. Either her mother had taken the marbles before she'd brought Saki to the doctor, or they never made it back from the spirit world at all. There was no time to fret over the loss. Marbles or not, she would make the climb.

Saki opened the sliding door to the walkway. The forest was purple in the last rays of the sun, and soon darkness would descend over the mountain.

The geta with the shadow straps didn't appear, and there was no guide to lead her up the hidden roads. A voice at the back of her mind told Saki that the door was closed forever, but she squashed the thought and began the hunt for a new pair of shoes. The garden slippers she'd borrowed from Maeda were two sizes too big, and her own shoes were missing from the front entrance.

At the back of the house, the bins of junk from their afternoon cleaning sat underneath the walkway. Saki leaned over and pulled out two mismatched straw sandals. They were worn out and some of their straps were shrunken, but her feet were small enough to fit.

The scratchy straw reminded her of the object spirits. They'd said that an object gained a soul on its hundredth birthday, and that the objects remembered the people who had been kind to them. She didn't know how long the sandals had been in Grandma's storeroom, but it was worth a try. Before she strapped them to her feet, she held the sandals to her chest and closed her eyes.

"Please," she whispered. "Help me get to the shrine. I need to make sure everyone is safe. I want to make everything right."

She tied the old straw to her feet. The fiber was itchy against her skin, not at all like the wooden geta, but they did the job. Saki slid off the walkway. With one last guilty glance at the house, she turned to search for a path up the mountain.

The tanuki's back road was gone, and Saki couldn't find the Pilgrim's Road either. Behind her, the way to town was quiet, but it was only a matter of time before the doctor noticed she was missing.

She hurried over to the path she'd taken on her first day in the village, the human path that led up to the plain, old, tumbledown shrine. Her trials had started there. That was where she'd seen the black tendrils for the first time.

After the fox had left her alone in the grove of the tree spirits, she'd seen them again. At the edge of the grove, through the forest darkness, the fallen tree's infection leaked from the real world into the spirit world. It lay dead on the hallowed ground of the shrine, tainting the purity of the entire mountain.

When her grandfather was still alive, nothing would have been allowed to rot so long on sacred ground. Even if the village only used the shrine once or twice a year, he had made sure that everything was in balance.

The Welcome Fire was supposed to invite the souls of the dead to share the world of the living, but Saki had picked the branch of a dead tree for the invocation. The evil spirit was right. She'd opened the gate.

Despite her fever, Saki loped up the mountain path. Any gate that was opened could be closed again, and an invitation could always be revoked. Tonight was the last night of Obon. If she couldn't save the spirits she'd already lost, at least she could stop the evil spirit from doing any more damage.

In the human world, the torii gates looked small and

frail. Whispers followed Saki from the woods, but she would not let herself be scared. She reached the last gate before her strength ran out, and she stumbled to the stone water basin.

She washed with shaking hands. After each palm was clean, she brought the ladle of water to her lips and rinsed her mouth. From the gate behind her, she sensed a heavy nod of approval, but when she turned her head, the movement was only a shadow of the leaves on the gate.

"It's you, isn't it?" she said aloud and smiled at the gate-keeper, invisible to her human eyes on this side of the veil. Saki bowed her head. "Thank you for your vigilance."

Moonlight filtered over the shrine grounds. She'd been here with the tengu. The buildings were smaller in the human world, but the style was the same. If she looked around a rock, she was sure to find a slug or a toad.

As Saki made her way to the back of the shrine, panic fluttered in her stomach. The branches of the healthy sakaki trees swayed in the wind, and an insect buzzed by her ear. She slapped the bug away, but the buzzing grew stronger, shaking her down to her bones.

"Relax," she told herself. "It's just a tree."

Her hand slipped into her pocket and rubbed her grandfather's charm. In another heartbeat, some of the fear fell back, and she pressed on through the grove.

Long before she picked the dead tree's form out in

the dark, she felt its malevolence rippling through the woods. It lay fallen at the edge of the grove, the space around it barren and lifeless. She forced her feet forward. The straps of the straw sandals dug into her skin, and the pain kept her from losing herself in the waves of fear. The silver spirit's words came to her again.

You must hold close to courage. Do not fear the night.

As if breaking through a nightmare, Saki marched straight toward the dead log. Age and termites had eaten away at most of its branches, but one still remained, wedged beneath the weight of the tree and the earth below.

She grasped the branch with both hands. The bark was slick with rot. She dug in with her nails and pulled, but the wood refused to yield.

Insects darted across her skin. They pricked and buzzed, taking her blood but not her nerve. She braced one foot against the log and pulled again. Part of the branch tore away from the tree. She heaved back once more, all of her weight behind her.

The bark under her foot crumbled with the pressure. Her leg plowed into the heart of the rotten tree, burying her to the ankle. She kicked to get it out, but something in the tree held her inside, the rot wet and cold against her skin. She didn't dare let go now.

With a cry, Saki pried her foot free. Filth soaked the

straw sandal, and a thin film lay over her bare foot. From the hole in the bark, a dark shape moved. A black tendril wriggled out, only a finger's breadth from her hands.

She dug her heels into the earth and pulled the branch with all of her strength.

"You don't belong here!" she shouted. She wouldn't let the darkness infect her world as well. The rot stopped with her.

Through the buzzing of the insects, the trees of the sakaki grove rattled their leaves. Saki blinked away tears of frustration. With her eyes half-closed, she thought she saw small white hands fall against her skin. A surge of strength rushed to her aching arms.

The rotten branch snapped off, and the force threw her back onto the ground. She scrambled to her feet, branch in hand, and wiped her hair away from her face. A streak of tree rot from her hands smeared against her cheek.

The black tendril in the bark was gone. The chill on her ankle prickled where the liquid rot met the night air, but all around her, the forest had quieted. Even the cicadas had ceased their endless cries. Saki took a breath and silently thanked the living grove for its help.

The stillness remained. Not a single leaf stirred. No sound met her ears but her own panting breath.

A noiseless figure snaked along the ground. A dozen more tendrils reappeared at the spot where she'd broken off the twig. As they built onto one another, they stretched out, groping over the earth to search for their missing piece.

Saki took a step back.

More tendrils poured from the sides of the log. From every rotten sore in the bark, every crack and crease, hundreds of slithering shapes appeared. They wove together until the mass grew tall enough to block out the moonlight.

Saki turned and ran.

The wave crashed behind her. The tendrils shot along the ground, running into the tiny buildings of the shrine. Saki darted back to the main path. The black tendrils cut her off. She changed directions so quickly that one of her straw sandals flew off into the woods. Without any weapons or any other way to fight, all she could do was flee. She had to survive long enough to burn the branch and end this.

The grove, the shrine, and the path were lost. That left only the woods. Saki turned downhill and charged. The tendrils followed, but as they moved farther from the shrine, their movements slowed. Saki spared a glance back and saw nothing but the still woods.

She turned down the mountain once more and slowed to a halt. Between two trees, another girl was waiting.

"You shouldn't be walking on that foot," Saki called, but the breathless reprimand was swallowed up by the forest.

She squeezed the branch and took another step when the wet, putrid smell in the air made her pause. "Maeda?"

The girl lifted her head. Saki met her own face, the dark brown eyes she stared into every day in the mirror, the same sweat-damp clothes. A perfect copy, except for the black veins twisting and writhing beneath the skin.

"How did you…" Saki flicked a glance over her shoulder for only a split second. In another instant, the creature's rotten breath brushed her cheek.

"You took a bit of me. It's only fair."

Saki jerked away. She scrambled back, her eyes never leaving the uncanny figure, until her spine slammed against the bark of a tree trunk. The living ghost followed with certain steps and a too-sharp smile.

"Where are you going? It's all gone," said the creature. It had taken her voice too. "That's the way of nature. Life to death, day to night…you to me."

"You're wrong. It was my mistake. Please don't punish anyone else for it."

The creature was close enough that Saki could see the tendrils pulsing under its stolen skin. "But was it really a mistake? Give up, little girl. You'll be—"

Saki shoved the creature away. It tumbled downhill and slid to a stop, facedown in the underbrush. Saki's whole body was trembling as she crept around the tree trunk.

The leaves began to stir. The creature sat up again and

stared at her with a face plagued by slick black tendrils. The wiggling worms wove the copy's jaw back together. It had not yet finished when the creature spoke again. The voice it had stolen rasped with layers of muted screams.

"You had the chance. Now after I've sucked the marrow from the spirit world, I'll taste a bit of yours." Its jaw opened, half-latticed with tendrils. A thick black sludge dripped down its chin and hissed onto the forest floor. "How many treats have you been saving for me in that big house down below?"

The house. Maeda was there, helpless. Her parents and her brother would return soon. Grandma... She couldn't live if she let anything happen to them.

Saki finally turned her back and ran uphill. She pushed again for the shrine and whatever desperate hope remained as a fresh, raw panic pumped through her blood.

The creature in her skin was waiting at the clearing. The black tendrils slithered along the ground near its bare feet, encircling the shrine. They looped behind Saki, cutting off her only means of escape. She skidded to a stop, her breaths in wild gasps.

She'd lost the marbles, but there was one last weapon she could use against a spirit. Saki snapped her grandfather's metal charm off the phone and flipped open the screen.

"If you're going to be me, you'll be needing this."

The phone cast a pale electric glow as she lobbed the

plastic at the imposter. The figure froze. The plastic case struck the darkness at its heart. In another instant, the human shape burst into a mass of inky tendrils. They recoiled but did not retreat.

Saki held the rotten branch in one hand and her grandfather's charm in the other. The metal was warm against her skin. It lit something inside of her, like the glow of the butterfly messenger.

The Path of the Gods…a road beyond the shrine…the sure of heart.

More than ever, she was sure.

Saki charged behind the shrine buildings and up toward the mountain peak before the tendrils had a chance to regroup. She was past the last boundary when a beam of moonlight shone through the forest onto the hidden path.

Leaves slapped her in the face, and branches scratched at her arms, but she ran too fast to feel the pain. She couldn't hear a sound outside the thundering of her own heart, but she could smell the stink on the air as the darkness approached from behind.

It took only one misstep. She stumbled and slid backward. She risked a glance over her shoulder, and her breath froze in her lungs. The black tendrils were in full pursuit. They'd chained together and flooded the path behind her like a swelling tide.

Still clutching the branch, Saki clawed her way back to her feet.

The path was steep. Every muscle in her body was on fire, and she felt no closer to the spirit world than before. If she stopped, the wave would overwhelm her, and that would be the end of everything. But the path couldn't go on forever. When it ended, there would be no place left to run.

Saki looked back and saw the black tendrils reaching toward her. One of them brushed against her arm, and a chill sunk into her bones. The ageless voice of the infection shrieked with rage and greed.

IT IS MINE. IT WILL ALL BE MINE.

In an instant, the earth dropped out from under her. She hurtled forward, wheeling in the air. A flash of stars, the moon through the trees, the sickening thump as her body hit the ground.

There was pain, then darkness, then nothing at all.

CHAPTER 21

S he was warm.

"You have come," a clear voice said. "I knew you would make it."

Saki sat on the floor of a grand reception room. The walls were white, trimmed in green and gold. The silver spirit knelt in front of her, her eyes gleaming.

"Where am I?" Saki asked.

The silver spirit rose to her feet and offered Saki her hand. "This is the Palace of Souls."

"I was running in the woods." There was no door behind her, no gate or road. "I tried to find the secret path, but…"

"You found it," the silver spirit said, though her voice was not happy. She nodded to the branch in Saki's hand. "You came from the grove."

As Saki held the rotten tree wood, miniature tendrils, like black worms, poked out from the bark. Saki dropped the branch on the floor, but the tendrils were too weak to do anything but flail.

"This small fragment cannot hurt you," the silver spirit told her. She handed Saki a light square of silk. "Here, use this."

Saki didn't reach for the silk right away. She looked back up at the spirit. "The darkness chased me. It was with me on the path. I didn't...I didn't mess up again, did I? By bringing it this close?"

"It could not follow you. Not this part of you." A flicker of concern passed on the silver spirit's face. "But we must hurry. Take what you've brought and come with me."

Saki picked up the branch with the square of silk, and the silver spirit led her to the only door in the room. It opened to a long hall. No lamps or candles burned to lead the way, but the pale walls shone with a light all their own, like the soft glow of the moon.

Saki caught the silver spirit by the sleeve of her kimono. "Last night, I was on the bridge in front of the gate. I lost my friends in the darkness. Please, do you know how I can find them?"

"I am very sorry, but I have not left this place since you were last expelled from our world."

"Then take me out now!" Saki pleaded. "I have to save them!"

The silver spirit stopped by another doorway along the hall. She raised her hand and showed Saki the edges of the door frame. A dark stain seeped through the gaps between the walls.

"Do you see the marks on these doors? Each door leads to a different part of the spirit world. The wrath of the infection has blocked them all."

Anger flashed in Saki's eyes. Her grip on the rotten branch tightened until the wood bent and splintered. She had come so close, without any guide, only to be trapped.

"They sacrificed themselves for me, but I can't do anything to help them?" Saki beat a fist on the delicate walls where the rot had seeped in. "This isn't fair!"

The silver spirit placed a hand on Saki's shoulder, not a touch of comfort, but a gesture of resolute strength.

"You found the Path of the Gods on your own, at great risk to yourself. There may still be something we can do. Do not throw away all hope, for everything is not lost. The Palace of Souls and the Midlight Prince still hold."

"Then take me to him," Saki said. "If he holds the power in this world, he must be able to do something."

The silver spirit stepped back. "This way. Follow me to the end of the hall."

The stains around the door frames lightened, and the walls shone brighter. By the time Saki and the silver spirit came to the final set of doors, a cool, clean scent drifted through the air.

The doors at the end of the hall were carved to

resemble a ripple running across the water. They were not lavish but had a quiet grace. As Saki and the silver spirit approached, the doors opened on their own.

They came into a spacious room with a low ceiling. Folding screens painted with scenes of the Night Parade were the only decorations set out on the floor. On top of a cushion in the center of the room sat a boy only a few years older than Saki. He was dressed in an old gray kimono that drooped on his slight frame.

With the rotten branch in hand, Saki stepped forward. "I'm looking for the Midlight Prince."

The boy gave her a soft smile. "That is what they call me."

Saki was stunned into silence. He had none of the splendor of the silver spirit, and his soft face showed no emotion beyond simple curiosity. His clothes were plain, and his hair, though longer than hers, was tied behind his head without any of the decorations of a lord or samurai. Saki couldn't call him a prince at all.

Her mouth drew into a hard line, and she brandished the tree branch like a sword. "Who do you think you are?"

The boy became confused. "I beg your pardon? I am called—"

"Yeah, the 'Midlight Prince.' You said that already. But a prince is supposed to take care of people. What have you done to stop this? It was taking over your shrine all this time, and you did nothing."

The boy did not retreat from her gaze, but his expression was muted. "I have no power over this world. I cannot affect its change."

"Then what kind of ruler are you?" she shouted. "The spirits said that only you had the power to make things right. Why can't you fix this?"

"In the days long ago, the spirits were correct. My office is not that of a sovereign but of an emissary; I am the channel between your world and the world of the spirits. What energy is gathered at the shrine in the human world can be used here," he explained. "In the time you walked the Night Parade, have you not seen the connection between the worlds?"

Saki looked down at the one odd straw sandal still left on her foot. The village of object spirits had come directly from her own world, and she had spoken to the spirits of the trees, which never had voices in the daytime. Though many things looked different in the spirit world, it was all a matter of perception. Saki took a deep breath to calm her temper.

"I have. I know they don't always have the same rules, but my world and this one are different parts of the same place."

"Yes," said the prince. "The fate of this world is tied to the world of humans. Though your world has little need of us, we have great need of you."

A thread had been tugged, and the tapestry began to unravel. If the spirit world depended on energy gathered from the humans, there was a reason the prince had no power to wield.

"You use the energy of the prayers from the shrine," she began. "It's deserted now, and no one comes. If people were around to notice that a tree in the grove had fallen, the infection wouldn't have started in the first place." Her hopes fell. "So it really is my fault... I even invited the dead tree back for Obon."

The prince bowed his head. "In death, the essence of the tree that fell in the grove was supposed to be cleansed. But that essence was recalled and brought back into the living world, and from the world of the humans, it came here. Though you must not be so quick to fault yourself. Your actions, however misguided, only hastened an inevitable conclusion. For this world, which lives only through belief, being forgotten is our ultimate death curse. Had you not come, we would have slowly faded until nothing remained. Do not blame yourself for the machinations of fate."

Saki shook her head. Again, she was helpless. "This is crazy. The dead spirit tried to tell me the same thing: 'hopeless,' 'lost cause,' 'just give up.' What kind of leader are you? You can't just resign yourself to die! Forget fate!" she cried. "I don't want this world to just disappear!"

A light filled the room. Stains on the walls, where the rot had leaked through, were gone in the blink of an eye. The silver spirit smiled, but the light was not hers. Neither did it come from the prince, though his face showed a new vigor. Saki looked all around the room before she realized that the light came from her own chest. After a brief moment, it faded, but the atmosphere between them was changed forever.

"A wish from the heart," said the silver spirit. "This place has not felt such power for a very long time."

The prince stood. He was more than a head taller than Saki now. "You are still part of the human world, so perhaps your prayers can help us banish this darkness. Will you lend us your power?"

"You want me to pray? Those words before just sort of…tumbled out of my mouth. I didn't even think about what I was saying."

"Lend me your hands," said the prince. "Do not be anxious."

"But what about burning the branch?"

"Place it between us. You must know by now that a task in this world can be fulfilled in many different ways."

Saki swallowed her doubts and touched her fingertips to his. They held the branch together, human and spirit united in hope. The black tendrils had retreated from the light from Saki's chest, but the darkness of the dead tree still lurked in the fibers of the wood.

The prince held her gaze.

"If thinking does not help, then do not think. *Feel.* Remember what brought you to this place. Hold those feelings close to your heart, but do not hide them from the rest of the world. Nothing can harm you as long as you believe in the strength you hold within."

Saki closed her eyes.

So much had happened in so little time. She'd felt the belief slowly settle on her shoulders like snow. That first terror in the graveyard and those will-o'-the-wisp eyes seemed like so long ago now. She'd conquered those fears, pushed herself past what she'd ever imagined she could do. She felt her connection to the spirit world in the deepest part of her being.

The person she'd been when she'd first come to the spirit world was not the same person she was now. She was prepared to take chances that she hadn't allowed herself before. Knowing the secret of the Night Parade made her feel a connection to the village that couldn't compare to anything in the city. She'd met loyal friends because of the spirit world. She'd become the master of her own fate. She'd ridden the wind and stared down the twisted face of death itself.

She couldn't let this place, which had given her so

much, be torn apart. She wouldn't surrender the friends who had done so much to help her. Her greatest wish was to see this world survive. Survive and thrive.

Through the fog of her thoughts, Saki opened her eyes. The branch she held with the Midlight Prince glowed with golden light.

Rather than bursting into flames or dissolving into flecks, the wood shifted against her skin. Saki breathed in and remembered the spirits in the sakaki grove. This branch, too, must have been part of a spirit once. How sad and lonely it must have been to be separated from its family… Was that why it clung to this world so desperately?

A sudden and unexpected tear streaked down Saki's cheek. The tear fell from her chin and burst against the golden glow of the branch. The light drew itself inside. When the illumination faded, the bark was supple and new. At the end of the branch, a patch of tiny white flowers bloomed. From life to death to life again.

When Saki lifted her gaze, the room had changed. The walls were set with windows that opened to the night sky. The moon hung so close that she might have reached out and touched it.

The Midlight Prince was also different. The color of his robes appeared like the indigo haze of the sky as the sun rose and set, and his sleeves and collar were embroidered with shining silver thread. Yet despite all of this, his face and his manner remained unchanged.

"You have done more than any of us could have hoped for," he told her with a smile.

"Will my friends be all right?" Saki asked.

"If you have kept them foremost in your heart, then I am certain that your feelings protected their spirits from danger."

Saki let go of the prince's hands and fell to her knees on the floor. Relief washed through her body, and she held the blossoming branch to her chest, the weight of the new life both beautiful and frightening.

The prince knelt down to meet her eyes. "You have given much of yourself this night. More than should be asked. Yet I thank you for all that you have done."

Saki brushed her fingers under her eyes. "I want to go out and see them. My friends. I have to apologize for all of this."

The prince's mouth dipped into a frown. "You must not stay here any longer than you have. I can return you to your world, but we cannot spare much time."

Saki shook her head. "No, I want to see them. If the infection is gone, there shouldn't be any danger left."

"Not to the spirits," said the prince. "However, you have risked your life to find this place. The Night Parade has ended, and the barrier between the two worlds has returned. If you do not leave now, you will never be able to return to the human world."

"Just for a minute, please. I promise that I'll—"

The prince placed a hand on her shoulder. "Saki, there is only one way a human reaches the world of the spirits outside of the Night Parade. Your soul passed through the barrier, but your body remains in the human world. The two must not be parted for long."

Saki looked to the silver spirit to confirm the words. That grave face on their reunion had not been only for the specter of the infection. The silver spirit wore her frown still, urgency in her sharp gaze.

"What does that mean?" Saki asked when the silver spirit reached out to take the blossoming branch. "Am I dead?"

The prince chose his words with great care. "Not yet."

Saki took a deep breath. "Then please tell them I'm sorry. And thank you. I want them to know that I didn't forget."

"I will make sure of it."

Hands trembling, Saki rummaged around in her pocket. She took out the broken charm and ran her thumb over the inscription.

"That is very powerful protection," said the prince. "Only a great soul would possess the knowledge to make something so potent."

"This was my grandfather's. He took care of this shrine before he died."

"Then we are in his debt as much as yours."

"He really loved this mountain. I think I'm starting to know why. He wanted this charm to keep the things he loved safe. My grandmother gave it to me, but I want to leave it with you." She took the prince's hand and pressed the charm into his palm. "I have to go soon, far away from this place. I want everyone to still be here if I ever get back."

"That is very kind of you. However, I cannot accept this as a gift. It is something far too close to your heart. I will keep it only until you return to claim it. Is that agreeable?"

Saki nodded, and the prince smiled once more.

"Now, we must send you back where you belong."

He touched one thumb to her forehead. In an instant, Saki's body became weightless, her arms floating up at her sides as he completed the silent ritual.

"We will always be around you, though you may not see us with your eyes."

Her vision blurred. She opened her mouth to thank him, but the taste of copper rushed into her throat and made her choke. Her lungs struggled for air to breathe. Her body felt lighter and lighter, no surface anywhere to grasp and hold. Everything around her went dark.

CHAPTER 22

She was cold.

A warm hand cupped her cheek and swept the hair out of her face. Water sloshed nearby, and a few ragged breaths carried through the air.

"Saki? Saki, can you hear me?" Her father's voice was gruff with panic.

She opened her eyes. Her legs were halfway submerged in pond water. Above them, the stars twinkled through the trees. The mountaintop was empty except for Saki, her father, and the sound of their breaths.

She heard her grandmother's shouts below them, but the voice didn't sound right. Her grandmother never lost her composure, and the shouts that Saki heard were frantic, searching. Perhaps it was someone else.

Her father pulled her up to solid ground. He cupped her face in his hand and looked into her eyes. A question lingered, but he could not open his mouth to say the words. Saki raised her fingers to her face and they came away red with blood. The cut stretched across one side of her forehead and throbbed in time with her pulse.

"Hi, Dad."

He smoothed the hair on top of her head, and his eyes never left the gash on her face. "You scared the daylights out of me. Don't ever do that again."

They were quiet once more until her father picked himself up with a grunt. He bent down to gather her in his arms, a feat he had not attempted since she was small. Tight in his embrace, she rested her head on his shoulder and felt the drumming of his heart in his chest.

Her father carried her down the narrow trail to the shrine. The spirits had called it the Path of the Gods, but as the branches brushed Saki's feet, it seemed like any other part of the forest. Or perhaps the road had never been an outside place at all, but somewhere inside. She sighed and let the unanswered question fade into the familiar sounds of the woods.

The fevered heat of her body had gone. Her skin felt cool but not cold. The leaves whispered as the wind passed by. Calm spread throughout the forest, and the same feeling of peace settled in her heart.

They passed the sakaki grove. The rotten tree was just a shell, all of its power over her swept away, and the shrine buildings had gained a new strength. They would be safe on the sleepy grounds now, no curse to hinder them. At the edge of the shrine, standing at the unpainted torii gate, a woman in disheveled clothes hurried to Saki's side.

Grandma must have been pulling at the neck of her yukata, because the lines were all askew. Her hair was fluffed out at odd angles, and the moon turned her face ashen pale. She held a pair of Grandpa's old prayer beads between her fingers and ticked them back and forth the way Saki always used to fiddle with her necklaces.

"Oh, thank the heavens you found her!"

Saki held out her hand as her father took her down the road. She caught the edge of Grandma's yukata for a split second, until the fabric slipped from her fingers.

"Everything's okay. You don't have to worry."

Grandma hid her face in her hands to hold back her sobs. She lingered by the gate as Saki's father lumbered down the path. Before Grandma followed them, Saki saw her turn back to the shrine. She pressed both hands together and closed her eyes. At the end of the prayer, she gathered up her yukata and stumbled along behind.

"How did you find me?"

"We heard a voice above the shrine. I thought it was a fox at first, but then I found you by the pond. You hit your head pretty bad, kid. What in the world possessed you to—No, never mind. First you see the doctor."

Saki buried her face in her father's shoulder to hide her smile. A fox, was it?

At the bottom of the path, the house had been over-run with visitors. A police car blazed its lights, and Dr. Maeda stood by his own car with a medical bag. Maeda's bike was tied on top, and Maeda herself peered out from behind the windshield. Saki's mother and brother stood in the doorway, paler than the waning moon.

"You're very lucky," the doctor told Saki after he checked her pulse and waved a light in front of her eyes.

"Yeah," she said. "I know."

CHAPTER 23

When she woke around noon, the deluge of people in the house had calmed to a trickle. Grandma's friends from the village, mothers and grandmothers, had all brought up gifts of food and sweets to show their concern. By the time Saki pulled herself out of bed, the dining table was covered in homemade dishes.

Her mother looked over her newspaper as Saki wandered in, following the delicious smell.

"What are you doing out of bed?" She tossed down the paper and tried to push Saki back to her room. "I can bring you something if you're hungry, but you should be getting rest."

"Mom, I'm fine." She'd slept longer in the last two days then she had the entire trip, and she was eager to get away from the sweaty futon in the corner room. Aside from the weakness in her muscles and the gash on her face, the fever was gone, and the rest of her body was healthy. "I'm just going to sit and eat. That's not going to give me brain damage."

Saki's mother must have seen the determined look in her eyes, because she held up her hands in surrender.

"Fine, but I expect you to be fully cooperative when Dr. Maeda comes back up to check on you."

Saki sat down at the table and started eating pickled cucumber slices off a lacquered tray. They'd kept her up long enough to make sure she didn't have a concussion, but they wouldn't let her out of the house, let alone out to the doctor's car. Maeda was probably in a lot of trouble for helping Saki sneak out, and she had nothing but a busted bike and a swollen ankle to show for it. Saki picked at a bowl of fried tofu and vegetables, eating only the carrots.

"Do you want some rice?" her mother asked, hovering near her shoulder. "I think that Grandma's still in the kitchen washing dishes, but I'll check. Stay here."

A moment later, Grandma looked in from the kitchen. She held out a rice bowl, but her movements were soft and hesitant. "There wasn't much left in the pot. I'll make another right now."

She placed the bowl on the table next to Saki without meeting her eyes. Before she hurried away, Saki tugged on the sleeve of her grandmother's yukata.

"Hey, Grandma? Thanks for everything." She hesitated and dropped her hand. "I'm sorry that I caused you so much trouble. I didn't mean to be a bother."

Grandma reached down to take Saki's hand, her eyes set and serious. "Never." Her voice wavered, and her face was strained with emotion. "Don't ever think that you're a bother in this house."

"So maybe I could come back next year?"

Grandma bowed her head. Only her eyes and the taut corners of her mouth gave away the smile she tried to keep from breaking loose. "You will always have a place here, whenever you wish."

Saki was still eating when the car rolled up the driveway. Her father led Dr. Maeda into the house as a smaller figure trailed behind wielding a pair of crutches. The doctor nudged his daughter into the room. Her foot was wrapped with bandages, and she had to juggle her crutches before she knelt on the floor and bowed deeply to Saki's parents.

"I apologize from the depths of my heart for putting your daughter in danger. It was my fault that you had to worry. I promise that I will never be so careless again." Maeda took a deep breath. She remained bowed over until Saki's mother reached over and set a hand on her shoulder.

"Thank you for your apology, Tomo. We know you didn't mean any harm."

Saki caught Maeda's glance as the other girl rose. They smiled at one another as if meeting for the first time.

After Dr. Maeda spouted out another round of apologies for his daughter's recklessness, Saki's grandmother rose and shuffled toward the kitchen.

"You must be thirsty after coming all the way up in this heat. Let me get you a cup of tea."

"Oh no, we don't want to be any trouble," the doctor replied.

Saki's father shook his head and waved the doctor to a seat at the table. "Not at all. Come, have at least one cup."

He looked down at his daughter. "Tomo, you go wait in the car while I do the examination. We don't want to cause any more of a fuss."

Maeda silently complied with her father's instructions. On the way out, she turned her head to Saki and mouthed a word that Saki didn't catch. Then she pointed outside before she pulled herself through the doorway with her crutches.

Saki waited until the adults were distracted by their tea, then excused herself to the bathroom. When they had their backs turned, she slipped out the front door behind Maeda.

The other girl sat on the walkway around the front of the house, dangling her feet above the ground with her crutches across her lap. She waved Saki closer, then grabbed Saki's arm and scanned her up and down.

"I'm really, really glad you're not dead. How many stitches did you get?"

"None, thankfully. But with my luck, I'm sure it'll scar," said Saki with a lopsided smile. "Sorry for roping you into this. Are you in a lot of trouble?"

Maeda sighed. "Every time my mom looks at me, she starts crying. I think she thinks I'm going to join a motorcycle gang after this."

Saki held a hand to her mouth to keep from bursting out in laughter. The expression on Maeda's face was too serious.

"I'm really, really sorry," Saki said. "If it helps, I don't think you'd do well in a gang. Especially not with that foot."

Maeda glanced back at the door, then she leaned her head close to Saki's and whispered, "What really happened up there? What possessed you to run all the way to the top of the mountain?"

"The easiest way to explain it is…" Saki thought hard before answering. "I found something important to me. When I thought that it was in danger, I had to do what I could to protect it. Of course, my parents think it was all the fever making me hallucinate. They're too worried to be mad, so that's the official story."

Maeda drew back and pursed her lips. "So you really did see spirits? For three whole nights?"

"I didn't just see them. I did all sorts of things."

Maeda's gaze wandered up to the mountain. Her breath hitched, and she turned back to Saki with an eager gleam in her eyes. "I want to know everything."

"Are you sure? It might take a long time to tell."

"I'll give you my email address, and you can tell me about it when you get back to Tokyo."

Saki bit her cheek. "I have a better idea. Can you tell me your home address instead? I'll write you letters. That way, I can draw pictures. Some of the things I saw were way too weird to explain in an email."

"Really? You promise?"

Saki held out her pinkie finger. Maeda hooked it with her own.

"Yeah, I promise. And if I can't get it all in the letters, I'll just have to tell you when I come back."

"And don't forget that you promised you'd take me too. I'm not counting last time because I couldn't walk, but next time—"

Before Saki could respond, the front door swung open, and Dr. Maeda appeared behind them.

"Tomo, I told you to wait in the car. You shouldn't be bothering Saki while she recovers." He frowned at both of them. "And you, Saki. I still need to do some tests. Running around the house before you're ready will only slow down your recovery."

Without argument, Maeda pulled herself up and hobbled back to her father's car with her crutches. She waved as Dr. Maeda herded Saki inside, in spite of Saki's insistence that she felt perfectly fine.

Inside, the doctor recorded all kinds of information: her heart rate, blood pressure, and the sound her lungs made as she inhaled. When the poking and prodding was finished, Dr. Maeda scribbled a few lines on a note and handed the note to Saki's father.

"She's remarkably well. As long as she keeps to only light activities, I see no reason why she wouldn't be fit for traveling."

"Thank you, doctor. How much do we owe you?"

The doctor patted sweat off his forehead with a handkerchief. "Please don't even consider it. It's the least I can do."

They were set to leave the next morning. Everyone packed for the trip, except Saki, who could only watch as her mother, father, brother, and even Grandma hurried back and forth from the house to their car. In all of the sorting, Saki still hadn't found her pouch of marbles. She cornered her mother in between suitcase runs, keeping her voice low in case Jun was lurking nearby.

"Mom, have you found any of my things around the house? I'm missing something important."

"I'm so sorry, Saki. Jun and I went up this morning to look for your phone, but we couldn't find anything except some old junk," her mother said. "We'll get you a new one before school starts again."

"Wait, what kind of junk?" Saki asked, the marbles forgotten. She'd lost the second of the old straw sandals in the pond, but she was grateful that they'd been able to carry her so far.

Her mother shrugged. "Just an old umbrella and a rag."

Saki clapped a hand over her mouth to hold back her cry of excitement.

"What's the matter?" Her mother scanned her face in alarm.

"You didn't just leave them there, did you?"

"Of course not. We put them in an old storage shed. Someone really should go up there and clean. Not to mention clear the path up to that pond. Even in the middle of the day, I couldn't see through all the weeds."

Saki relaxed. At least now she knew. They'd find their way back to the village of the object spirits somehow, she was sure of it. "You shouldn't just throw them away. They were probably put up there for a reason."

"Well, we won't have to worry about it, at any rate. We won't be back until the year after next." Saki's mother put a hand on her shoulder. "But I would understand if you don't want to come back. You've had a tough couple of days. Maybe we can find a way for you to stay with a friend next time."

"No!" Saki jumped. "Um, I mean, I don't mind coming. I think Grandma's a lot happier when we all come together."

Her mother smiled. "You know, I think you're right. She really loves to see you kids. I know it was boring, but I think she really appreciated spending time with you."

"Well," said Saki. "It wasn't always boring."

Her mother raised her eyebrows, but Saki left the remark at that.

❦ ❦ ❦

The car wound down the mountain. Sunlight streamed through the windows from the west. Though she'd slept so much the past few days, the warmth and the rhythm of the car lulled Saki into a sleepy daze.

She leaned her head against the window as the car breezed past a long line of trees. For the first time since she could remember, she felt a quiet part of her reach back for the mountain. She still missed her room in Tokyo and the smell of her own pillow, but she was also starting to miss the shuffling of leaves beneath her feet and the way the trees made their own secret paths through the forest.

Her brother looked up from his video game to frown at her.

"What are you smiling about?" he asked. "You're in a lot of trouble, you know."

Saki grinned and poked him on the cheek. "Maybe I'm smiling because your face looks funny."

He gave her an odd look and stuck out his tongue before he returned to his game. Her mother and father were both silent in the front seat. Saki enjoyed the moment for as long as she could, because she knew that when her family got back to Tokyo, none of them would have time for pauses like this.

The car was almost at the base of the mountain. The forest thinned and gave way to rice fields and the village houses. Saki turned to catch one last glimpse of the trees through the rear window.

At the edge of the forest, a small animal sat by a road sign. The tanuki reached up to scratch his ear with a hind leg. A dark bird landed on the sign and pointed his beak toward the car. Tall grasses by the side of the road stirred. A pair of pointy ears appeared, but Saki couldn't tell what kind of creature they belonged to.

The car drove farther down the road. The shapes of the animals grew smaller and smaller. Saki pressed her nose against the glass of the window, hoping to keep the image in her sight for just a few more seconds.

Before the car turned down another street, a fox's tail slipped between a line of trees.

ACKNOWLEDGMENTS

Words cannot reflect the true depth of gratitude I owe to the people behind these pages. The journey to this book lasted much longer than three days and nights.

To Thao Le, my amazing agent, and to the wonderful team at Sourcebooks.

To Saori Moriizumi, Yumi Kusunoki, Maaya Ikeda, and Jess Hisamoto. To all of my classmates at Knox, some of whom were kind enough to read the very first drafts of this novel and not immediately tell me to burn it.

To my professors: Ryohei Matsuda, Barbara Tannert-Smith, Gina Franco, Chad Simpson, Nick Regiacorte, Robin Metz, and Cyn Kitchen.

To my friends from Sunset, who supported me from the very beginning. To my friends in Gunma, who supported me no less near the end. To Jackie Morgon, Natalie Bennett, and Peter Frazer, my brave beta-readers. To Nick Knoske for talking me down the query letter cliff. To Julie Israel, my lifelong friend and inspiration.

To Hiromi Oike, Setsuko Miyata, Akane Suto, and all of the other teachers at Omama Higashi Junior High School. To Kunihiko Shimizu.

To my students, who taught me more than they'll ever know.

And to my family, whose love and support let me follow my dreams half a world away. I hope my mother knows just how much I adore and admire her.

ABOUT THE AUTHOR

Kathryn Tanquary grew up in Portland, Oregon. She attended Ridgewood Elementary School, where she had the chance to visit its sister school: Katoh Gakuen in Shizuoka Prefecture, Japan. She has a BA in creative writing from Knox College and spent one year abroad at Waseda University's School of International Liberal Studies in Tokyo. After graduation, she taught English as a Foreign Language at a junior high school in Midori City, Gunma Prefecture. She currently resides in Tokyo.